ROUGH

INJUSTICE

DAVID N ROBINSON

CROSETS PUBLISHING

978-1-8380055-5-9

Cover designed by BespokeBookCovers.com

Published by Crosets Publishing

To everyone who has suffered, especially those unable to tell their story

1

'This one's a Latvian. Goes by the name of Alisa.'

Grace hands me a thin manila folder. She's been standing by the open door, waiting for me.

'Been working at a club near Stratford. A bouncer there, a man called Besim, has a thing for her, it would seem.' She looks at me in that sceptical way of hers, half-moon glasses down her nose, eyebrows raised. All our clients are female. Most of them arrive distressed or on the point of breakdown. It is Grace's natural Ghanaian warmth and larger-than-life personality that draws them, ever so gently, across the threshold.

I skim the contents of the file, its single sheet of paper fluttering as Grace's desk fan oscillates back and forth. It's yet another steamy, airless August day, the kind that makes me wish I'd found a place with air-conditioning.

'How did she hear about us?'

'Word of mouth, so she says.'

'Perhaps we're starting to make an impact?'

'You may be, for sure, Mister Rick.'

I'm always Mister Rick to Grace. She has this cadence in her voice, which I find soothing yet full of authority. As if speaking from personal knowledge about the worst aspects of human behaviour, shaped by her own experiences in the grim realities of life. We haven't known each other long. Already we've become life members of each other's fan club.

'We're a team, Grace. Never forget that. Is she settled?'

'More or less. I presume you want me to sit with you?'

'Please.' When we started the charity less than a month ago, I made it an unwritten rule never to see distressed clients on my own. 'Lead the way.' Given that it's a Friday, I had been planning on leaving early and going for a run. I guess those plans are now on hold.

Immediately, I sense Alisa is vulnerable. She's been crying, and there is a hint of a bruise beneath her left eye. She's dressed in torn jeans and a T-shirt, with a denim jacket around her shoulders. The latter seems superfluous, given the temperature. There again, what do I know about these things? Grace makes the introductions, and we sit.

My first thoughts with a new client are usually about Cath. *I'm doing this for her,* I tell myself. Even now, after all this time, I tense up when I think about what happened.

'Alisa, I'm sure Grace has explained. We want you to feel safe here with us. Everything we discuss is confidential. Grace and I might make handwritten notes, but that's it. We make no recordings or keep electronic records of any kind. Also, we never discuss our clients or their circumstances with anyone. Not with lawyers, not with the police, not with anybody. Are you happy with that?'

Alisa nods but otherwise sits in silence. The only sound is from another fan whirring. This one, perched on the far corner of the desk, is not as big as Grace's. It has a precarious wobble as it moves from side to side.

'Also, we never take money. As a charity, we offer support and guidance: a place where you can safely come and talk with people who will be sympathetic. On occasions, I might try to help in other ways. Ways that need not concern you – but the aim generally being to make problems disappear. Otherwise, we're here to support you in whatever way we can. Does that sound fair?'

Again, Alisa nods.

'In that case, you may have covered some of this with Grace already, but why don't you take your time and tell me what brings you here today?'

I let her tell her story in her own words, with no interruptions. She wobbles, tears in her eyes, when she reaches the part about the security guard, an Albanian, grabbing her in her dressing room and thrusting his fingers deep inside her panties. Grace, as ever, is ready to soothe and smooth.

'Take your time, darling,' she says. 'Trust me, and I'm sad to have to tell you this. We hear about these kinds of things all too often.'

She tells the whole grisly tale, and it isn't pretty. Yet one more story of blatant sexual abuse of a vulnerable woman. Only when we are about through do I ask about the bruise on her face.

'Was it this Albanian, Besim, who did that to you as well?'

To my surprise, she shakes her head.

'It was his manager, Tarik.'

'What happened?'

'I complained to Tarik about Besim. He refused to believe me. Told me to stop spreading lies and filth. Said if I wanted to keep my job, I should keep my mouth shut. I started explaining what had happened, which is when he got angry and hit me in the face.'

Grace and I exchange glances. She is rolling her eyes. It is her '*go, sort the bastards, Mister Rick*' expression.

'Are they handing out the happy pills?'

Alisa shakes her head.

'We don't do drugs. None of the girls at the club do.'

I'm not sure I believe her. However, if she's not dependent on Besim or Tarik for supply, that's a bonus.

'Here's what I suggest.' I speak in a soft, authoritative voice. 'I think it would be safer if you tried to find work elsewhere. That's not always straightforward. However, Grace can introduce you to one or two people who like to be helpful. In finding our clients somewhere different to work, that is. Do you have anywhere else you can stay? Somewhere the club doesn't know where or how to find you?'

'It may be possible for me to share a room with a friend of my cousin. She lives over Hackney way.'

'You should call. Assuming she okays it, I suggest you move out of your current place immediately. By this evening, if you can. We are not a wealthy charity, but in situations like this, we offer a small grant of up to five hundred pounds in cash. To tide you over. How does that sound?' Five hundred pounds is usually a life-saving sum of money to people trapped in the system like Alisa.

It is the one moment she smiles.

'That would help a lot, thank you.' She looks fatigued, as if the exertion of telling someone about her traumas has drained her. I am about to leave her with Grace when she grabs my arm. 'They've got my passport.'

I glance at Grace. Once more, she rolls her eyes behind her reading glasses. We have both been in this territory before.

'Where is it?'

'Tarik took it from me when I started work.'

Which is all I need to know.

2

The nightclub is on a busy street, sandwiched between a minicab office and a takeaway kebab joint. I drive directly from the office, wanting to arrive before the place gets going for the night. In this part of East London, parking is a nightmare. Bus and taxi-only lanes are everywhere. Patrolling wardens are in plentiful supply, ready to pounce on miscreant parking offenders. There are few perks in being disabled I get to enjoy, but unrestricted parking is one of them. Guilt-free, I slot my carefully adapted car into a loading bay a hundred metres from the club's entrance. No longer the Porsche, sadly. I could have customised it but decided not to. Old life versus new life, I guess. Rummaging in the glove compartment, I place a 'disabled' badge on the windscreen and set the blue cardboard timer to the correct hour.

Getting out of a car is no longer the challenge it used to be. I've learned to rotate my hips and pelvis, swinging the legs around so they are out the door, both feet on the ground, before standing up. It's a little more laboured than hopping out on one foot, as most people do. But not impossible. A kind of two-step tango, whereas before it was just the one. That I can walk so easily is a modern-day miracle. People rarely notice as long as they don't stare at my ankles. They might think I move oddly from time to time, but otherwise they don't know. It is the reason I tend not to wear shorts.

The time is shortly after six in the evening. Business should be slack so, with luck, this shouldn't take long. I am already buzzing, feeling the adrenalin pumping.

A thin, puny man is standing by the door. He looks like a bouncer-in-training. Not the guy you'd have standing on the pavement at ten o'clock at night, for sure. Someone to put on the graveyard shift early in the evening, in a role designed to toughen them up. To see if he had what it takes. Which I doubt. This one's unlikely to turn out to be a pussy-grabbing, Besim-type. Nor is he likely ever to become Besim's face-slapping boss either.

'You open?' I ask.

'Sure,' he replies, and tugs at the door handle to let me in. It's almost too easy. The guy gets a 'fail' in my book.

The club turns out to be a pole dancing venue. No surprises there – I had guessed as much from what Alisa hadn't told me earlier. The music is pulsing as I scan the small set-up. There is one lone, scantily clad girl going through her routine. Probably another East European. I bide my time, heading to the bar and ordering a beer. From a bottle, since, although I'm sure no one will be likely to spike drinks at this hour, old habits die hard. I wince at the ten-pound bottle charge.

'You've got to be kidding,' I say to the barman as I hand over a note.

'It's free entry from six to eight, mate.'

'Shouldn't there be a happy hour at this time of day?'

'You got in for nothing, didn't you?'

I ignore him and perch on a stool, watching the evening shift crank into action. There are two other male punters in the house, both sitting at tables near the stage, drooling over the dancer. Another bouncer emerges from a side room and heads outside to check on the puny guy at the entrance. When he comes back in, he clocks me, the recent arrival sitting alone at the bar. He's my height, stocky, with a thick neck. Classic bouncer material. I signal the barman.

'Is that Besim?' I ask, nodding towards the man by the door.

'Sure,' he says, surprise in his voice. 'You know him?' But by then I'm already on the move.

As I approach, the man registers I want to talk and turns, hands clasped together in front of his groin.

'Hey, it's Besim, isn't it?' I move to stand in front of him. With the music blaring, closer-than-normal proximity is necessary, so I get away with it. For the moment.

'What about it?' he asks. English is not his natural language.

'I've heard a lot about you,' I say, beaming, my manner friendly. My left hand touches the collar on his jacket. I am about to invade his personal space, so I hold back, just a tad, which confuses him. 'I'm told you have a delicate touch with the ladies.'

Which is when I do two unexpected things. First, I drive my knee into his groin. Followed by a swift, right-handed uppercut to his jaw. Both connections are on target, each delivering satisfying sounds of crunched body parts. As he slumps, dazed, to the floor, I drag his limp body into the shadows at the back of the room. The barman is too busy ogling the pole dancer to have noticed anything.

Besim is not in a good space. I am about to make his life a lot worse. I grab hold of his right hand by the index finger and, with a sharp downward motion, dislocate the knuckle joint. Same for the middle finger. Both fingertips now hang at unsightly angles. I do the same with the index and middle fingers on his left hand, then squat down beside the whimpering man.

'Listen, you piece of shit.' Besim is on the floor, in a lot of pain. 'If you go throwing your weight around, sticking your grubby fingers inside ladies' knickers, you've only got yourself to blame. For the consequences, I mean. Do we understand each other?'

He looks at me through watery eyes but shows no sign of comprehending. I bunch all four fingers of his right hand inside my fist and squeeze. Bones and knuckles are close to splintering. When I grab his jaw in my other hand, I have his full attention.

'Take my advice. Don't ever come back to work in this place again. If you do, I promise I'll be back for round two. Do I make myself clear?'

The man nods, and I let him go. If the joints in my feet were more substantial, I'd have kicked him for good measure. However, whilst my knees are more than able to crush a man's testicles, a thin metal spike is all that attaches each of my prosthetic feet. So, this time, Besim gets off lightly. He has enough damaged body parts to contend with.

The side door leads to a narrow corridor, with a fire exit at the far end. I open the first door on the left and discover two women preparing to head out on stage. One has platinum blonde dyed hair, and the other short, dark hair.

'Sorry to intrude, ladies. Just a quick question. The bouncer, Besim. Has he been trying it on with either of you?'

The two look at each other, their expression fearful.

'Listen. I'm an investigator. There are rumours that bouncers at this place are coercing sexual favours from women working here. Would that be your experience?'

'All the time,' the dark-haired one says, eventually. From her looks, I can't believe she's a day over eighteen. Given the murky migrant world she's likely to be part of, she probably isn't. 'He's disgusting, a pervert. Tarik, the boss, is worse. I had to give him oral before he paid me last week.' The other girl nods in agreement.

'Well, I have news for you. All that kind of shit is going to be history. Besim will not be giving you trouble, I promise. In a short while, I suspect neither will Tarik. Does Tarik have your passports?'

'Yes.'

'I'll try to get them back before I leave. What about drugs?'

'We don't do drugs,' the second girl says, her face expressionless.

'Seriously?'

'Nothing we get from here.'

The same thing, at least, that Alisa had told me.

'Good. Tarik's office is next door?'

Both girls nod.

'Don't go anywhere for five minutes. I'll be back.'

Tarik's office is larger than its neighbour. It's a square, windowless space with two desks, several television monitors and a large filing cabinet next to a wall safe. Tarik is on the phone when I burst into the room. As he gets to his feet at the unexpected interruption, I notice one of the TV screens behind where he is sitting. It's a direct feed from the women's changing room next door.

I hate this perverted shit. It makes me see red, which is why I ignore the pleasantries with Tarik and get straight to the point. The point being a massive, nose-busting fist thrust directly into the man's face as I approach his desk. The phone drops from his hand, and Tarik falls back, slumping dazed into his executive chair. I did a little karate in the evenings years ago when I was a brickie. Learning how to punch without breaking knuckles has served me well. Occasionally, I might confess to enjoying doing things like this – what Grace describes as my rough injustice approach. I grab the mobile, disconnect the call and put it in my pocket. I am not yet done with Tarik.

I notice black plastic cable ties in an open desk drawer and grab a handful. I use them to bind Tarik's wrists to the chair's armrests and then stoop to tie his ankles together. With these wretched prosthetics, I can kneel okay, but getting up is a pain. Hence, I prefer bending rather than kneeling. Tarik is going nowhere, courtesy of the cable ties. I feel pleased with my improvised handcuffs and make a note to ask Grace to get me some. I watch as he regains consciousness, his face a bloodied mess. The man's a smoker. I pick up a zip lighter from the desktop, roll up a shirt sleeve and apply a little heat to his forearm. That usually gets people's attention. Tarik is no exception.

'You must be Tarik?'

'Who the fuck are you?'

'Like your friend Besim, I gather you enjoy playing around with the girls too?'

'You don't know what the fuck you're talking about. You're a dead man, whoever the fuck you are.'

'Think again, dickhead. You've been abusing your position. Demanding sexual favours from the girls who work here. Paying them a pittance, taking their passports, making them your little sex slaves. Well, now it's payback time.'

'You're a piece of shit.'

Which is when I notice the kettle in the corner. I fill the jug from the sink and switch it on, all the time saying nothing, watching Tarik struggle to get to his feet but fail.

'Let me go, or I'll kill you, do you hear?'

'There's one thing people soon learn about me,' I say, my face up close to his. 'I do not negotiate.'

Tarik rants, but I ignore him. First I want to look at the CCTV set-up. No point leaving evidence of my visit to this place on the tape. I'm familiar with most of these bits of equipment, soon discovering that I only appear in two camera angles. I fiddle around with the recordings, deleting various bits of footage. Satisfied that I have erased all evidence of my visit, I open the filing cabinet and peer inside. It contains account ledgers and various items of stationery. No passports or anything interesting.

'How do I open the safe?'

Tarik switches tactics, now saying nothing. He looks seriously pissed as he glowers, writhing against the cable ties.

'You'll tell.' As if to make the point, I pick up the freshly boiled kettle and bring it across to Tarik's desk. 'Question is, do you want to do things the easy or the hard way?'

He again says nothing, trying to remain calm but unable to hide his growing anxiety.

'Suit yourself.'

With Tarik squirming in his seat, I grab the waistband of his trousers and pull hard. Given my condition, the muscle strength I've built up in my forearms allows me to lift him easily in one hand. With the other hand, I undo his waist button and zip, and yank down his trousers and sordid Y-fronts. It is not a pretty sight.

'Get the fuck off me,' he screams, but I ignore him.

'The code to the safe, Tarik. Last chance.' The jug of boiling water is back in my hand.

'Go fuck yourself,' is what he mutters moments before I pour scalding water onto his privates. His reaction is immediate and hideous.

He screams, his body writhing against the cable ties, his bloodied face contorted. Like the nice guy I claim to be sometimes, I stop. 'Top left drawer,' he gasps, his face wracked with pain. 'Clipped to the underside. A piece of card.'

I put the kettle down and open the desk drawer. The card is exactly where he said it would be. Written on it, all crossed out except the last one, are rows of six-figure numbers. I put the card back and try the code. It works, and the safe opens. Inside are a few interesting items. A handgun, which I leave well alone; several bundles of twenty-pound notes, one of which I sneak into my jacket pocket to cover Alisa's expenses, plus another to pay the girls working out the front that night; and a small collection of passports.

I pick these up and look over at Tarik.

'Time to give these beauties back to the girls, don't you think?'

'You're a dead man.'

I walk towards him, the passports now safe in my jacket pocket. On a hunch, I pick up the kettle once again.

'How do you find the girls, Tarik?' If my hunch is right, this could be like prising open the oyster. 'Who sends them to you?'

Tarik says nothing, but his eyes give him away. He's scared. No longer angry, he's woken up to the reality: this one, he's already lost.

'Last chance.' I am on the verge of pouring when his resistance caves.

'I'll tell you!' he yells out. 'His name is Gregor. He sends me girls. I send him cash each month. That's the truth.'

This piece of information is a lucky strike. I'd come across someone called Gregor a few weeks back. It was in connection with a bar hostess who claimed she'd been raped. She'd told Grace and me that a man called Gregor had been responsible for her recruitment. I'd done some digging, stopped by the place she'd been working at, and sorted a few things out. However, all roads leading to Gregor had so far had drawn a blank. It had been bugging me for a while.

'How do you contact him?'

'Phone.'

I reach into my pocket and pull out Tarik's phone.

'This one here?' I say, holding it up for him to see.

He nods, and I scroll through the recent call list. Sure enough, there are several calls to someone called Gregor.

'Thank you,' I say, pocketing the phone. 'That wasn't so bad, was it?' I turn to go, then stop and return to the desk. 'One more thing. In case you're minded to abuse any more of the girls, take this as a warning.' With that, I pour the rest of the jug of water into his lap. Then I head out the door, leaving Tarik sobbing and wailing like a baby in my wake.

The two girls are still in the changing room. I take out the passports, and they each find their own.

'What about the girl on stage?'

'This is Eva's,' one of them says, picking up another passport.

'How much money should you be making tonight?'

'In theory, about one-fifty each. Plus tips, minus deductions. Usually, there are plenty of deductions. We'll be lucky to take home anything much at all.'

I remove one bundle of cash and hand it over.

'It's your lucky night. Split the money between the three of you and head home. I'd find someplace else to work from now on. Neither Tarik nor Besim will bother you again.'

Spontaneously, both girls step forward to hug me. Tears in their eyes, they look as happy as Alisa had earlier.

'Thank you,' they say in unison.

It's time for me to get going, the fire exit suddenly feeling a safer way out than heading out the front.

3

I arrive back at my ground-floor apartment, ready for a beer. The temperature in London remains in the high twenties, and the early evening air is humid. I take a bottle from the fridge and twist the cap, only realising at this point that the knuckles on my right hand are raw and gashed, courtesy of Tarik's teeth.

It's Friday and tonight I have a date. A work contact, Inés Keller, has been keen to try this new Italian restaurant she's heard about. Based on Inés's dogged persistence to drag me on a date, I suspect she wants more than just a shared restaurant review. It sounds just what I need after the nightclub visit.

Before heading out, I need a shower. In my condition, this is more complicated than it used to be. I carry the beer with me into the bedroom, sit on the bed and roll up my trousers. First, I press a button to release both prostheses before removing the elasticated liners that fit over each leg stump. With that completed, I feel more human again. Certainly cooler. I drain my beer and swing myself into an electric wheelchair I keep by the bed, heading straight for the bathroom. In the middle of the night, if I need to pay a visit, more often than not I do this chimpanzee-like crawl across the floor on my hands, bum and feet stubs. It looks weird, but I can be fast that way. If I did this now, I'd only get dirty again as soon as I got out of the shower. Hence the wheelchair. I use grab bars to swing out of the chair and across to a bench seat inside the shower cubicle.

Later, much refreshed, I get dressed. I put on a clean set of stub liners, with their long, metal spike at the end, before stepping into each prosthesis and hearing the reassuring 'click' that means they are locked in position. I've just finished when I remember Tarik's phone in my jacket pocket. I reach to grab it, scrolling through various messages, in particular those to and from the man Tarik referred to as Gregor. The abusive language in the texts confirms my belief that both are sick people. I jot down Gregor's phone number on a notepad before disconnecting Tarik's phone from the network. No point in sending Tarik's Albanian friends a 'come and find me' location message by leaving the phone on. I move to the kitchen and file away the piece of paper with the number written on it in the disorderly stack of correspondence I keep at one end of the kitchen table, which is when I notice the answerphone light flashing. I have a message. It's from my mother. Since our falling-out, we've hardly spoken.

Perhaps this is the moment to say something of the Baxter family backstory. Not too much, since I'm not that much of a rear-view mirror type of person. If you're driving the bus, you're watching the road ahead. You can't be watching behind you all the time.

The clock started ticking in my life about thirty-eight years ago, on a farm close to Bulawayo. At the time I appeared from my mother's womb, I became baby brother to my only other sibling, Cath, two years older. When I was two, my parents sold the farm and moved to England. I guess they got the timing about right, given what was about to happen in the country today known as Zimbabwe. My father bought some arable land in the East Anglian Fens, and Cath and I both went to schools near Ely. She excelled at her studies while I wasted my time. Story of my old life, some might say. Cath enjoyed drama and the arts. I enjoyed messing about.

My rather aimless teenage purpose in life was doubtless influenced by my parents receiving an offer on their Fenland farm. Overnight, it was as if they'd won the lottery. They suddenly had enough money in the bank to set aside a cool million each for Cath and me. The cash, however, was locked up in some impenetrable trust until our twenty-fifth birthdays. As a result, I didn't bother with university. Whilst Cath was off at drama school, making her parents proud, I was signing on at the Job Centre, trying my hand at useless odds and ends. I was a hefty lad, well able to stand up for myself. I knew how to pick a fight and usually come out on top, which is why I opted for manual labouring jobs to begin with. I became a brickie on an Ely housing development for several months before having a go at plastering. I never could get the hang of it. Finally, I took up landscape gardening. I quite enjoyed that, if truth be told. I would have done more if Dad hadn't keeled over and died from a stroke. He was only sixty-two, and it was a shock to us all. Life seemed to slam into the buffers without warning. Since selling the farm, Dad had set up a cut flower business out towards Norwich. My mother was desperate for someone to take over. Would I help out? Well, I could hardly say no, could I?

Actually, it was all right. I got stuck in and developed a taste for running a business. In time, the trust fund paid out, I bought a Porsche and developed something of a party habit. To my mother's regret, I led a varied – and sometimes complicated – social life: lots of female companions, but nothing ever permanent. Meanwhile, Cath was making a name for herself. Bit by bit. First on television and then one or two minor roles in films. She just needed that one big break, she kept telling me. It would come, I would say. Little did I realise at what cost.

The falling-out with Mum happened a few weeks before I had my skiing moment of madness on the infamous Swiss Wall above Champéry. My darling sister's death had precipitated it. Until the moment I learned she'd taken an overdose, I thought Cath had been going through a rough patch. She hadn't been getting the prominent film roles she'd craved. I put it down not to her acting skills – or lack of – but to a rolling of the dice. Do older sisters confide such things to their younger brothers? Perhaps not, but until the moment she left us, she and I had always been close – or so I thought.

She'd been speaking to our mother, however. Quite a lot, as I discovered. To this day, I don't know whether that included all, or only some, of the grisly details. That was the reason for the schism. Somewhere on Cath's ambitious journey to get the film part she always wanted, some media mogul had crossed the line. Demanded favours in return for a boost to her career. That was all Mum had been prepared to tell me. It made me so angry. I tried every which way to persuade her to say more, but she refused. I was totally in the mood to do something about it, most likely in a Besim-and-Tarik kind of way. I lost my temper, said a few things I probably shouldn't have. Mum, in return, clammed up. Refused to speak. She had been all too aware how much that would irritate me. Hence our prolonged period of familial silence.

Ever since then, we've been on this childish Christmas card and birthday card communication-only routine. The last time I saw her in the flesh was when she came to visit me at Stoke Mandeville hospital. It was when I was in rehab. There were plenty of hugs, a lot of tears, followed by the brick wall coming back up and the two of us resuming our radio silence. A few weeks later, when I was on the road to recovery, she wrote a letter, explaining that she was moving nearer to Cambridge. She'd found another man – a retired businessman. That didn't help matters between the two of us. Still, the presence of the new man allowed me to cross her off my worry list. Who was I to stop the pair of them from flying and sailing their way around the world, spending my father's legacy and this chap's meagre pension? I had other things to worry about. So why the phone call now?

'Hi, Ricky. It's your mother. I need to talk to you about something. Please call me as soon as you can.'

Not 'whenever convenient', or 'sometime soon'. This was 'as soon as you can'. She didn't sound panicked, however, so I resolve not to call back right away. It would make me late for my date with Inés. I'll call in the morning.

4

The restaurant is in Spitalfields, a trendy spot near the City. When I get out of the taxi, the pedestrian-only area is heaving with lawyer types and young professionals. I spot Inés at our table as soon as I walk through the door. Like me, she's also not come straight from work. Instead, she's opted for a low-cut blouse and tight jeans combo. It works for me. Her chestnut-brown hair looks great too. Frizzy locks, scrunched in a bun at work, are this evening untied and flowing. We give each other a warm embrace.

'Tough day at the office?'

'Not any more, Ricky. It's good to see you. How are things?'

We've been bumping into each other from time to time as the charity's first clients have crossed the threshold. Inés is a senior investigating officer in a department of the Home Office's overstretched operation against human trafficking. The modern-day slave trade. It turns out we're both interested in similar groups of vulnerable people. Although she and I are not always coming at solutions from the same side of the law. I've fed her a few leads. In return, she keeps promising to send vulnerable women in my direction as and when. Not a lot has happened on that front, but it's early days. There's been some nice chemistry between us. Just nothing serious. So far, that is.

We order a bottle of red wine and chat about this and that. As the wine flows, Inés is all smiles, and I'm relaxing, finally.

'What happened to your hand?' She touches my grazed knuckles as I'm picking up a slice of salami from the sharing plate of antipasto.

'Oh, it's nothing. I fell in the shower. When my pegs are off, I can be a right old liability.' She looks at me dubiously.

'Want to tell me what really happened, Ricky?'

I chuckle, she smiles and we change subjects. I discover she's a single mother, a result of marrying the wrong person at too young an age.

'Tell me more.'

'My daughter's almost fifteen now, can you believe? Her father and I met at police training college. You know how it is,' she sighs. 'Two youngsters fall in love, the woman gets pregnant, produces a lovely little girl, then three years on discovers the man she married is no longer the person she thought he was. The little shit was playing away from home. When I found out, he got rough.'

'Pity our paths hadn't crossed sooner.'

She gives me a wide-eyed smile, and I can feel her knees against mine under the table.

'There's no excuse for abuse,' I add.

'We all make foolish mistakes.'

'We do. I have no lower legs, thanks to my stupidity.' At this, we both laugh.

'How did that happen? You never told me.' She's toying with the rim of her glass as she asks. She's probably wanted to know about this for a while.

'About fifteen months ago, my sister killed herself. Her suicide left me feeling angry, though I didn't realise how much. I found consolation in bottles of beer and wine. I drank too much and became a grumpy, moody waste of space. On a whim, I headed to the ski slopes of Switzerland to escape from it all. It was a boys' trip. We partied too hard, drank too much, and along the way, I ended up getting legless. Literally. I skied off the edge of a precipice on the longest and most difficult mogul field in Europe. Snapped both pins to shreds.'

'Ouch!'

'It was my own stupid fault.'

'No spinal injury?'

'In hindsight, I was so lucky. I didn't think so at the time, but there we are. Life moves in a mysterious way. I stopped drinking, and my hospitalisation and subsequent long and painful period of rehab gave me time to reflect. As you say, my spine was undamaged, meaning that my chances for a good recovery were high. Plus, my sister had left me all this money, way more than I'd any right to expect. My injuries gave me months sitting around thinking about life, trying to get fit and rebuild my idea of what a normal life was going to be. Flushed with cash, wanting to atone for Cath's death: it's what caused me to set up the charity.'

We both order the filled pasta special with a dark, creamy meat sauce. It arrives eventually and tastes delicious. By now, the wine is flowing, and it's turning out to be a lovely evening. The restaurant is full of the sounds of people enjoying themselves.

'We should have done this before,' I say in between mouthfuls. 'Making the time for a dinner date.' She places her hand on mine and flashes a generous smile. In combination with the wine and her low-cut blouse, the evening is working its magic.

'Tell me about the office.' We've finished eating, and they have already cleared our plates. 'Working on anything interesting?'

She shakes her head in a *what sort of dumb question is that?* way. 'Oh, this and that, you know. Human trafficking stuff, mainly. Then there's the county lines drug scene, modern slavery … want me to go on? It's a nightmare. Sometimes, I sense we're not even scratching the surface.'

'I know the feeling.'

'The migrant crisis is the bane of our lives. One massive, impenetrable wave of humanity flowing into Europe from all across the globe. Forget Brexit and the EU and all that supposed free movement rubbish. The gangs fuelling the migrant flow are the ruthless ones. They are run like slick businesses: some big, some small, many of them interconnected.' She looks at me, eyes wide. 'Some are even at war with each other.'

The waiter arrives bearing two plates of the house tiramisu to tempt us. I decline, but Inés takes one and is soon tucking in.

'Want to try some?' She scoops up a small portion and places her spoon in my mouth. I pretend to like it, but she sees through this and wrinkles her nose at me. It's not my kind of thing.

'Where there are gangs, there's usually abuse,' I say as she eats. 'Why we all seem prepared to turn a blind eye to what's going on, beats me. We had this Latvian girl today. A pole dancer, being abused by bouncers at the club she's working at. What can we do on a case-by-case basis? Listen, offer to help find her a new job, give her money to tide her over. It's nothing lasting, only a reprieve. Like you, we're not even scratching the surface.'

'Word on the street, Ricky, is you're already making quite an impact.'

'Nothing substantive.'

'Two bouncers at a nightclub in Stratford might feel otherwise.'

I raise my eyebrows at her, and she goes all coy on me.

'It was something I saw in my emails before you arrived.'

I smile but say nothing.

'Listen. My little unit may be part of the Home Office, but we're not the police. We investigate. We do our research and then let the courts sort it out. It can be slow and cumbersome, but we can't just waltz in and administer the odd bit of rough justice, however much we'd like to. You, on the other hand ...' she says, stroking the back of my hand with her index finger, 'can do whatever you think appropriate.'

'So,' I say, taking her fingers in mine and squeezing. 'Perhaps we ought to join forces? You know, you scratch my back, I'll scratch yours.'

'Now we're talking my kind of language. I so like the sound of that. Do you have coffee back at your place?'

'One unopened packet of Colombian special roast. Plus, some decent red wine, as it happens.'

'What are we doing here, then?'

'I really don't know. If you sort out a taxi, I'll get the bill.'

5

Perhaps this is an opportune moment to introduce Baz. I owe Baz. Without him, I would most likely still be in a dark space. He's unbelievably quiet. Unbelievably unassuming. Yet one of the most courageous, inspiring men I know. The bond between us is something we never discuss. You think I'm overstating this? Try this scenario for size and tell me I'm wrong.

Imagine you're a hard-working, peace-loving young Iraqi of Kurdish background. You have been brought up in simple, rural traditions with few demands or needs. Because of endless wars in your country, your family has spent years on the move, trying to escape the fighting. When ISIS declares itself a caliphate and captures Mosul, a city close to the village of your birth, your parents send your younger sister, Samira, and you on a circuitous journey to a safer life in the West. Your elderly parents pay most of their life savings to a friendly go-between who promises to smuggle you both to safety in the UK. Passports and work are guaranteed. Or so your parents believe. They know little about gangs or how they operate. Neither, at that stage, do you.

The journey you embark on is full of trauma, suffering and terrible abuse. Things go from bad to worse when you reach the UK. The gang leaders send you to a small town in Lincolnshire where you work in the fields. Samira is sent somewhere you've never heard of: a place called Leicester. Briefly, it's possible to text each other. Then everything goes silent, all contact lost. You try calling people you believe might know her whereabouts, but you hit a brick wall. When you ask those looking after you, you are beaten and they confiscate your phone. They also threaten to do unspeakable things to your parents back in Iraq unless you forget about your sister and work harder. Later, they tell you she is dead. They even show you photographs of a body you think might be hers; you can't be sure. This is when you hit absolute rock bottom.

You contemplate suicide, but there's a part of you that has to be sure. Deep down, you have this glimmer of hope. Which leads you to contemplate this idea. It's crazy, but the more you consider it, the better it sounds. You will suffer an accident at work, something which will place you in hospital for a long time. There you will be safe: you'll eat and sleep without harassment and be able to plan your escape. You will even have time to think through how you might go about learning the truth about your sister. What have you got to lose?

Welcome to Baz's world.

To date, this courageous young man has achieved only fifty per cent of his overall plan. He had some luck along the way. He found me. However, I had some luck along the way, too. I found him. By complete chance, we had adjacent beds in Stoke Mandeville hospital. I had lost two legs below the knee. He had lost just the one. In his broken English, he told me his story. His passion and courage moved me more than I ever imagined. Would you be able to contemplate jumping into the path of a combine harvester? Because you could see no other way to escape your servitude. Let alone find the time or space to discover how your sister had died? If she had died. I couldn't. I was having enough trouble dealing with the fact I had let Cath down. This double amputation I'd had was part of my atonement, remember? Baz's straightforward honesty and courage touched me. When I learned his story, it moved me to tears. I instantly understood what I would do with my new legs in my new life. I wanted to help Baz find his sister, and for that, I needed Baz to be part of the journey.

When we were both ready to leave hospital, I asked Baz if he wanted to take a spare room in my house. I suggested that this arrangement could last until we had both got our lives back into better order. Out of typical Iraqi politeness, he declined. I badgered him, and he still refused. Finally, after what seemed like hours, if not days, of dogged persistence, he relented. Only on the condition that he help me convert my London property to make it fit for use by a double amputee.

In Cath's memory, my aim in setting up the charity was to provide support and some measure of relief to women who are being abused. I wanted to get things done, in a way that – and this was my particular spin on things – traditional law enforcement wasn't able to. Or prepared to. I had enough money in the bank, thanks to Cath's generosity. Why not set to work and do something good for a change? My mother, if we'd only been speaking about these things, might even have been proud. At least I think she might. I'm not convinced she'd be a massive fan of the rougher elements of my new life, but what do I know? These days, I'm trying to live my life helping others. Those less fortunate than me, people who've suffered along the way. Which is why I need Baz around me. So I can be reminded of why I'm doing all this.

Unlike me, who's just this blundering, tough guy who lost his legs in an angry fit of drunken stupidity, Baz has lived in the real world. He and his sister have both been victims of abuse. He knows how the gangs work the system. He's got personal experience of how they prey on the vulnerable. Baz is a man on a real mission, needing to learn Samira's fate. Whereas I have been on this meandering, long-term journey that, until my accident, hadn't really got me anywhere. Baz has made me see the world differently. He's made me realise that I yearn to do something positive to atone for how Cath died. Something practical. Something that makes a difference and stops abuse where it starts. In this way, our two missions have become aligned.

I tell Baz from the outset I want to do three things to help. First, if he has any legitimate debts, I will clear them. Second, I want him to come and work with me. I will pay him in cash, and he will help me with projects. Third, I promise that I will try to help him find out about his sister, as much as I can. As much as he'll let me. I say this because Baz is a proud person. He's desperate to find the truth, but only on his terms and in his own way. To date, we haven't made a lot of progress on this third thing. However, it was this resolve to find Samira that was the practical impetus I needed to get off my backside and get the charity started.

It's still early days. At times, I feel that I'm making stuff up as we go along. Like using cable ties on Tariq. Part of me wants to believe that finding a man such as Gregor could be a useful starting point for making progress on our charitable objectives. As I mentioned, I'd come across his name only recently. Tripping over him again at the club today feels like a gift, especially now that we have a mobile number. Not for the first time, I'm wondering whether Inés could help. Maybe she or her colleagues have heard of him? Or better still, know something about him.

As she and I share a taxi back to my place, her head resting on my shoulder, one hand resting near a place full of promise, I am trying to work out when might be the best time to ask.

6

It's next morning by the time I raise the subject of Baz's sister. You might wonder why I haven't done this in the days or weeks before Inés and I had our dinner date. The answer, quite simply, is because of Baz.

You would be forgiven for imagining that Baz and I had long since made the journey back to the village in Lincolnshire, where he first began working. To visit his former gang leaders. The ones who helped him find work. The people who treated him like a slave and beat him up. The same folks who might still know how to connect with the people controlling Samira. You might even imagine a Besim-and-Tarik type of interrogation. Even before my newfound love affair with cable ties.

The fact is, Baz hasn't let me. Baz has been, and remains, fearful for Samira's safety. He bases this worry on the slimmest of chances she might still be alive. He says he knows how the gangs operate. How one false move by him – or me – could bring disaster. The thing to understand about Baz is that, at heart, he's a simple, peace-loving Kurd. If it's possible to say this and not offend him, he's too nice. Too polite. Unlike me, who's become this angry, blunt instrument, Baz is a meek and mild person. Someone who wants to believe in the good in people. He might visit the gym, and have gained muscles he'd only been able to dream of previously, but in his heart of hearts, he'd have trouble killing a fly.

'These men evil, Ricky. They do terrible things. Maybe Samira is dead, maybe not. If not, I must be careful. I need disappear. Best think I'm dead.' Baz's English is never fluid, but the sentiment is clear. I respect that.

'You can't just do nothing, my friend,' I said to him early on. 'Not after all you've been through to break loose.'

'I don't do nothing,' he had answered, his tone and manner hurt. It was as if I was insulting him. 'I ask people back home. See if any contact. Samira always Viber her cousin. Sometimes message, sometimes video. I've been asking. Nothing. Not even Viber.'

'What's Viber?'

'In Iraq, we use all the time. Like WhatsApp, but better.'

'And?'

Baz shrugged. With him, it is always something of a helpless, disappointed gesture.

'So far, nothing.'

'Nothing as in no reply or nothing as in they haven't heard from her?'

'The same.'

'Then let's visit your old gang in the Fens.'

'No!' His tone, as ever, saying it all. At that moment, it meant 'end of conversation'. Even though he might often appear meek and mild, Baz can be more stubborn than most. On this issue, his feet have remained glued to the spot. He refuses to budge. 'These evil people, Rick. Trust me. We do this my way.'

Time, however, is the judge of all things. Baz's way has not yet produced firm leads. Attempts to make enquiries through distant Kurdish relatives back home have drawn a blank. Baz's parents are no longer in communication. Baz tells me he fears they, too, might be dead. A mortar attack, or worse. In that part of the world, it is not uncommon for entire villages to be wiped out in a single air strike. The time has come for us to step this whole enquiry up a gear. It's time to ask Inés for help. She's smart enough to know ways to approach this with sufficient care and caution.

Inés and I are sitting around the breakfast table, sampling yet more of the Colombian special roast. It has a lovely nutty flavour, and the French press is half empty. When my pins are off, I struggle to bring myself, let alone any guests, coffee or tea in bed. The early morning routine has had to change. I could have asked Inés to make us some, but that's not my style. Perhaps the old me might have done. These days, it's not the way I treat my house guests. I don't need anyone taking pity on me.

'Fun night, last night?'

She grabs my hand in hers and squeezes. Her head is propped up by her other arm, bent at the elbow. She has this bleary, freshly awoken look which I find sexy.

'Not a bad morning, either,' she says, smiling. I blow an air kiss across the table.

'What are you doing this sunny Saturday?'

'Me? Oh, I don't know. Bits and pieces. No, I tell a lie. My daughter and I are going clothes shopping this afternoon. Want to come?'

'Thanks, but I'll pass.'

'What about you?'

'I'll be heading to the office. We sometimes get walk-ins over the weekend.'

'Does Grace work weekends?'

'Grace would work every day if I let her.'

'She's like gold. How did you find her?'

'Pure fluke. A few weeks ago, I'd just located what I felt were suitable premises. They were nothing grand, but at least they were on the High Street in Bethnal Green. The place had felt right. Plus, it was only ten minutes from here. I'd always known I would need someone to help run the charity. Now that we were so close to opening, I had no idea how to go about finding such a person. In a quandary, I was on my way back to the office from the bank, having just signed the lease on the property, when I passed a branch of the Citizens Advice Bureau. Hang on, I said to myself: the CAB might be a referral source for the charity. Then it also struck me they might know of someone suitable. On a whim, I went in. Next thing, I'm meeting Grace.'

'What's her story?'

'I've only found out fragments. She's Ghanaian, born in the UK, married a Nigerian but now divorced. For many years, she suffered at the hands of an abusive and violent husband. Being Grace, she suffered in silence. Until one day, the husband came home and announced he was running off with a much younger floozy. There was a blazing row. He punched her in the face and scarpered, taking most of her jewellery and all of her money. A few days later, Grace, struggling to come to terms with it all, made her way to the local branch of CAB to seek help. Out of the blue, she met me.'

'At which point, the "would you like to come and join my charity, helping to protect and support female victims of abuse" struck a chord?'

'That's about the sum of it. Grace became my second employee. Well, my first official one.'

'Remind me, who's the other one?'

'Have you not met Baz? It's a long story. Officially, he's not on the payroll. He will be, assuming that one day soon I can get him a passport and make him legal. He's one reason I set up the charity.'

Now I have Inés's full attention.

'Tell me more.'

Which is my cue to recount the story of Baz and his sister. The combine harvester episode brings tears to Inés's eyes.

'You need to get closure about Samira, is that what you're saying? Or rather, Baz does.'

'Dead or alive. Either way, we must tread carefully.'

'Would you like me to help?'

'God knows how. She was last known to be in Leicester. She could be anywhere. I don't have the guts to air my real worry about all of this to Baz. Namely that, by now, she might well be dead.'

'If she's alive and without a passport of her own, the gangs will have given her a new name. Finding her is going to be nigh on impossible.'

'Any bright ideas?' I ask.

'Wave a magic wand and make all these gangs disappear. That would help. Seriously, finding someone like Samira is going to be needle-in-a-haystack stuff.'

'How many gangs are we talking about?'

'Licensed gangs? Several hundred.'

'That many? I'm amazed. What about unlicensed ones?'

'You tell me,' she says. 'A fair few.'

'I'm guessing the trafficking gangs are all unlicensed?'

'What do you think?'

'Someone's got to stop some of this shit from happening, that's what I think.'

'There's quite a lot of interest in one or two of the gangs, currently. For the reasons we've been talking about.'

‘Slip me some names, and I’ll pay them a visit.’

She gives me a warning look. ‘These are not nice people.’

‘I can be unpleasant when I need to be.’

‘Let me think about it.’

‘A name or two is all I need. Especially people you feel might be abusing women. While you’re at it, if you come across anyone called Gregor, I’d be particularly interested. I’ve got his phone number here somewhere,’ I say, and hunt around in the pile of post on the kitchen table. ‘Yes, here we are.’ I hand her the paper with the number I’d found on Tarik’s phone.

‘How did you get hold of this, Ricky?’

‘Let’s just say, someone gave it to me.’

‘I can’t promise, but I’ll see what I can do,’ she says, writing the number down and handing back the piece of paper.

7

Grace wants to know chapter and verse. At first, I assume this is about my visit to Alisa's club. It is only when she remains sitting by my desk, eyebrows still raised, that I get it.

'The Italian place was good.' It is a feeble attempt by me to shut down further enquiry. 'Thanks for making the reservation.' Grace remains rooted to her chair. She isn't fooled by my amateurish attempts to deprive her of gossip.

'Did you and Inés have a nice evening?' She flashes her broadest, all-knowing smile.

'Great, thanks.'

'I like Inés. She's very –' she pauses, searching for the appropriate word '– suitable.' I should have realised from day one that my choice of female companions would always be subject to Grace's approval. 'What country's she from?'

'I've no idea.' Her question puzzles me. It's never crossed my mind. Now I think about it, I wonder whether Inés's family might have their origins in one of the Caribbean islands. Her dark-honeyed skin and frizzy hair are the clues. It's not something I've considered.

'Not a one-off, then?'

I smile at Grace's persistence.

'There's no need to cross her off the Christmas card list yet.' It is a joke we share between us. She worries I need someone more permanent in my life. Maybe she's been talking to my mother. Which reminds me, I need to call her.

'By the way,' I say just as Grace is getting to her feet. 'Are you able to get a supply of cable ties? You know, the nylon zip tie things. I've discovered they're good makeshift handcuffs. I think I should carry a few around with me in future.'

'That's easy. I can get those in the hardware store down the road.'

'One other thing,' I say, reaching into my pocket as Grace is manoeuvring her heavy frame off the chair. I hand over Alisa's passport. 'This belongs to Alisa. See if you can contact the other girls at the club. I'd like to meet all three of them together. I suggest we keep the passport in the office for the moment. It'll act as an incentive to get Alisa to come back in.' Grace is doing her eyebrow-raising thing at me again. 'I need to know more about who's been running their little operation.'

'I'll send Baz to make contact and set up a meeting. He's good at that sort of thing.'

'Mum, you rang? It's Ricky.' Odd as it sounds, I had to brace myself to make the call. Family dynamics can be a challenge.

'Ricky, darling. I can't tell you how lovely it is to hear from you.' Her voice cracks as soon as she speaks. For a while, we blather around aimlessly, talking about stupid bits and pieces: her health, my health, how we're both keeping. Something's not right, though. I can tell from her voice.

'What about you, Mum? How are you and that man of yours getting on? Howard, isn't it?'

A nose is being blown, and tears are welling. I realise what's coming.

'That's why I called,' she wails, and the story tumbles out.

Howard is no longer the love of her life. It turns out he was a gold digger. Seeing a wealthy widow in his sights, this self-proclaimed 'former investment adviser' has spent the last few months befriending my mother. He set about to beguile her, deliberately, with his charms. This full-on assault included persuading my one remaining parent into allowing him to manage her not insubstantial investment portfolio. Love, it would seem, makes the best of us gullible.

'He's disappeared, Ricky. We had this trip all planned and everything. I had even booked and paid for the flights. Two days ago, the day of departure, he never turned up. He hasn't answered my calls or anything.'

'Have you been to his house?'

'There's no one there. The place is all shut up. Completely deserted. I've tried calling his mobile, but he's not answering.'

'Perhaps he's ill or something. Have you checked the hospitals?'

'I was about to. Then I realised there was no need. It gets worse.' Her voice trembles and I can sense the punchline.

All her money's missing.

'I didn't believe it at first. So I checked. Again and again. It's gone. All of it.'

'How much?'

Once she calms down enough for her words to be audible, I learn the staggering size of Howard's swag. Three million pounds.

'Have you called the police?'

'They're no help.' More nose-blowing and tears at this point. 'They sent someone junior. All he did was ask ridiculous questions. I need you to help me, Ricky. How am I going to live? How am I ever going to get my money back?'

What I had thought would be a ten-minute chat eventually takes nearer an hour. Finally, with various names and details noted, I end the call. I did my level best to console my mother, but I am not sure I helped much. She is not aware of the charity I run. I've never spoken to her about it, nor has she ever enquired. Naturally, I'll try to help. It's the least I can do.

'Where's Baz?' I ask Grace a little later.

'Out, trying to find Alisa.'

'Tell him I've got something urgent for him to do. I won't be in tomorrow. I now have to visit my mother.'

'Finally found the tongue in her head, has she?'

I explain about my phone call. Grace's attitude changes in a heartbeat. Instantly, she's full of forgiveness and compassion. Something which, hitherto, has been absent in any conversation I've had with her about my mother.

'Well, that makes her a client, Mister Rick.' The implication being that this places Mum under Grace's care and attention, which in itself should be interesting to watch.

8

After an amputation, there's this genuine sense of loss. You don't realise it, but you're grieving. I found it all too easy to get into this downward mental spiral. I had some pretty dark days. Some never pull themselves out of it. I don't blame anyone who leans on the booze or medication for support. It so nearly happened to me. My good fortune was that I found Baz and he found me. Then, together at Stoke Mandeville, we found the gym. Since then, our workout routine with the weights has become as much a part of our daily lives as eating and sleeping.

My party trick is powerlifting. On a good day, I can bench-press over three hundred pounds. I don't do drugs, so I reckon that's not bad. Because of my condition, I also need to focus on my upper leg strength. The quads, as us gym junkies refer to them. The leg press machines are an excellent workout for toning these muscle groups. Baz and I lie, side by side, and count the reps. I like to wind him up by accusing him of cheating: after all, he's only missing the one leg below the knee whereas I'm missing two. We try to do five rounds of twenty reps. In the old days, I found it rubbed and hurt my stumps on both legs. Now, I'm used to it. Pain is good. It reminds me of how lucky I am to lead a near-normal life.

The gym has helped Baz. Whereas I was always a big lad, Baz, when I first met him, was skinny with little muscle tone. He undoubtedly had stamina and bravery by the bucketload: just not a lot of muscle mass. All that has changed with regular work on the weights. He's not the aggressive type, but the old Baz would never have felt confident in a fight. These days, if provoked, who knows what might happen.

'Did you find Alisa?'

Baz and I are drinking water from the cooler, our workout at an end. We have this routine. When we are on the machines, we focus only on our reps. Besides, Baz is not usually a fluent talker.

'Yes. She happy to know you have passport.'

'What about the other girls?'

'She call them.' Baz sounds affronted. I smile at him. 'They come to office Monday. In the morning.'

'What are you doing tomorrow?' True to his Sunni Muslim roots, Sunday is more often than not a workday for Baz.

'I think maybe go see cousin of a friend. He knows people now working on farm. Near Peterborough. I think this one is good contact. I think working for similar gang as mine.'

'Are you sure?'

Baz has been working his way through his address book. Relations, friends and contacts: fellow Kurds he hears about who are in the UK, trapped by debt, just like he was. He is desperate for snippets about Samira but terrified about creating ripples. Hence, he's been sniffing around, but cautiously. Too gingerly, in my opinion, but there we are.

'I've been thinking,' I say, and pick my words with care. This is an important conversation, one I can't afford to screw up. 'Perhaps the time has come for me to visit your old gang. They can't connect me with you, not after all this time. Why don't I go and see them? It's time someone had a conversation. The kind that makes people feel obliged to help. Who knows, they might even point us to the person who can tell us something about Samira.'

Baz considers my words but says nothing.

'Come on, Baz, what have you got to lose? You're desperate to find out about your sister. What do you think?'

Baz maintains a stony silence. He rubs sweat off his face with a towel, staring at his cup of water.

'I just want to talk to your old gang bosses. The longer you leave it, the more difficult it becomes.' We both know what I mean by this. The time card is the one weapon I have remaining, the weakness in Baz's argument.

'Maybe,' he says with great reluctance. 'But I come with you.'

'Not to meet them, you won't.'

'I want to see their faces after you visit.'

'It may not be pretty.'

'I'm okay with that.'

I change the subject. 'Meanwhile, I need your help. I have to visit my mother tomorrow. Can you see this cousin of your friend another day? I'd like your help in tracking down a man who might have stolen my mother's money. Grace has his name and mobile number. Would you do that for me?'

'Yes,' he says. 'I speak with Kels.'

I haven't yet mentioned Kels, which is remiss of me. Kels – I think short for Kelly, though I've never been sure – is one of life's troubled yet gifted. Someone who travels the rollercoaster of life enduring more than most. She is both joy and nightmare in one combined package. Bubbly and enthusiastic one moment; mood-dampeningly negative the next. Kels lives close by the office with her caring companion, an Alsatian stray she calls Freds. She too has a troubled past. She lived with a musician for several months. Someone older than her, like about thirty years or more her senior. Into all sorts of weird and unpleasant shit. One day he overdosed on heroin and killed himself. Kels discovered the body. To give her credit, she found out about the charity almost the moment we opened our doors. She walked into reception one day in pieces. Lost and confused, she fell into Grace's welcoming arms. Since then, we seem to have adopted her. Or she us, I am never totally clear which way round it is.

Never one to worry about appearances, Kels has more facial piercings than you'd find in a rivet factory. Last time I saw her, she'd cut her own hair and dyed it dark green. I adore Kels. In return, this unpredictable individual grunts at me occasionally, speaking only in monosyllables whenever she drops by the office. Which happens regularly. She seems drawn to Grace and has a special smile reserved for Baz. I suspect all three of us are the closest thing to friends and family that Kels has. Besides Freds, of course.

Kels's age is a mystery. I think she's about thirty, Grace thinks she's younger. Beyond doubt is that Kels has unique talents with anything concerning technology. When she's not playing on her game console, Freds at her feet, she's writing computer code for some hi-tech gaming business based out of Seattle. From time to time they send her money. Most of this, it would seem, is spent not so much on living but more on funding an expensive taste in the very latest, high-spec computers and software.

Grace has allocated her a coffee mug all her own. That fact, more than anything else I could do or say, makes her one of us. Kels, plus mug of coffee, is frequently to be found adorning the run-down sofa that sits in our reception. Freds will be nestled in beside her, drooling. This smart canine has long since known about Grace's fondness for the biscuit tin. In return for our hospitality, Kels is often on hand and willing to help where we need it. Usually, it's technical questions: the more challenging, the better.

When I get home, I call Inés before taking a shower.

'How was your day?'

'Not as good as last night. Not by a long way. Anyway, shopping with a teenager is never straightforward. What've you been up to?'

'This and that. I'm actually just back from the gym. Wondering what you were doing this evening, to be honest.'

'I promised to take Jess to the cinema. Sunday's looking clear, though.'

'Fancy a trip to the country? I've got to go and see my mother.'

'Where does she live?'

'Outside Cambridge.'

'As long as I won't be in the way.'

'Hardly. I can drive by and pick you up en route. How about ten-ish? That should get us there well before lunch.'

'Sounds perfect.'

9

The village of Bottisham lies to the north and east of Cambridge. On a Sunday morning, the traffic out of London is light, the journey taking about an hour. This is arable farm country, and most of the wheat crops have already been harvested. Circular bales of straw wrapped in green protective plastic lie scattered across barren stubble fields. I prefer the old, rectangular variety. Maybe I'm showing my age.

Inés is good company. We talk about everything and nothing. She makes me smile. She even laughs at my jokes. Occasionally. Somewhere along the way, she tells me she's been thinking about my offer, to help each other. In her case, by giving me some names. She's still undecided, she tells me. She'd have to break a few office rules – a line in the sand she's not at all happy about crossing.

'It's up to you.' I glance across at her whilst navigating the car around a gentle bend on the dual carriageway. 'There could be a way. Where you gave me what I wanted without breaking any rules.'

'Such as?'

'Say you had to work at home. You know, you've got the gas man coming to fit a new boiler. You bring a few files from the office, leave them scattered around the kitchen table. One or two might just have a few names inside. I call by your house unexpectedly. You offer me a coffee and head off to fill the French press. You wouldn't have told me anything. Plus, you'd never know if I'd sneaked a look inside any of the files.'

'You're devious, Ricky Baxter.'

'Not so much devious as determined.'

'I'll think about it.'

My mother has aged since I'd last seen her at the hospital all those months ago. We hug for several seconds on the doorstep, and I can feel her tears on my cheek. Bringing Inés turns out to have been a genius idea. Any mood of recrimination, any temptation to revisit lost arguments: these dissipate in the presence of Inés. Besides, my mother has other worries on her mind.

'Look at you, Ricky,' she says, holding both my arms in hers. 'You've been to the gym. More like your father every day. He'd have been proud.'

Whether this resemblance is real, or in her mind's eye, I don't know. My recollection of my father differs from the image that stares back at me in the mirror each morning.

'You look great, too, Mum.' She can sense I'm being polite. She's not only aged but also looks tired. *Emotionally drained* is the term Inés uses later, which about sums it up.

We sit in her drawing-room, and almost immediately we're going back over the same ground we spoke about on the phone. This is mostly for Inés's benefit. Howard, it seems, has been a devious piece of work. He saw the wealthy widow coming and took her for a ride. He moved in with her, and they went on expensive day trips and holidays together. It was only a matter of time before he offered to manage her money. He had been an investment adviser, after all. His words, not mine.

'I don't know how I could have been so stupid. I was so gullible.'

'We all like to see the best in people,' Inés says. I find myself in need of coffee and head off in search of supplies.

'Can you manage, Ricky?'

'I think I can boil a kettle,' I call out.

'You'll find mugs in the cupboard next to the sink.'

I catch snippets of their conversation whilst I'm waiting.

'Tell me about you, dear,' I hear my mother quizzing Inés. 'How long have you two been together?' I try to tune this stuff out, using the time while the kettle boils to have a nosey around. It is not an enormous house. More compact than our old family home.

'What is Ricky doing these days? He and I don't talk as much as we used to. It's all been silly, I realise now.' I find a jar of instant coffee in a cupboard.

'A charity, you say? Well, that's nice. Doing what?'

It's helpful that Inés is softly spoken. All I've been able to hear is my mother's strident voice.

'Helping abused women.' I time my reappearance to perfection, armed with a tray, three mugs and a packet of biscuits.

'Good, you found the biscuit tin. I thought we might go to the pub for lunch. There's not a lot of food in the house. I've been distracted.' My mother looks up at me. A light bulb has switched on. 'Is the charity because of Cath?'

I grab a mug of coffee and take a sip. Peering at my mother over the rim, I nod.

'Then, Ricky, I have to say I'm proud of you.'

Taken aback, I mumble an awkward 'thank you' and offer the biscuits around.

'Let's talk about Howard,' I say. 'We need to find him if we're to stand any chance of recovering your money. I'd like to know more about him. The house he was living in is empty, you say. Are you sure?'

'Positive. I peeked through the windows. All the furniture has gone.'

'Can we see for ourselves?'

'What, today?'

'If you're up to it? How far away are we talking about?'

'It's over towards Newmarket. It wouldn't take us long.'

'When he used to call you, did he ring the house landline or your mobile?'

'Either one. Usually the house number. Sometimes he might text me on my mobile.'

'Any video calls?'

'Never. We haven't been apart much these last few months. Until a few days ago.'

'No final "adieu"? No "parting is such sweet sorrow" message or email?'

'Nothing.'

'Can I look at your mobile phone?'

'Why?'

'I want to see if he ever used a different phone other than his normal mobile when he contacted you.'

'Some messages are private, Ricky.'

'I'm a grown man, Mum. If you want me to find this gold digger, I'll need to poke my nose into bits of your recent history.'

She wanders out to look for her phone, and I glance across at Inés.

'You okay? Not too bored?'

'I'm having a ball. She's lovely, your mum.' She stops talking as footsteps approach.

'Here you are,' my mother says, handing over an old iPhone. 'I've unlocked it. Just don't read any of the texts out loud. I couldn't bear it.'

I scroll through her emails, texts and call history. Howard has been smart enough not to contact my mother using anything other than a single mobile number and email address. The ones she gave me yesterday over the phone. Both of which, according to her, are now not being answered.

'Do you have a picture of him?'

'Not many. He didn't like his photo being taken.'

'Perhaps now we know why,' I say, looking fleetingly at Inés who raises her eyebrows.

'I can find one, if you like. Hand me back the phone, Ricky, can you?' I watch as she scrolls through the device, soon passing it back with a hazy selfie of the two of them walking on a beach. It's not crystal clear and it was taken on a windy day with hair flying here and there. However, it's enough for me. I take my phone out and snap a quick picture to remind me later.

'It was taken when we were in Norfolk, a short while ago,' she starts telling me when I feel my own phone vibrating. It's a text from Baz, the message brief.

Howard's mobile phone is no longer active. What a surprise. By now, he'll be using a different identity altogether.

We pull up outside Howard's former house. It is smaller than what I'd expect for a wealthy former investment adviser. I mention this to my mother.

'He told me he'd been through a very messy divorce. Twice, in fact.'

'Dad always said marriage was the most important investment decision we ever make. Perhaps Howard wasn't so good at managing investments, after all?'

We have hardly got out of the car before noticing an estate agent's signboard. It's a local firm, based in nearby Newmarket.

'That wasn't here two days ago,' my mother pipes up.

Inés and I exchange glances.

'Think they'll be working on a Sunday?'

'It's worth a shot.'

'I'll call them.'

This proves to be a lucky strike. The offices are open until one o'clock, giving us a little over an hour. Ten minutes later, we are parked up outside. The place looks small. I figure one, two members of staff maximum will be working the Sunday shift.

'Now Mum,' I say, in the imperious tone offspring use when trying to boss their parents around. 'If we're to stand any chance of getting your money back, here's what I need you and Inés to do.'

Ten minutes later, we are sitting around a small circular table with Josh, an over-eager junior agent in his early twenties. My mother, after some initial reluctance, is sitting in my folding wheelchair, playing the disabled card. It is an unusual role reversal for her and me. Inés finds our subterfuge amusing. We are each peering at a glossy brochure on the table in front of us. Josh, it would seem, is working on his own this Sunday.

'Are you the potential purchaser, Mrs Baxter?' Josh asks my mother.

'In a manner of speaking. I'm thinking of buying a property for my son, Ricky, and his girlfriend. It seems such a delightful house. We went for a drive past on our way here.'

'It is a fabulous property,' Josh purrs.

'Why is the current owner selling?' I ask.

'It's a sad story,' Josh says, in confiding tones. 'The owner died a while ago. A firm of solicitors in London is handling the sale.'

'Which firm?'

'If you or Mrs Baxter makes an acceptable offer, you'll get all that information in due course. I met the man handling the sale myself. The good news is he's keen to find a buyer quickly. If you like the place and were to make a sensible offer, I am sure he'd be happy to come to a rapid decision.'

Which is when I nudge my mother. It's her moment of glory.

'I'm so sorry to interrupt. I wonder, do you have a toilet I could use? It's just that I've been stuck in the car all morning.'

'Sure,' Josh says, then hesitates. 'You can use – well, there's one out the back if you're able to manage?'

I wink at Inés.

'You stay here with Josh,' I say to Inés. 'I'll deal with Mum. Ask about the garden. Also, I need to know about broadband and stuff like that.'

I unlock the parking brake and wheel my mother clumsily through the small office.

'I'm sure I could cope doing this on my own,' my mother says, playing to the gallery.

As we pass Josh's desk, his desktop computer is still on, the screen active. I nudge the mouse as we pass, to prevent his screen saver from kicking in.

'Here we go. Can you manage?' My mother struggles to her feet and shuffles into the small toilet.

I stand by Josh's desk, watching as Inés works her charms, keeping the agent distracted. She's kind of cute is Inés. She plays with her curly hair. Touches Josh on the forearm a few times. Meanwhile, I pretend to take a call on my mobile. Actually, I'm moving Josh's mouse and scrolling down a spreadsheet to find the property in question. Bingo! I snap a few photos of Josh's screen with my phone before checking the images. The sale is being dealt with by a solicitor called Duncan Murray of Murray & Co. Their address is some PO Box in central London. Most likely an accommodation address. There is an email and mobile phone number, all now captured on my phone. I move the mouse to change the image back to what it was when Josh had left it and call out to my mother.

'Are you finished in there?'

Josh glances across at me, and I shrug. I guess our business with him is about done for the day. Besides, I now need to ask Kels for her help on this one.

10

Once back in the car, there's one particular call I'm keen to make before we set off. I check the photo image on my phone, memorising Duncan Murray's number before pressing the required digits. The call is on loudspeaker by the time the phone at the other end rings.

'Not a word, anyone.' Moments later, the phone is answered.

'Hello?'

'Is that Duncan? It's Mike here, one of Josh's colleagues at the Newmarket estate agents. We haven't spoken before. Is this a good time to talk?'

'Sure. I was about to have lunch, but it can wait.'

My mother is shaking her head in disbelief. She recognises the voice. I raise an eyebrow at her, just to check. She nods, her face lacking any expression or emotion.

'I'm pleased to say we have an offer on the house in Newmarket.'

'Really? That was quick.'

'Yes, and at the asking price, too. A couple, in their thirties, cash buyers both of them and no chain.'

I let the conversation dribble on for about a minute, before hanging up.

'It was Howard?'

'Oh, I'd know that voice anywhere.' My mother sounds dejected.

'The good news is that we're one giant step closer to getting your money back.'

She turns to look at me, her expression puzzled.

'How will you do that, Ricky? How did you even find Howard's number?'

'It's what I do, Mum. It's a side of me you've not seen before. I'm good at this stuff. It's why I started the charity.'

I switch on the ignition, the cool from the air-conditioning welcome. Before driving off, I text Kels. Since the company maintaining the accommodation address will have electronic records, I want her to find Duncan Murray's actual address. Electronic records are, after all, Kels's speciality.

'Take care, my darling.' My mother gives me an enormous hug on the doorstep as we prepare to leave. 'We've both been childish since Cath's death. Me especially, I'm so sorry.' She pauses a moment to wipe away a tear. 'If you come face to face with Howard, please make him realise how his actions have hurt me.'

'Do you know, I think you might even mean that.'

She nods whilst reaching for a handkerchief.

'Do come back and visit soon,' she says, one hand gripping my bicep.

I tell her I will and also promise to call with news as soon as I have any.

Whilst Inés and I drive back to London, Baz is busy checking out a specific property in Muswell Hill, courtesy of information supplied to him by Kels who, it would seem, has lost none of her techie flair. I drop Inés at her house and agree to meet Baz at the office. Inés asks whether I'd like to stay for a drink. It's tempting. If I do, one thing will lead to another, and I'll miss Baz. Instead, Inés and I agree to talk later.

It's not far off our gym hour by the time I arrive at the office. Grace asks about my mother, and I tell her about the outing to the property agents.

'I doubt she was happy being in a wheelchair, Mister Rick.' Grace has this whole-body laugh. Everything shakes and it's infectious.

'There was grumbling at first,' I say, laughing with her. 'That all changed when I pointed out how important it was. If we were to stand any chance of tracking down Howard.'

There's a knock on the door and Baz steps into the room.

'Baz! Come and tell us both what you found.'

Baz leans his forearms against a chair back.

'It's private house. Very smart. Nice neighbours. Expensive.' Baz talks, as ever, in fragments. When he says the word 'expensive', it sounds as if he's being respectful.

'Not a big firm of lawyers, then?'

Baz shakes his head.

'I took lots photos,' he says as if remembering. He digs his phone from his pocket and passes it across for Grace and me to peer at it.

'Number sixty-two.'

There's a large black BMW parked in the drive. Not the Audi convertible my mother had said Howard was using for conjugal visits to

Bottisham. That's no surprise. Assuming he'd been planning the big con, he'd hardly be parking the Audi out the front of his Muswell Hill house for the world to see. I swipe through various photos. The house comprises three floors and has what appears to be a small alleyway down one side.

'Not a terraced house then.' I say this more to myself than Baz, who looks at me nonplussed. 'Is that a small alley down the side of the house?'

'Yes, I looked. Nice garden.'

'Was anybody at home?'

'Maybe,' Baz says vaguely. 'One window open here.' He enlarges one particular photo and points. 'Yes, I think maybe.'

'The two of us should pay him a visit, then.'

'After the gym, right?'

I smile. These days, Baz is becoming even more of a gym junky than me.

It's still broad daylight at seven in the evening when we park up a short distance from the property. Baz and I are both pumped, showered and ready to go. We've discussed the little routine we are planning, and it feels good. First, we check Duncan Murray is our man Howard in disguise. If we have the wrong person and the wrong property, then we must switch to Plan B. Plan B is looking thin, currently. We'll cross that bridge if necessary.

Plan A, however, feels exciting. It's nice to have a project where Baz has a crucial role. I ask him to take the lead for two reasons. One, as an Iraqi with poor English, he's one hundred per cent cast in character for what he's about to do. Two, I don't want to run the risk, however slight, that Howard, if it is him, might recognise me from my mother's family photos. So, I stay in the shadows, across the street from the black BMW, camera phone ready for me to play paparazzo.

Baz approaches the front door, bucket in hand, the turtle wax and some cleaning rags visible. What my mother would have called a chamois leather is slung over one shoulder. He rings the bell and we both wait.

'Hello?' Baz's distinctive voice carries across the street. 'I do very good car wash. Special price first time.'

Remembering the selfie my mother had shown me earlier of her and Howard on the beach, I know we have found our man. Howard, or rather Duncan Murray, is the same person, no question. I'd put him in his early sixties. There's something comical about this pathetic creature. The archetypical con man who's hit the jackpot in the early stages of retirement. Wineglass in hand, he shuffles stiffly on the doorstep, a large pot-belly visible through a cheap mail-order T-shirt. Plan A it is. I ping Baz a brief text to that effect as Murray dismisses the pesky migrant car wash guy with a loud 'no thank you', slamming the door in his face.

The second part of Plan A is almost too easy. Inching my way down the alley beside the house, I spot Murray in the back garden, clambering back onto a recliner. Glass of wine still in one hand and a fat, smouldering cigar in the other. Time to ping Baz another text. To let him know I'm ready.

It's an old con, but it seems to work every time, especially with trusting people who least expect it. As the doorbell rings once again, Murray, swearing, puts down the cigar and takes his wineglass with him to see who it is. Meanwhile, yours truly slips into the house from the rear. I take the precaution of closing and locking the terrace doors behind me. I even draw the curtains. There's little point in the neighbours seeing what might be about to happen.

'Didn't you hear me the first time?' The angry tirade resumes on the doorstep. 'I told you, I don't want a bloody car wash. Get lost. Go away, or I'll call the police. You're a damned nuisance, the lot of you.'

Which is when he senses my presence, turns around and clocks me emerging from the living room. Time stands still for a few seconds. Next thing, he's advancing towards me, about to remonstrate, when he pulls himself up short. His brain has cranked into gear, despite the booze. I'm bigger, younger and fitter than he is. The sound of the front door closing makes him turn around. You can almost hear him asking: *What's the car-wash guy now doing inside my house as well?* Time to put him out of his misery.

'You must be Howard,' I say, in my most polite voice. 'Or perhaps it's Duncan? No matter. I'm Ricky. Edwina's son. She's sent me on this little mercy mission. She'd very much like to have her money back.'

As you might imagine, we are forced to listen to a stream of angry denials and abusive language. After a few seconds of waiting, I feel compelled to step forward and grab him by the nuts, squeezing hard. That shuts him up. More accurately, the onslaught of verbal abuse ceases, replaced by howls of pain. The wine glass drops to the floor and smashes.

'You have a choice,' I say in a low voice, my vice-like grip unflinching. 'We can make this easy and quick, or slow and painful. Your decision.'

When I get no answer, I conclude that a headbutt to the face is what's required to bring this to a swift conclusion. Duly delivered, the sound of splintering nose cartilage echoing in the hallway, Murray sinks to his knees. Which is when Baz steps forward, he and I hauling the dazed, confused and now bloodied pensioner into his darkened living room, a trail of crimson blood smearing the cream carpet in his wake.

I hand Baz some of my new, trusty cable ties and he quickly gets to work. Grace bought a load for me from the hardware store. Rather conveniently, a packet fits snugly inside my jacket pocket. Baz ties Murray to a sturdy wooden chair, one of a number arranged around the glass dining table. He straps each ankle to a chair leg and then both wrists to the wooden uprights behind Murray's back.

'Been planning the big con on my mother for long, Murray?'

'It wasn't a con. I planned to give it all back, I promise.' His pathetic lies only make his guilt worse.

'Spare me the bullshit,' I say, delivering a gentle right hook to his face. The force sends the chair tipping backwards. I feel in familiar territory, a Groundhog Day re-run of the Besim and Tarik show. I look at the pathetic creature lying on the floor. If I had my legs back, I'd be giving him a kicking, there and then.

'It was a big-time con. You spent months planning everything. The rich, lonely widow. You, the wealthy investment adviser with a second or third home near Newmarket. That was dumb. Take a tip from me. Next time, try renting. Much harder to trace a tenant than an owner or landlord.'

'You've got this all wrong,' he bleats. 'Your mother was charming. Is charming, I mean. We were in love.'

I move right up close to him, bending down to peer into his face from close quarters.

'So much in love, you piece of shit, you steal all her money and then disappear. That was how it went down, wasn't it?'

'I was having financial difficulties and simply borrowed the money. I fully intend to pay it all back.'

'Like you were about to change your name back to Howard and go knocking on her door with some flowers, you mean?' I look at Baz. 'Why don't I leave him in your care for a few moments? I want to search the house. Don't be too soft on him.'

In time, I find a laptop and a briefcase in one of the upstairs bedrooms. Inside the case are bank account and brokerage statements, credit cards and a mobile phone. I carry them all down the stairs and back into the darkened room. Baz has, by now, finished heaving Murray's body into an upright position.

'He call your mother a whore.'

Murray's right eye is swollen, bleeding from a cut to the brow.

'Good job it was you who heard that, not me. I might have killed him.'

'First, the money. Maybe we kill him later.' Baz shrugs, as in the old gangster movies. Maybe he's been watching a few, honing his technique. Has the peace-loving, quiet Iraqi I met all those months ago finally disappeared? Whether it's my influence or maybe it's the confidence given by his new physique, the one he hones and refines at the gym each day – who knows? I fleetingly wonder whether Baz might be capable of giving as good as he gets after all.

'So, Murray, we'll need a little co-operation if you're really in the mood to pay my mother's money back.' When I flash him a fake smile, he doesn't react, so I move in closer. 'You will be co-operative?'

'If you untie me, I'm sure we'll be able to work something out.'

'Big mistake, Murray.'

'What's that?'

'I never negotiate.'

'I only asked you to untie me. I'm trying to be helpful.'

'Listen, slimeball. I don't need you to be helpful. We're way beyond all that. I just need you to unlock your electronic banking for me.'

'Go to hell!'

Which is a foolish thing to say since it causes me to punch him hard in the stomach.

'When I mentioned I needed you to be co-operative, it was a statement, not a question. You say you're minded to give all my mother's money back. Let's make it happen, shall we?'

Accessing Murray's online banking records requires not only passwords but also the use of Murray's fingerprint, both to unlock his phone and to allow entry to his bank account. Murray decides to be helpful. In the way a handcuffed man with one eye swollen and blood dripping from his broken nose ever can be. A satisfying pool of red liquid on the glass table in front of him serves as a warning of worse to come for misbehaviour.

After a few wrong turnings and false starts with the fingerprint process, we find ourselves in the money. Literally. A shade under four and a half million pounds in cash, sitting in a sterling deposit account held in Murray's name.

'Any plans to invest any of this?'

Murray ignores my taunt.

'How much money did you steal from my mother?'

Murray seems to prefer silence to any admission of guilt.

'How does north of three million sound? Plus, of course, there were the expensive holidays you took together. The cruises, the first-class airfares. Who paid for these?'

Murray stays faithful to his vow of silence, but the sight of Baz clenching and unclenching a fist causes a rethink.

'She did. Your mother.'

'So, perhaps a figure of three and a half million would be nearer the mark. What do you think?'

Murray blinks, trying with great difficulty to keep his composure. His retirement plan is heading for the rocks. Baz steps forward, but I hold out a restraining arm. We seem to be developing a nice good cop, bad cop double-act. Secretly, I'm delighted.

'I suppose,' is all Murray manages under the circumstances.

'Before damages,' I continue.

'Damages?'

'Sure. The emotional stress caused by your cruelty. These are not trivial amounts of money. Damages of at least half a million seem justified to me, do you agree?'

Despite the question, I don't care what Murray thinks. I have already navigated to the bank's payment screen and entered an amount, reducing the four and a half million balance down to just shy of one hundred pounds. I enter my bank name, number and sort code as the payee and then just need Murray's finger on the mobile phone touchscreen to authorise the payment. I take care not to show Murray the exact amount on the screen. He can enjoy that surprise a little later when he's all by himself and licking his wounds. He can try suing me, if he likes. I don't give a shit.

Who says money doesn't talk?

Samira's Story

Part 1

These days when it happens, I screw my eyes tight shut. Like the seasoned slave I have become, I transport my mind to a different place. I imagine myself floating mid-air above our ramshackle home in Iraq, looking down from above. I pretend to see my mother, sensing her shame and anguish: tears streaming down her face and that mournful, helpless sobbing. In my mind's eye, I can never find my father. Yet his torment hounds me. I know it would tear his soul to shreds to learn the brutality of these unimaginable acts. I wonder, more and more, whether I am losing my mind, such are the ordeals I continue to suffer, day in, day out. Horrors that began one dark and cloudless night somewhere near Turkey's border with Bulgaria.

They smuggled Baz and me out of Iraq in a filthy minivan. We crossed the border into Turkey through little-known dirt tracks in the scrub close to where Syria, Iraq and Turkey all meet. To the east lay impassable mountains, to the west the border with Syria. This was the centre of what might yet become the country of Kurdistan, our homeland that keeps failing to gain its independence. They squashed six of us in the vehicle like chickpeas in a can. I was the only woman. For us Kurds, a draped headscarf is customary. In the heat, I had little choice but to remove it. I felt ashamed and, for the first time, vulnerable. They allowed us one small bag, the rest of the space taken up by plastic soda bottles filled with petrol. Periodically these were emptied into the tank through an opening behind the driver. As a result, the van reeked of fumes. In the oppressive heat, it made us nauseous. We were human cargo in a human chain, our stop-start journey across Turkey causing us to be tossed from one set of minders to another, each new handler more hostile and less pleasant the nearer we got to the border with Europe.

Our fortunes changed for the worse once we were beyond Istanbul. It was after nightfall, and we had stopped for water at a remote station in the middle of nowhere. Our vehicle became surrounded by people. There was a lot of shouting. Next thing, the van's doors were flung open, and all six of us were dragged outside and bundled into different cars. Baz and I kept together, crammed into the back of a battered Mercedes smelling of stale urine and sweat. The driver and one other were in the front, both male and barely older than teenagers. In the rear, I was sandwiched between my brother and a woman in her late twenties, perhaps older. She was in charge, yelling infrequent directions to the youthful driver in a language I didn't recognise. She had cruel, steel-blue eyes and a harsh tongue. Every time Baz or I asked what was happening, she would shout at us to be silent. She spoke to us in English, a language I had learned from watching videos on the internet. Baz's English was less good but, somehow, we muddled through.

We left the carriageway and began weaving our way through dark country roads with no streetlights and little sign of life. The other vehicles had long since gone their separate ways. At one point, we briefly joined another main road, and my heart lifted. I spotted a sign for a town called Hamzabeyli, somewhere I knew from maps to be a crossing point into Bulgaria. My euphoria was short-lived. We quickly turned off again, once more taking tiny back roads. For an age, we bumped along increasingly uneven roads until, at the woman's urgent command, we pulled off onto a dirt track and came to a sudden halt. Silhouetted in the car's headlights was a stone building. Even from the safety of the vehicle, the place felt ominous.

'Crossing borders is dangerous.' The woman grinned, a sneering, sadistic smile. 'Crossing borders is complicated. Very expensive.'

The other two from the car were standing either side of her, looking at the floor, shuffling their feet. Lurking in the shadows were two others who had been waiting for our arrival. These men were older: unshaven and dressed in black. We went inside the building. It might once have been a home, but it had long since been abandoned. The air smelled rank and fetid, as if the only inhabitants these days were vermin. A few worn candles had been lit and placed here and there. In the half-light, I could make out a rickety wooden table and a few packing crates on the dirt floor. Otherwise, there was not a lot else. Remembering these details: the flickering candlelight; the two scruffy men; the filth and stench everywhere; and, worst of all, the unspoken menace that hung in the air. Even now, the memory makes me quake to my very core.

'All money given. This big mistake,' Baz's pleading voice sounded weak and apologetic. Without warning, the woman stepped forward, slapping him across the face. My poor, darling brother. Kind-hearted and always generous, he wouldn't have been able to comprehend such behaviour from a woman. I muffled a scream, and the woman barked orders at the two older men.

'Tie them up.'

Looking back, this was the moment. At every point until then, Baz and I might have believed that we had some semblance of control. Our parents had spent their life savings buying our freedom, or so we thought. Immediately our hands were tied, everything changed. The actions and behaviours of these despicable people were about to brand us in a manner which would alter everything.

This was the moment when Baz and I became enslaved.

Time ceased to function. Events became so hideous, so sadistic and so barbaric that survival instincts compelled me to abandon any concept of reality. Submission took hold. What option did I have? As an innocent and reasonably devout Sunni Muslim, finding grown men staring lustfully at my nakedness was beyond comprehension. I was in shock. When the abuse began, the brutality was unbearable. The only way I found to cope was to transport my mind to a different place. To this day, I continue doing this, the scars from that night so vivid they still haunt me.

Deep down, I know it will never be as bad as that first night. I have convinced myself I am over the worst. That I can cope. That I am coping. Maybe I am deluding myself? Perhaps I have already lost my mind? Dear God, if so, I beg you. Save me from this recurring nightmare. Look after my darling Baz, keep him safe and let me die.

11

The first thing I notice when I open my eyes is Inés lying beside me. She's watching me in the lazy way people do when one partner wakes before the other, staring in what she thinks is silence.

'I thought I could hear you watching,' I say as I come to the surface. Without waiting for her response, I manoeuvre myself off the bed and spider-crawl to the bathroom.

Inés and I caught up again once I was back from Muswell Hill yesterday evening. Once on the phone and again when she appeared on my doorstep a little later, bearing an expensive bottle of wine as a celebratory gift.

'I was being silent. You couldn't possibly have heard a thing.'

'That's what you think,' I say, gargling some mouthwash and returning to the bedroom. 'What time do you need to be at work?'

'It's a Monday,' Inés says. 'Come back to bed. I have a feeling there'll be delays on the Tube this morning. I might just have to be late into the office.'

I'd rung my mother yesterday as soon as I'd got home. I'd checked to make sure the money was in my account before calling. She cried when I told her the news.

'I don't know what to say, Ricky. You're amazing. I've been so stupid these last few months. I don't know what I was doing, I'm so sorry.'

'No amount of money will ever bring Cath back. Besides, it takes two to quarrel, Mum, and you and I are talking again. Who cares?'

'Where's the money right now?'

'I've got it. I cleaned him out. You tell me how much is missing, and I'll wire the funds to you in the morning.'

'Are you going to keep the rest?'

'Not me, it's all going to the charity.'

'Come and see me soon, Ricky. Stay the weekend and bring that girl of yours. I liked her. We should talk some more.'

I agreed to call soon to arrange a visit and rang off.

Usually, I'm a coffee-and-porridge sort of breakfast person. I don't need fancy cereals or anything with sugar in it. In summer, like now, I mix oats with hot water, add a few seeds, grate a bit of apple on top and that's me done until lunchtime. Enough to stop me, most days, raiding Grace's biscuit tin. Inés, it would seem, is a tea-and-toast person. Thankfully, I've some sliced bread in the freezer.

'I've been thinking,' she says at one point, staring at the last corner of toast in her hand. 'Maybe I need a new boiler fitted after all.'

Perhaps it's the remnants of the wine in the system, but I'm slow on the pickup.

'It was your idea, Ricky. I'll give the gas people a call and see if they can come on Wednesday. Then I can work from home.'

The penny is dropping.

'As long as the office lets you bring a few files home,' I say.

'I can't see it would be a problem.'

'Maybe I could find some time to drop round for a coffee during the day?'

'What a neat idea, I'd like that,' She pauses. 'In fact, I'd like that a lot.' We beam at each other. We have crossed a line together. It's our little subterfuge.

'Why the change of heart?'

'It's not a change of heart. It's just as time goes by, the more I get to see the way you work, the more I see how we complement each other. On many levels.'

'You'll help, then? Finding this man, Gregor, and people like him?'

'Put it this way. If we have a file on him in our system, it'll be coming home with me.'

12

I am standing by Grace's desk in the front lobby. It's been two hours since she and I had our early morning catch-up. I sense Grace was a little put out to learn my mother had so rapidly and effortlessly been removed from the client list. Her mood changed, however, when she learned of the Baxter family rapprochement. Grace has always been determined to meet my mother, perhaps now more than ever.

'Have you seen Kels?'

'Not yet. She was in yesterday, whilst you were visiting your mum.'

Which is the precise moment I feel Freds sniffing by my feet. Next thing, Kels appears in his wake.

'Speak of the devil.'

Kels has pulled out the stops in the wardrobe department. The weather outside may be warm and sticky, but Kels sports tatty denim dungarees, rainbow socks and a faded brown sweatshirt bearing the logo of a rock band I've never heard of. Draped around her shoulders is a scruffy leather jacket.

'Hi Ricky,' she says and flumps down on the sofa. 'Did you find your man?'

'We did, thanks to you.'

She shrugs, her piercings in danger of clashing like cymbals. Today, Kels's green-tinged hair has undergone a crimson rinse. It hasn't worked. The resultant mishmash verges on a hideous brown in places.

'I'll get the coffees,' Grace says, walking stiffly towards the small kitchenette down the corridor. 'Do you want one, Mister Rick?'

I decline, instead sitting down beside Kels.

'How's the gaming world?'

'Good. Gamescom is happening soon.'

'Where's that?'

'Germany. Cologne.' Kels's economy of words can make me seem like a blabbermouth.

'Is it a big show?'

'Only the world's biggest.'

'Will you be going?'

'Nah, it's too difficult, what with Freds and everything.'

'We could look after him. I'm sure Grace would be happy to.'

'I'm not that bothered.'

I change tack as Grace returns with Kels's coffee. Freds knows this usually heralds the opening of the biscuit tin. The animal is already on his feet, sniffing hopefully.

'Thanks to you, I recovered all of my mother's money.'

'Good.'

'On a different tack, I was wondering whether you might have time for another project?'

'Depends.'

'I need a mobile traced. I'd like to know where its owner is located.' I want to get a reaction from Kels, but all she gives is a deadpan look. 'A download of recent calls and texts would be amazing.'

'Now that is humongously difficult.'

'I know. But you're the best, Kels. If anyone can find a way, you can. I'll pay you for your time.'

'No, you won't. You'll pay me if I want you to pay. Right this moment, you're in credit. Whose number is it?'

'A man pimping women to seedy nightclub owners. His name's Gregor. I don't have a surname, as yet. He mustn't know we've got his number.'

'I'm not that stupid.' She runs her fingers through the fur on Freds's neck as she thinks about what I've asked. 'Tell you what, let me have a go. I'll see what I can do.' She holds out her hand and I pull out the piece of paper I'd picked up off the kitchen table.

'Don't go scaring the horses.'

Kels tucks the paper inside the back pocket of her dungarees while I head to my desk, Grace in pursuit.

'We had two new cases yesterday,' Grace tells me. 'A Latino, housekeeper to an American banker living in a fancy apartment in Canary Wharf. Her name's Renata. It seems the wife's back in Florida and the husband's started hitting on the maid. In more than one sense of the word, I might add.' I look at her and she gives me the eye-roll. 'Poor girl had bad bruises on her arms and torso.'

'What is it with these people, Grace?'

'I don't get it, Mister Rick. If someone tried to do that to me, I'd be reaching for the bread knife.'

'Sounds like an out-of-hours house call is warranted. Do I need to talk to the woman first?'

'She's coming by later this morning. I thought you ought to meet her.'

'Very good. And the other?'

'The other's more of a domestic issue. Certain parallels with my past life. A Jamaican couple. I don't think you need to get involved.' She studies her hands in her lap as she speaks. 'I think I was of some help.'

'Great job. Well done!' She looks up at me, beaming with pride.

'Why, thank you, Mister Rick.'

It proves to be a busy day. Later that morning, Grace and I meet with Renata. After overcoming some initial reluctance to tell me what's been going on, we eventually agree on a plan. I will come by the apartment later this evening. The plan will have consequences for Renata, but I assure her it's for the best. Not least, her mental and physical well-being. I tell her she's a client and promise we'll look after her. That seems to do the trick.

After lunch, there are female voices in the front reception. I go to investigate and find Grace talking to the two ladies I met in the nightclub changing room on Friday evening. Even allowing for the warm weather, no one could describe either as being overdressed. Skimpy T-shirts, tight shorts and plenty of jewellery is their hot weather off-duty dress code. They see me and come in for a hug. I cast Grace a fleeting glance and see a hint of disapproval on her face.

'Hi ladies, come on in.' I turn to Grace. 'We'll go to the meeting room. Are you joining us?' Grace is already on her feet and walking before replying in the affirmative. I call out to Baz. Soon all five of us are settled into the cramped space Grace and I like to call our conference suite.

'What happened after I left on Friday, ladies?'

It is the dark-haired Estonian, Sofia, who speaks first.

'It was pretty much chaos. Besim was hurt real bad. We were leaving our room when he staggers past, in a lot of pain. So much so, he says nothing to either of us. Next thing, we hear screaming from Tarik's room. Lisandra here,' she says, pointing to her friend, 'went to see. Tarik was all tied up with his dick exposed, howling like a baby.'

'It was a mess,' Lisandra adds. Her voice is softer, the accent better educated. She's the one with platinum blonde dyed hair. I sense Grace disapproves of her. 'Sofia and I didn't hang around. We went out front, grabbed Eva, the girl on stage, and told her to get her stuff. We all left as soon as we could.'

'Have you been back since?'

'Not really,' she says, cagily. It feels an odd remark, but I let it pass. 'Thanks to the money you gave us, we should be fine for a few days.'

'Anyone tried to contact you?'

'I got a call.' It is Lisandra once again, still sheepish. 'Someone I didn't recognise. He told me to get back to the club or there'd be trouble.'

'What did you do?'

'Told him to fuck off.' She looks up, pretending to look proud, but my radar is twitching. 'I think I might get a new phone.'

'I've had mine off since Friday night,' Sofia chipped in. 'Apart from one quick call with Alisa over the weekend.'

'You should both get new phones. Is yours still on, Lisandra?'

'Sure.'

'Best to turn it off right now.' While she is fiddling with her phone, I turn to Baz. 'I thought Alisa and Eva were joining us this morning?'

'They told me they were coming.'

'Alisa told me she'd be here,' Sofia pipes up.

'What about Eva? We've still got Alisa's passport, haven't we, Grace?'

'Sure,' she replies, taking a burgundy document from a pile of papers in front of her and waving it around.

Which is the moment we hear some kind of commotion out the front. Male voices shouting for attention. Grace is out of her seat, on her way to find out what's going on. I give Baz the nod too. He follows in Grace's wake. Sofia, Lisandra and I sit in silence, listening. It sounds like two men, their tone aggressive. Grace and Baz will do their best, but I sense this is going to need my help. On a whim, this feels like a moment for the invalid in me to make an appearance.

'Stay here and don't make a sound,' I whisper quietly, moving to the spare wheelchair that sits permanently beside my desk. The two girls watch in fascination as I click off both prostheses and shove them under the desk. Then, grabbing a baseball hat off a peg by the door, I put it on back to front and roll my way out the door. It's my faintly ridiculous outfit, as Grace later calls it. If it makes me look stupid and defenceless, so much the better. Time to face the enemy.

Standing in the front reception area are two men. One I recognise. It's the puny, wiry guy from the nightclub. The other is muscle I haven't seen before. Unlike his buddy, the muscle guy would pass my bouncer credentials test. Over two-fifty pounds, toned body, thick neck, and arms like tree trunks. This would be someone to stay on the right side of.

'That's him,' the puny guy says as soon as he sees me coming towards him. Then he checks his excitement. He's clocked the wheelchair and is re-evaluating.

'What's the problem?' I turn on my fake Zimbabwean accent. It's something I learned from Dad – one of my party pieces. I turn to look at the puny guy. 'Have we met before?'

'Sure. Friday night. You came to the nightclub.' He says this with dwindling conviction. I roll my wheelchair towards him so he can see I have no legs.

'Really? In this condition? I think you must be mistaken.' I roll my eyes at the muscle guy and shrug. It's a look that says *your chum's a dickhead.*

The two men glance at each other, the puny guy confused.

'We're looking for two girls from the nightclub.' It's the muscular guy speaking, his voice deep and authoritative.

'Listen.' It's been a while since I used my fake accent and I enjoy taking it for a spin. 'We run a charity here. In case you hadn't noticed, it's for abused women. We don't discuss our clients. Not with you, not with the police, not with anybody. I don't know what nightclub you're all from, but it's of no interest to me. Do we understand each other?'

'We think they're here.' He's persistent, and I know Grace is bristling. Out of the corner of one eye, I notice she's still on her feet, positioned next to her desk, blocking the path to the conference suite. I can't see, but I know her arms will be crossed in a defiant *get past me if you dare* kind of way.

'And I think I need to repeat myself. We never discuss anything to do with clients. Not with you, not with anybody.'

'Just tell us if they're here or not.' It is the puny guy again. I'm delighted to see Baz step forward, positioning his body so that he's right up close to the man. When Baz feels in the mood to square off, it can, if you're on the receiving end, feel intimidating.

'You not listening?' This is a side of Baz I rarely see, and I'm enjoying this. The puny guy steps back a little.

'We think the two girls are there,' the puny guy says defiantly, nodding behind Grace. His tone, although aggressive, lacks confidence. Definitely a 'fail' in the bouncer practical exam. 'We track their phones, see?' He holds up a device in his hand as if it's incontrovertible proof we're lying.

'You're barking up a different tree, buddy. I don't know what you think I've done, or not done. You have the wrong guy and the wrong place. We run a simple charity. Me and my friends here: we don't do nightclubs. Can you see me dancing in this thing?' I slap my hand on the side of the wheelchair.

'I think we've made a mistake.' It's the muscular guy, his voice deep and growly. He speaks with authority, stepping forward and placing his thick hand on the puny guy's arm. It's a *back off* kind of gesture.

'I hope so, for my sake.' My attempt at lightening the mood doesn't work. As they both head for the door, the puny guy turns for one last shot.

'Listen, smartass. Give the girls a message. Tell them their two friends, Alisa and Eva, say hi.' With that, they both turn and leave the building.

'You must have ruffled a few feathers the other night, Mister Rick.'

We watch as the men get into their Chevy sedan and drive away.

'See?' I say, turning to Baz and thumping the side of the wheelchair with my hand. 'Disability can have its positives.'

'Let me relieve you of this hat-thing right away,' Grace says, snatching the baseball cap off my head.

'I think they take Alisa,' Baz says. 'And the other girl.'

'I should have warned her to keep her mobile turned off. This is my fault.'

'That big guy. He's scary.'

'One of Gregor's men, doubtless. Let's talk to our two visitors, see if they know of a way to find him.'

Hours later, Baz and I are at the end of our daily gym routine, once more by the water cooler. Today, the place isn't busy, the heart-pumping rhythms blasting from the music system playing mainly to idle machines. We've pushed ourselves hard, my stubs feeling uncomfortable in their sockets. This is rarely a good sign.

'The girls tell us nothing, right?'

I nod, lost in thought. Baz is right. The two girls didn't tell us a great deal. Nothing that is about to lead us to Gregor. They had been brought into the country by a trafficker. He was long gone, and they had no way to contact him. They'd been told initially they would get a waitressing job. When nothing materialised, and with their debts beginning to rocket, they had little choice but to take the only job on offer. Working for Tarik and Besim. They were installed in a small apartment in a decrepit tenement block near to Mile End. The rest, as they say, is history.

'Let's hope Kels comes up with something.'

'She will. Kels very good.'

On that score, Baz is right. Kels can be slightly weird but is hugely talented.

'You okay to come with me tomorrow?' I ask. 'We said we'd explore some Lincolnshire farms.'

Baz gives me a reluctant half-smile, half-grimace, but says nothing.

'The clock's ticking, my friend. This quest of yours is only getting more difficult.'

I don't always understand Baz. If our roles had been reversed, I'd have gone knocking down doors several months ago. I think it's because Baz has been a migrant himself. He knows what these people do when they get angry. Me, I most likely wouldn't have given a shit. Maybe that's the problem. Baz does – and he knows the risks. If we make any progress tomorrow, one thing's for sure. I'm going to need to tread carefully. Otherwise, I risk losing someone who's become a dear friend.

'What about Alisa?' Baz asks. 'And the other girl.'

'I thought I'd pay another visit to that nightclub tonight.'

'You think she's there?'

'Maybe. What do you think?'

Baz considers this, then shakes his head.

'Gangs moving people. She somewhere else now.'

'You think? Why?'

'They threaten. Say they do terrible things to her family.' He shrugs, as if a painful memory is nagging. 'Maybe they have photos. These very nasty people. To be sure, they move her. Now her friends can't find.'

'I want to see for myself.'

'You want I come?'

If the muscle guy or the puny bouncer is working the evening shift, I don't need either of them clocking Baz and linking him back to the charity.

'I've got it covered. But thanks for offering.'

There's a different bouncer on the door when I arrive. Maybe the puny guy has the night off. Either that or with Tarik and Besim out of action, perhaps he's been promoted. I find the prospect bizarre, but then again, I'm not running the place.

Today's doorman is a more impressive make and model. He has his eyes on me the whole time I'm making my approach. Unlike the puny guy, this one has a Bluetooth earbud and microphone looped over one ear. I turn on my best Zimbabwean accent for him.

'Evening, my friend. Are you open?'

'Sure,' he says, watching me carefully whilst pulling the door wide.

The place is busier than before. Two girls are on stage and nearly a dozen gawping punters leer at them from tables around the room. There is another group of young lads gathered near the bar. The barman is the same, but he's too busy serving customers to notice me. A professional-looking security guard, one I haven't seen before, is monitoring proceedings whilst patrolling the perimeter of the room. He's sporting a similar Bluetooth earbud and microphone. Not that it's going to be doing him much good with all the music blaring. I spot a new keypad lock on the door out the back, the one leading to the girls' changing room and Tarik's office. The place has had a modest security upgrade. I'm impressed. It's time for me to speak with the replacement security guard.

'Different girls tonight.' I have to shout, given the noise. The man nods, trying his level best not to engage me in conversation. 'In fact, the entire crew seems different from the last time I was here. Apart from the barman.' My father would have been proud of my fake accent. 'Why's that?'

'All change,' is all I get.

'What, even the girls?'

He repeats himself, this time more slowly as if talking to a complete moron.

'I was hoping to see Alisa. She was great last time. She not here either?'

The man stares into the middle distance, trying his best to ignore me whilst at the same time shaking his head. I am tempted to knee him in the nuts like I did to Besim. On balance, this is likely to be counterproductive. It is tempting, I have to admit.

'Is she at a different club now or what?'

This provokes no answer other than an indifferent shrug of the shoulders.

I change tack and go for the jugular.

'What about Besim?'

This gets his attention.

'What the fuck do you want with him?' His eyes widen as he revs up a few notches.

'Is he coming back or is he gone as well?'

'You ask too many fucking questions.'

'Whereas you, my friend,' I say, stepping forward. 'need to polish up your customer relationship skills.' We square off at each other, each sizing up the moment. Ready for action and reaction, not quite sure yet how this might end.

'Besim's gone,' he says eventually. 'Alisa's gone. I don't know the fuck where. Unlike you, I don't ask stupid fucking questions. Now piss off.'

Which is all I need to know.

As I make my way out of the club, I have to hope Kels hasn't lost her touch. Otherwise, Alisa's in trouble. And since she's now a client, I feel more than a little responsible.

Talking of clients, I'd agreed with Renata I would come by the apartment at around nine o'clock. Driving there directly from the nightclub, I check my watch as I park: I am a few minutes late. Thankfully, Renata is waiting by the front entrance, pacing back and forth. When she sees me, her face conveys mixed emotions: mostly fear, but she manages a brave smile.

We ride the lift to the twenty-third floor together.

'You're happy to go ahead with this?'

She nods but says nothing.

'And he's back from work and definitely at home?'

Again, a silent nod.

'Remind me. His name is Dan, is that right? Dan Watson?'

The lift is slowing to a halt as she nods again.

'Remember what I want you to do. Your phone's working?'

She removes a device from her pocket to show me. The battery is fully charged.

'Then lead on. Let's get the show on the road.'

Renata lets me into the apartment and closes the door. It's a duplex penthouse, with views over the Docklands. As she leads me inside, I hear voices in another room: one is male, an American, talking to an American woman on speakerphone.

'That's his wife,' Renata whispers.

I stand by one of the floor-to-ceiling windows, waiting for the call to end. The view is spectacular. Aircraft on their final, steep approach into City airport glide silently past the window. The call finishes and a slender man in his thirties, about five-ten and not long out of the shower, bursts into the living area with a towel around his waist. He's calling out

Renata's name when he does a double-take, seeing me standing there.

'Who the fuck are you?' He turns to Renata, a look of anger flashing over his face. 'Did you let this man in?'

'I came in by myself,' I say before Renata can reply.

'Do I know you?'

'Not that I'm aware.'

'Did I invite you?'

'Not that I'm aware.'

'Then, if you don't leave right away, I'll call the police.'

'Fine by me,' I say, a trifle belligerently, but I'm beyond caring. 'Then we'll be able to show them all of Renata's injuries, shall we? The bruises in particular. They are horrific, but I'm sure you're fully acquainted with those. Maybe we should mention the sexual assaults at the same time. The ones you've been subjecting Renata to whilst your wife's been away.' I have his full attention now, inching closer as I continue speaking. 'It was her you were speaking to on the phone? Did you mention you were dressed in a flimsy towel? That once the daily call ritual was over, you were planning to screw the maid once again. Perhaps beat her up afterwards, just for good measure?' I grab the towel from his waist. Underneath, he's stark bollock-naked. 'Presumably, you get a thrill parading in front of the maid like this, Dan? It's probably like wearing a kilt. It keeps the tackle nicely aired and ready for action, isn't that right?'

I leave the apartment with Renata, having waited for her to pack her suitcases and gather all her belongings. The time is just after ten. To my disappointment, I never had to use a single cable tie. Strong, manly, over-confident Dan Watson soon morphed into a weak, pathetic creature. I get no pleasure from seeing grown men cowering naked on the floor.

Begging me not to tell his wife. Pleading with Renata not to press charges. All the while, Renata capturing all of this on video on her phone. The deal we struck was fair. These deals are never great because some woman had to suffer. However, Renata walked away with five thousand pounds in cash, money taken directly from Dan's safe. Plus, while we watched, Dan wired another ten thousand pounds to Renata's bank account. Finally, I forced him to type out and sign a glowing employment reference. Told him what would happen if he ever bad-mouthed Renata again to anybody, including his wife. Mentioned in graphic detail what I would do to him personally if I ever heard of any more abuse happening to anybody he had dealings with.

I take Renata to a hotel near Tower Bridge, paying for one night's lodgings out of charitable funds. She hugs me, tears in her eyes. We say our goodbyes and I head home. She'll be fine. If need be, Grace will support her in finding a new job.

All in a day's work. It's what we do these days at the charity. It's what I do, and what Grace does. All because of Cath. May she rest in peace. Renata may be sorted. I'm more concerned about Alisa.

As for finding Samira, we haven't even moved off first base.

Samira's Story

Part 2

Before daylight, numb, battered, violated and broken, we were abandoned. Discarded like a dirty rag upon the floor. My knees hunched against my naked body, I felt so dirty, so unclean. At some point, they had untied my hands. It felt such an irrelevance given everything else I'd had to endure. Somewhere close by was Baz, bound and tearful. Beaten physically but also defeated mentally, having been a helpless spectator to the torment and abuse his sister had been subjected to. I could hear him and he could hear me. We whimpered to each other in the dark, the candles long since extinguished. Daylight arrived with a sudden force. I was beyond being worried about my nakedness and hurried to my brother, loosening the rough hessian rope that bound his wrists behind his back. I am not ashamed to say we held each other close for a long while.

Baz struggled at first to get to his feet. No bones were broken, though his arms and legs were livid in places with thick red welts. My physical injuries were internal. I felt raw, defiled and humiliated. Tentatively we explored the house. There was little to discover, although Baz spotted our bags, abandoned in a heap on the track outside the house. There were other pockets of better news. We appeared to be alone, which was an immense relief. I'm not sure either of us could have taken more abuse. A short distance from the house, down a simple dirt path, was a lake. If we could have run, we would have. Instead, we part-walked, part-hobbled to the water's edge, Baz carrying clothes for us both to change into. The water was like balm: clear, cool and soothing. For several long minutes, we lay still in the water, basking in the simple pleasure of feeling soothed and clean once more. Recording fragments of these memories now, I realise if it hadn't been for that lake, for the cleansing, cocooning effect the water had on my body, I'm not sure I would have felt strong enough to face another day.

In time, we dressed and made plans. I knew we weren't far from the border with Bulgaria. If we walked in a northerly direction, it surely had to be possible to cross into Europe? Innocently, we set off. Perhaps we were naïve, but what other option did we have? After slowly, painfully, and at times aimlessly traipsing through the scrub, we heard voices. It was an off-road vehicle stopped on a small section of dirt track. Two men were talking, struggling to mend a puncture. Local Turkish farmers, earning a living working the fields in and around the border area. They took pity on us, looking shocked and appalled to hear of our treatment, vowing, in broken English, to get us across the border into Bulgaria. They would connect us with friends who, they assured us, would find us safe passage to the UK. We told them we had no money, but they waved their hands dismissively.

'Don't worry. When you get to England, you pay later, it's okay.'

'Is crossing border difficult?'

They had finished changing the wheel by this stage. Baz and I were sitting in the back, the vehicle bumping its way along an apology for a road. My question caused both men to laugh.

'Nowadays, impossible. Come, we show.' The driver veered the vehicle down yet another side track. We rattled and rolled along a near-impassable road full of boulders and potholes until we stopped on the brow of a small hill. Gleaming in the distance, stretching left to right as far as the eye could see, was a steel fence. Roll upon roll of razor wire lay strewn along the top, occasional strands glinting in the sunlight.

'Bulgaria!' one of them said and then laughed. 'Old days, we drive there often. See our friends. Now, not possible.' My heart sank. After everything we had been through these last twenty-four hours, this felt as if we had slammed into a brick wall. As if sensing my mood, the driver turned to us both in the back.

'No problem!' he said and winked at me. 'We find a way. Everything okay, I promise.' He then turned the vehicle around, and we set off once more.

We drove mile after mile through yet more meandering back roads, never once seeing another vehicle. The countryside morphed into flat prairies, with fields on both sides brimming with crops. Next thing, we rounded a bend and everything transformed. One moment, we were on our own, the next we were at a junction with what must have been the same main road we passed the night before. All we could see in both directions was a long line of lorries, parked up and waiting to cross the border into Bulgaria. The driver beamed when he saw the look on my face.

'Bulgaria no problem, trust me.'

We crossed the main road, wriggling in between two lorries to get to the other side where a signpost pointed to the village of Hamzabeyli. We eventually came to a halt near a small cluster of houses. The whole place felt barren, a forgotten world. Next to where we had stopped was a nondescript house with a run-down open barn to one side and two grain silos out the back. Inside the barn were several combine harvesters, all different shapes and sizes. The driver switched off the ignition and swivelled around in his seat.

'Bulgarian combine harvester,' he said proudly, pointing to an old red machine with its side panels off. Two men in short-sleeved vests and with grease all over their hands and arms were hard at work.

'Come,' he said, getting out the car and waving us to follow him inside the house. As we were taking our shoes off, his wife appeared and spoke to us in good English.

'You are God's guests. Please feel very welcome.' They offered us Turkish coffees and, out of politeness, we accepted. The woman then disappeared to talk to her husband before returning a while later.

'My husband tells me what happened. These are unforgivable things. On behalf of my country, I'm sorry. Now we try to help. We have good friends in Bulgaria. People who get you to the UK. My husband calls them right away. The plan is dangerous, but not too much. Our Bulgarian farmer friends bring their combine harvesters to Turkey for repair. Here, we can get the parts: sometimes, across the border, it is difficult. This one,' she said, pointing to the red machine, 'will soon be ready to return. We know the border guards. They are happy to help us farmers. For tractors and farm equipment, there is usually no problem. Our drivers take a shortcut to frontier ahead of the lorries. They go through with few delays or investigations. The machines are big, so they make a different route through the border area, avoiding the body scanners that check the lorries for migrants. We can make space inside the grain tank for you. Don't worry, we cover the tank, you will be safe. When it reaches the farm in Bulgaria, our friends will arrange your journey. Okay?' She beamed at us, proud of her language skills.

After all that we had been through, this sounded amazing. I translated what she had said so Baz could understand it, his face breaking into the first smile I had seen for days.

'How much will this cost?' I ask, translating Baz's question for her.

'For now, nothing. Our friends in Bulgaria will explain the arrangements once you arrive.' If I had been a little sharper-minded, I might have challenged this notion of an ill-defined debt to be repaid in the future. Our minds were in a state of mental fog, traumatised by the events of the previous night. I was just keen for us to do whatever it took to get as far away from this dreadful place as quickly as possible.

I would have said yes to almost anything.

13

'You filed that report yet, Sarge?'

'I'm working on it, boss. Bloody paperwork, takes forever.'

'I've just had a look at the case notes from the hospital. Made me wince, reading it.'

'Reminder to self. Must keep dick away from the kettle in future.'

'Poor bugger's going to be lucky to get away without a skin graft.'

'Not to mention the mashed-up nose and face.'

'You're sure there's no video footage from inside the club? Normally, a place like that has cameras everywhere. Bloody perverts, the lot of them.'

'Nothing, boss. We checked the camera system. Whoever it was knew what they were doing. The tapes had been wiped. We have a reasonable description from the two who were attacked, both of them bouncers, both Albanian. The first chap was the one who'd been given the boiling water treatment. The second had also been on the receiving end of our man's attentions. Doesn't sound like he'll be playing the piano in a hurry.'

'What's the motive?'

'That's the odd part. The attacker made away with only a small amount of cash from the office safe. Other than that, it seems not a lot else.'

'Someone after the petty cash, fuelling a drug habit, is that what you think?'

'God knows. Doesn't seem likely. The violence doesn't fit that pattern.'

'A lone nutter, then? Someone with a grudge against the skin business?'

'Could be, who knows?'

'What do you make of the use of cable ties?'

'In what way, sir?'

'Well, it makes it all feel a bit premeditated. How many people wander around carrying cable ties?'

'Maybe they were lying around the manager's office.'

'It's possible. Did you get anything out of the girls working there?'

'Scarpered, the lot of them.'

'Seriously? Have we tried contacting any of them?'

'Tried, sir, not succeeded. The club had no records that we could find telling us either who they were or where they lived. Nothing that either bouncer was going to admit to, at any rate. Not in their condition.'

'Now hang on, they have to have records. Even for pole dancers.'

Both men look at each other in silence for a few seconds. The older man, a DI in his late forties, raises his eyebrows and shrugs. The young sergeant mimics the gesture, a look of resignation on his face.

'Tell me about the "reasonable description" you mentioned,' says the DI.

'White male, about six-two, close to one hundred kilos and works out at a gym.'

'So that narrows it down only to, say, about three or four million people.'

'Give or take.'

'Is there no good news? Any glimmer of a breakthrough that might allow our supervisors to believe we haven't completely lost our basic policing skills?'

'We lifted a set of prints off the kettle. Same ones we found on the door of the office filing cabinet and also the safe. They're not brilliant, but enough to let us run them through the system.'

'And?'

'Not known to us.'

'Checked the entire spectrum, including the military?'

'The complete works. They've all drawn a blank. The dabs at least give us a link positively identifying the person who did this. Something that could be used at a later date, if and when.'

'I'm not holding my breath. What else?'

'I'm looking into whether there might be any street cameras in the club's vicinity. I'm not hopeful. The location is not exactly a crime hotspot.'

'Fair do's. In summary, you're telling me we have a pretty unhelpful description and a few token fingerprints connecting an unknown male to the crime scene, is that right?'

'Correct.'

'Let's not waste any more time on this, Sarge. We've got our work cut out on Blacksmith as it is. This feels like a one-off. I don't feel sorry for nightclub bouncers at the best of times. Usually, they're pimping the girls to punters and doing all sorts of illegal shit. You never heard that from me. I suggest you file your report, put the dabs on file, and if they show up in the future, then we can always reopen the case. Fair enough?'

'Sounds like a plan, boss.'

14

Pick your choice of poor country. The maximum a labourer is likely to earn is the equivalent of about three hundred pounds a month. Absolute tops – and then only if they can find work. Which they usually can't. So, along comes a recruiter from a local gang and offers this person guaranteed work in the UK. The salary offered – not three hundred pounds per month but the same, or more, a week – seems too good to be true. In their rush to sign up, the recruiter skates over the small print. There's a finder's fee to be paid from future wages for getting them the job. That will only hit home later. Accommodation is also promised – again, at a non-negotiable price. They will only learn once they are here that they have little option but to pay rent for housing, which is often unfit for habitation. Plus, there's the cost of arranging transport to the UK, arguably one of the biggest deductions of all. These labourers are desperate. Why wouldn't they say yes? By the time they arrive – often smuggled in – they are trapped and have enormous debts. The recruiters are smart. They know the communities they're recruiting from. If a worker causes problems, the gangs apply pressure on the families back home.

Welcome to the modern-day slave trade.

Whether because of history, our tolerance or the very essence of what might or might not be Britishness: many of these underemployed, low-earning people still crave to come and work in the UK. Where, to their surprise and my perpetual disgust, we treat the arriving Bazs, Samiras and Alisas of this world like shit.

Baz and I are in the car, heading towards the town of Boston in Lincolnshire. This is farming country, the landscape flat and monotonous. The soil is rich, the harvests – whether cereal or vegetable – bountiful and, for an arriving migrant at certain times of the year, there is work. Plenty of work. Often, more than enough to share around. On occasions, at peak times, labour can be scarce. Which creates yet another opportunity for the slave trade to flourish. According to Inés, it's the big farms who use the licensed gangmasters to help organise pickers and harvesters of the right calibre and experience. The smaller farms are the ones sometimes struggling to get what they need. It explains why people like Baz, arriving in debt and seeking work, can end up working one or two of these smallholdings. Living in squalor in hovels barely fit for habitation.

Baz's memory of the area from many months ago is scant. He arrived with little spoken English into a country that felt alien. Even as we drive around, he can hardly remember anything. We've been on the road for almost two hours since leaving London early this morning. As we approach Boston town centre, I'm in need of coffee.

It may share a name with the vibrant city in the US, but this small town has the look and feel of a place lacking energy. Nail bars, tattoo parlours, and vaping shops have muscled into the High Street fringes. Low-priced European food outlets are everywhere. I'm struggling to find a coffee shop until Baz points out one on a street corner near the end of the High Street. I park up on a yellow line and put the blue badge in the windscreen.

We sit huddled at a cheap plastic table drinking coffee from chipped mugs. Or rather, I do, because Baz always drinks tea. His comes in a thick white china pot with a cracked spout that deposits a proportion of its murky-looking contents onto the table when poured. Baz continually fiddles with his teacup, twirling it one way, then back the other. When he looks up and catches me staring at him, his eyes are sad. Today, they have this scared look about them.

'Why we here, Ricky?'

His question catches me off guard. He knows precisely why we're here.

'Trying to find anyone you might recognise from your old gang. Hoping they can lead us to others up the chain. People who might tell us what happened to your sister.'

'How we do this?' He scowls as he speaks. Baz knows my methods. Perhaps he just wants reassurance.

'We track down people running the local operation. They'll be in contact with gang members higher up the chain. They'll take calls, send emails, that kind of thing. We have two options. We lean on them and persuade them to be helpful. Or we find a technological solution. One bad guy's mobile phone may well tell us all we need to know. Remember, we have a secret weapon. Her name's Kels.'

If Baz is soothed by my words, he doesn't show it.

'Any of this feel remotely familiar?' I ask, nodding out the window and wincing. The coffee is a cheap, instant variety and tastes like bitter floor scrapings.

'Maybe.' Baz deploys this worried shrug that he uses a lot. Partly it means *no,* or *I'm not sure*; partly it tells me he's embarrassed at not being able to answer the question properly. Then he smiles, and all is okay once again. 'I live close, I think.'

'Was it totally crap?'

Another shrug, this time no smile.

'Very bad. Always no money. When I start, it was much, much worse. We lived in caravans. Actually on farm. Sometimes five or six in one caravan. We start at five in morning, sometimes earlier, working all day. Later, we move to shared house. Better. Much better.'

'What did you do for food?'

'When living here in house, I use Indian thali restaurant. Maybe we find?' His eyes light up as if remembering. 'Yes, we find, I show you house.'

‘You like Indian food?’

This provokes the worried shrug. The smile arrives as an afterthought.

‘Five pounds, one tray thali. Special price. Food okay, but I don’t that much like.’

‘Did you never cook your own?’

Baz shakes his head.

‘Too tired. Besides, I no cook. Many workers the same, like me. No cooking.’ He stops mid-sentence, staring out the window.

‘That man.’ Baz’s face looks incredulous. ‘Minibus driver!’

An overweight, bald man ambles slowly past the window in front of us.

‘You sure?’

‘Yes!’ His tone suggests he’s affronted by my question.

‘Come on,’ I say, already on my feet, ready to abandon our drinks. ‘Let’s follow and see where he takes us.’

It turns out what is required is not active pursuit, but a gentle stroll. We meander through the back streets just to the north of town. Our man, the minibus driver, is in no hurry. Baz and I follow at a comfortable distance without fear of losing him.

‘Tell me about the minibus.’

‘Each morning he comes to house and takes us working. Same after working, he brings us back.’

‘Always the same man?’

‘Yes. I remember. Very serious, no smiling.’

We meander past a large park edged with red-brick Victorian terraces. Zigzag left and right across a junction next to an imposing courthouse. Again, Victorian red-brick. Then, turning into a narrow residential street lined with houses, about halfway down, the man fumbles in a pocket and slows. The buildings here are much more run-down: cheap double-glazing units; mortar missing in the brickwork; satellite dishes set at wonky heights and angles; and doors that don't match any of the neighbours'. The man unlocks one and disappears inside. There is a battered white minivan parked a short distance along the street.

'Do you recognise the house?'

Baz shakes his head.

'These houses nice. Ours not so good.'

'Time to say hello, don't you think?'

I get the worried shrug, but no smile in response. Seeing this man once again is taking Baz back to memories I sense he'd rather forget.

'Don't worry, I'll do the talking.'

I press the doorbell once, holding the button for several seconds. When this gets no response, I thump on the door loudly with my fist. The door feels solid, the former builder in me guessing it to be medium-density fibreboard topped with plasticised paint. I hear no answer, so I bang again with one hand and press the bell with the other. Eventually, I hear muffled sounds of a toilet flushing and a man's voice yelling that he's coming. Sure enough, moments later, the door opens. The man we saw earlier stands there, looking furious.

'I've never heard such a bloody racket.' His oversized body fills the frame. 'Can't a man have a shit in his own house without being interrupted?'

'You're the minibus guy, right?' I deploy my Zimbabwean accent once again.

'Yes.'

'It's just that my friend here remembers you,' I say, flicking my head in Baz's direction. 'Says you were an excellent driver.' I watch him as he stares at Baz. If he recognises him, he doesn't show it.

'What about it?' His temper is dissipating.

'My friend spotted you in town just now. I wanted to come and meet you in person.'

'Is he an Iraqi?'

'Your point being?' I give him my most righteous expression.

'Nothing. I do a lot of ferrying back and forth with those kinds of people. To the farms and back.'

'That's what I gather.'

'I don't recognise him. There again, I pick up lots of different people. Why are you asking?'

I give him a cock and bull story, the whole nine yards.

'I've inherited a farm in this neck of the woods. It's near the sea, near a place called Butterwick.' I pick a name at random from the map earlier.

'I know Butterwick.'

'I'm sure you do. Anyway, I'm going to need to find some workers and a driver. I thought you might help. Given my friend's recommendation.'

He gives me the once-over, back and forth with the eyes, followed by another glance at Baz for good measure.

'You'd better come in.'

He leads the way down a narrow corridor, his thick arms almost touching the walls on each side. The air smells stale, full of the wrong kind of odours, the sort hinting at poor hygiene and infrequent usage of cleaning products. We end up in a kitchen out the back, Baz and I squeezed around a small, square table. One glance tells me all I need to know. This man is a junk-food and ready meals kind of person: someone who eats from the same dirty plates, cooks in the same pan, and never puts things away.

'Sorry about the mess.' It's the nearest we get to an admission of his poor living habits. 'How can I help?' He stares again at Baz. 'Have we met before? I don't remember.'

'Some time ago, yes,' Baz says in his best English, smiling fleetingly.

'I need to find hard-working, reliable labourers,' I say. 'Pickers and farmhands. Having seen the accounts of the farm, we're going to need a lot of help to turn a profit. When my friend here recognised you, I figured you might know a way to put me in touch with the right people. Given you and your minibus seem so much in demand.'

It's hot and airless in the kitchen. Beads of sweat are quick to appear on the man's face and bald head. Periodically, he brushes them off with a swipe of his hand. Other times, he uses a forearm across the brow.

'For about six months, the work is nonstop,' he tells me. 'Yes, I do a lot of ferrying around. Very early morning pick-ups, afternoon and evening drop-offs, that sort of thing. This is my quiet time of the day. I did all my ferrying earlier. There are people I know who could help. They're not cheap, but they're reliable. You'll have to pay in cash. If that's okay, then I suggest you speak with the person I do most of my running around for. A lady called Tanya.'

'A woman?' He catches the surprise in my tone and laughs.

'Sure. Tough as nails. Runs a tight ship. You don't mess with Tanya, for sure.'

'How do I contact her?'

He grabs a large smartphone from his rear trouser pocket, fiddling around with it before finding what he's looking for.

'Got a pen?' he asks and then reads out a number. I note it down in my phone and call it back to check.

'Is she here in Boston?'

'Yup. Tell her Gordy Lennox referred you.'

'That's you, right?'

The man grunts in the affirmative as he wipes his head and brow once again.

'Very helpful, thanks. Assuming she can find me the people I need, you'll be asked to help ferry them to and from, is that right?'

'That's how it works. You tell her what you want, the pair of you agree a price, she contacts me. Couldn't be easier.'

'Thanks for your time,' I say, standing, keen to be out of this shithole. Baz follows as I lead the way back to the front door.

'You got a problem with your leg?' the man asks as we head down the narrow passageway. Baz's prosthetic foot is more evident than both of mine. I've offered him an upgrade on many occasions, but he's too proud to accept anything more from me.

'It's fine,' is all Baz says as I reach the front door and step out into the welcome fresh air. I turn around as Baz steps past me.

'Thanks, bud,' I say in my best Southern African, comradely manner. I'm keen to deflect more questions. 'Appreciate your help. I'll look out for you in and around Butterwick.' Then, my hand resting on Baz's shoulder, together he and I walk away from the property, back towards the High Street where the car is parked.

'God that place was a shithole,' I mutter as soon as we are out of earshot. 'That man has bad personal hygiene issues that need attending to.'

These days, it takes a lot to surprise me. Perhaps it's middle-aged arrogance, that time of life when we think we have life sorted. Then something happens when you're least expecting it, and the wind disappears from the sails. Like what happened back there. With Gordy Lennox. I guess I wasn't expecting to come across women involved in running the slave trade.

There's no logic to this presumption. I had assumed treating people like shit was a testosterone-driven male thing. Maybe it is, and this is just an anomaly. My brain wants to believe that in the skin business, abuse is a male-led activity. Perhaps not in other walks of life, like agriculture, where gangs providing low-paid and often-mistreated foreign workers could be led by either men or women. But in the skin trade, it would be men running the show for sure. Or have I got this wrong? I find the notion unsettling. It's going to worry me, I know it is. What if – and this is making my head spin – women could be even more cruel and unpleasant than men?

'You very quiet, Ricky,' Baz observes as we march past yet more Victorian terraces on our way back to the car. 'You calling this woman, Tanya?'

I come to a halt and Baz stops beside me. I was grappling with another issue in my mind. What would I have done differently if Besim and Tarik had turned out to be women and not men? Would I have still punched them in the face and poured boiling water over their boobs and bits? I am struggling with answers to these questions, and I'm not comfortable about what it's telling me. It's like I've just seen a flaw in the paradigm.

'Sure,' I say, distracted. 'Let's call her once we get to the car.' We set off again. 'You ever heard of or seen a woman called Tanya?' I ask, trying to distract myself from the uncomfortable questions I'm grappling with.

'No.'

'Did you come across many women running the gangs?'

I can tell by the expression on Baz's face he doesn't like this question.

'Not much,' he says eventually.

'Not so much or not at all?'

'Once. Yes,' he sighs, his face sheepish. 'When crossing Europe. Very bad woman. She do terrible, terrible things. To my sister too.'

'Such as?' I ask, but Baz doesn't answer.

'What was she like, this woman?'

This provokes another worried shrug.

'Bad person,' is all he says. I know him better than to keep pressing. It's a subject I'll have to return to another day.

Up ahead, a traffic warden is examining the disabled badge on the dash. To be fair to her, by the time we arrive she's quick to spot Baz's prosthetic and, with some juggling of my trouser legs, both of mine.

'Nothing wrong, I hope?'

'Nothing at all. You seem to have good mobility, if you don't mind me saying?'

'Thanks. Both me and my friend here: we work at it.'

'I'm sure you do. You have a good day. Take care now,' she said and begins walking away.

'Nice lady,' Baz says. I've not heard him talk about other women before. I look across at him, one eyebrow raised. He smiles, bashful. 'Happy eyes.'

I'm still chuckling about this as we get in the car. In the glove box, I keep a burner charged and ready to go. In my line of business, you never know when one is going to come in handy. Like now. I power it on and, while waiting for it to connect, I look up the number Lennox gave us for Tanya.

Tanya agrees to meet at midday at a place called Fishtoft, a village to the east of Boston. Thirty minutes before noon, I park in a side street, a short distance from the small cricket pavilion, our agreed meeting point. Baz and I leave the car and scout the area, choosing a small bench in a corner of the large village playing field to watch and wait. The bench gives an unrestricted view of the car park beside the pavilion.

At five minutes to noon, a Mercedes saloon rolls into the parking lot. A man is behind the wheel, and sitting next to him is a blonde-haired woman. Hard to say from this distance, but I put her age about the same as mine. She gets out of the car and heads towards the pavilion. She strides out with purpose and an impatient athleticism, her shoulder-length hair bobbing in the breeze behind her. The man stays in the car.

'Recognise the woman?'

Baz shakes his head, but with a frown on his face.

'Maybe, maybe not,' he says, before surprising me. 'The man, definitely.'

'You sure?'

'Yes!' Baz always sounds hurt, as if I might doubt him. 'Many, many times he comes our house. Violent man. He hitting often for being late. Sometimes for no reason.'

'Come on then,' I say, an idea forming. 'Walk directly towards the car and knock on the driver's window. Ignore me, I'll appear in good time. Whatever you do, say nothing, just stand and stare at the guy. With luck, he'll recognise you. When I make a move, help me in whatever way you can.'

I leave Baz and head via a circuitous way around the edge of the playing fields to approach the parked Mercedes from the passenger-side rear. Meanwhile, Baz is striding towards the driver's door as instructed. The time is three minutes to twelve. There will not be a lot of time for this.

Baz doesn't even get to rap on the car window when the man buzzes it down.

'Hey, don't I know you?'

Which is the moment I spring open the rear passenger door, perform an ungainly slide-across manoeuvre courtesy of my two less-than-useful legs, and grab the man around the throat with my right hand. I squeeze hard on his larynx, pinning his head back against the headrest.

'Any sudden moves, I have a gun,' I lie in my best Bulawayo brawl. My other hand is busy grabbing the driver's left wrist, struggling to drag it rearwards. He tries breaking free, but my gym work is paying off. Baz, meanwhile, grabs the man's other hand through the open window and twists it into an armlock. This brings our victim up short. I release a little pressure on his throat and whisper into his ear from behind.

'If you don't want to get hurt, grab the headrest behind you with your left hand. Nice and slow, now.' A deliberate twist on the wrist from Baz forces the man to comply. In seconds, I have one of my trusty cable ties out of my pocket and around his wrist, securing him to the headrest pillar. I slide out of the car. With Baz still holding the man's arm, I tie the other wrist to the door handle.

'Trussed up like a chicken,' I mutter before getting in behind the driver once more and searching his jacket pockets. I discover a mobile phone and a wallet, both of which I transfer to my pocket before scrambling out again. Then I have a rethink and take out the phone.

'What's the pin to unlock the phone?'

The man tries to blank me, so I ask again, my head halfway through the open window. He spits at me but misses. So, I punch him on the nose. Enough to cause a stream of blood to pour down his face.

'You, my friend, have got to learn to be nicer to people,' I say with more than a hint of irony. 'Shall we try again?' This time he mutters a four-digit code through gritted teeth. I swipe the digits on the keypad, and the phone unlocks.

One minute past noon.

'If he makes a sound, punch him in the face again.' I then draw Baz to one side, out of earshot. 'Wait five minutes, then disappear. Meet me at the car, got that?'

Baz nods, and I head to find Tanya.

15

Tanya turns out to be the day's second big surprise. I want to dislike the person I think her to be, but find myself conflicted. This woman possesses a raw energy and a sharp-minded focus I find instantly attractive. Which is unfortunate, given what's just happened to her minder back in the Mercedes. Doubly unfortunate, when you consider the shit folks like her are piling on scores of people like Baz and his sister.

'Tanya?' Today I have returned to my Zimbabwean roots. 'Rich Somers.' Over the phone, I gave a variant of my name. The Somers is from my mother's side of the family. It's a decent half-truth. One, like my fake accent, I use when it's convenient.

She swivels around, standing to shake my hand, her eyes giving me the complete once-over.

'Rich.' This is a statement, not a question. Hers is a firm handshake, businesslike and brusque. My hand is dismissed the instant our two palms are getting to know each other. She speaks with an accent. I have this sudden desire to learn more: where she's from; what makes her tick; and even see how easy it might be to hate her. Which is what I want to do with a passion. Off the bat, I confess to be making little progress on the last objective.

'You don't sound from around these parts.' It's a crass opener, but it's all I can think of.

'Funnily enough, neither do you.' Touché. 'Let me guess. South African.'

'Close,' I say, taking a seat opposite her. 'Actually, I grew up on a farm near Bulawayo.' More half-truths, but there again, I was there for a full two years of my life.

Tanya seems a cool customer. I can feel her piercing blue eyes on me. As I turn to look at her, I notice the short, angular nose, firm jawline and uneven front teeth. She wears no make-up, no jewellery, but has nice lips, something I'm trying hard not to think about. 'How about you?'

'Slovakia. A long time ago, but that's irrelevant. You said you had a farm, Rich. You need some workers. How many and when?' She flicks strands of blonde hair from her eyes as they flutter around her face in the gentle breeze. Her eyebrows are a different colour.

'I have a load of salad vegetables I need harvesting. About ten hectares. My farm manager's an unknown commodity. He says I need a dozen pickers in a week's time. I guess I have to trust him. Are you able to help?'

'I can always help, Rich. Question is, can you pay?'

'What kind of hourly rate?'

When she tells me the number, I try not to fall off my seat. This is one hell of a money-printing operation.

'Where are your workers from?'

'All over, but that doesn't concern you. We take care of visas, permits, everything. You just pay the hourly rate in cash in advance. We bus the workers to you every day. We pay their taxes, feed them lunch, everything. It's all taken care of.' She has this way of licking her bottom lip once she's finished a sentence. I'm finding it distracting.

'Is this all legit?' Her eyes turn to slits when she hears me ask this.

'We run a successful business. We pay our taxes and we treat our staff well. We do everything so that you don't have to worry. Of course, it's legit.' Just as Gordy Lennox said, this one's a tough cookie.

'Okay, how do we proceed?'

'Simple,' she says, licking her lip once again. 'Confirm the details with me by close of business today. Let me know the exact number of people you require, when you need them, what time you want them to start and finish, and where. Also, any specific skills. I'll then tell you how much it'll cost. You mentioned Butterwick, right?'

I nod but say nothing.

'So, the first morning, I'll send Gordy Lennox with your gang. You give the cash to Gordy, you get your workers for a week. Simple as that.' She searches in a pocket for a card and hands one over. It is plain white with her name, Tanya Kocianová, her email and phone number printed on it, nothing else.

'I guess we're about done then,' I say, standing, but Tanya is already on her feet.

'I guess we are.' Without saying goodbye, she's already on her way back to the car. Time for me to head off, fast, in a different direction – before she finds out the state her driver's in.

We're heading south on a dead-straight stretch of road toward Peterborough when my phone rings. The call connects through the car's audio system. It's Kels.

'Hi Kels, thanks for calling back.'

'What's up?'

'I need your help.'

'You already gave me something to do. I'm on it.'

'This is different. I have in my possession one mobile phone and a man's wallet. Let's say they weren't given voluntarily. I'd like them gone over with a fine-tooth comb.'

'How long have you had them?'

'Twenty minutes,' I say, checking my watch, 'give or take.'

'Are you driving?'

'Yes, Baz and I are on our way back to London.'

'Stop the car and take out the phone.' The urgency in Kels's tone makes me obey without further questioning. I spot a sign for a small lay-by up ahead.

'Okay, I'm pulling over. Why the hurry?'

'Can you unlock the phone?'

'Yes,' I say in that sing-song manner all of us use when what we really mean is *I'm not that stupid.*

'Disconnect the phone. Otherwise, someone may wipe it clean remotely.'

'Remind me, how do I do that?'

Kels guides me through the procedure.

'Bring the phone and the wallet to me,' she says once I'm done. 'Don't even think about looking at them.' With that, the line goes dead.

16

It's seven in the evening. I arrive home in need of exercise, having missed out on the gym yet again. Baz had to go on his own, which is rare. After heavy traffic on our way into London, it had been later than planned when we got back to the office. Then we had to wait for Kels to turn up. Finally, Grace presented me with a pile of urgent stuff she told me needed attending to. You'd think running a charity, rather than a commercial enterprise, would mean the admin would be lower. Think again. In some ways, it's worse. There are so many rules and regulations, forms and declarations. What an American friend of mine calls the *administrivia.*

I'm desperate to clear my head and go for a run. It's an excuse to use my favourite prosthetic of all time: carbon fibre blades. These lightweight babies are terrific. They enable me to run faster than I ever could before the accident. They also cause a great reaction from others as you pass them by, looking as alien as they do. Plus, they're fast. It's like being on an electric bike, powering past someone pedalling furiously. The old-tech cyclist might grumble as you overtake them. Secretly, they're hankering after what you've got. You would if you saw me zoom past you on these blades, trust me.

Putting them on can be a bore. First, I have to click out of my ordinary prosthetics and change the socket. What the hell does that mean? Pressing the button on the side of the prosthetic, sliding the foot off, peeling off the rubberised sleeve with the long metal spike at the end, and replacing it with a different sleeve with a padded, rounded end. This then fits snugly to a cup at the top of the blades and that's it, job done. What's the big deal? The big deal is it takes time. I also have to be careful to avoid trapped air in the socket. It might take an able-bodied person two or three minutes to change into their gym kit to go for a run. Me, it takes four or five times as long. All said and done, when I'm locked and loaded with my blades on, they feel amazing.

London is a fabulous city, full of green parks and open spaces. Near to where I live is Mile End Park, a great place to take the blades for a spin. I lock the front door and head out, only realising about fifty metres down the road I've left my phone behind. Cursing, because in my condition I never like to be without some means of communication, I turn back. It's when I'm beside the car, fumbling with my keys, that I remember the burner in the glove box. I unlock the car, grab the phone, switch it on and set the blades in motion once more. Minutes later, I'm entering the long, thin ribbon of familiar parkland just as the sun sinks below the horizon. My usual route is across the narrow width of the park to the towpath beside the Grand Union Canal. This waterway runs north-south along the park's western edge. Blades are a joy. The carbon fibre makes them light, super-springy and comfortable to run on. I was never the world's fastest runner, but with these beauties, I'm in with a fair shot to be as good as the next person.

My mind fills with thoughts of Tanya. Not in an 'I fancy her' way, though I confess the blonde hair, blue eyes and that routine of licking her bottom lip grabbed my attention. I'm struggling with the notion of women running gangs. Why hadn't I seen that possibility coming? It's doing my head in. How I would have dealt with Besim or Tarik if they'd been women? I am no closer to an answer. Twenty minutes later and well into my running stride, it's still bothering me.

I head north towards Hackney and turn into Victoria Park. With the sun going down, the light is fading. My regular routine would be to do two, maybe three circuits of the park, each a couple of miles long. Given the time, I decide this evening to do just the one, taking a circular loop which will bring me back on the last leg alongside Hertford Union Canal, a feeder waterway to the bigger canal I was running past earlier.

I'm two-thirds of the way around, still beating myself up, when the phone in my pocket vibrates. I slow to a standstill and answer the call.

'Hello?' I say, shuffling from side to side on my blades. They may be great to run on but are useless when you're trying to stand still.

'I don't know who the fuck you are, Rich Somers. After what happened to my driver today, you'd better watch out. London parks can be dangerous places to go running. Especially at nightfall.'

With that, the line clicks dead.

I realise immediately I've been stupid. How dumb to be using the same phone I'd called Tanya from earlier. Cursing, I ditch the phone in a nearby waste bin and set off running. But straight away, I come to a grinding halt. Ahead of me, directly blocking my path, is a stocky black African with a lot of biceps showing under a close-fitting white shirt. He, too, has been running. Sweat glistens on his face, and there are blotchy, damp patches visible all over his shirt.

'Are you Rich Somers?' The man's voice is deep, his breathing not yet under control. From his looks, I guess him to be West African. Perhaps Côte d'Ivoire. Or Nigerian, maybe.

'Not me, mate, sorry. You've got the wrong guy.' I deploy my best British accent as I shake my head. If he's looking for a fit and able-bodied white Zimbabwean, I am going to make this difficult.

He grunts in derision.

'I'm not sure I believe you,' he persists. 'I think you and Miss Tanya may be acquainted.'

I'm revising my assessment. His accent suggests he's from a former British colony, not French. Perhaps Nigerian? Grace would be able to tell in a heartbeat.

'I don't know anyone called Tanya.'

'Bad things happened earlier today. To Miss Tanya's driver. Things that are going to be causing someone a lot of difficulty.' He says these last words nice and slow. A second man approaches, running fast and only slowing when he gets near. A younger, fitter, more European version; less stocky, more lean muscle. A physique that comes from hard graft and gym membership. People like him used to work with people like me when I was a brickie. Carrying hods up and down ladders. Usually full of bricks. Sometimes mortar. Either way, it was a good way to keep the body in trim.

'Is this him, Samuel?' he growls. East London accent. A local boy, no mistake.

'He says he's not Somers.'

'Well, let's ring the number she gave us and find out.'

The story until that point would have gone something like this. Tanya urgently wants me found. She knows from the burner I'm no longer in the Fenland farming belt. So, she's had to sub-contract to a London-based crew. People who don't know me, but know about me. I am supposed to be this tough guy from Zimbabwe who beat up her driver. Someone who needs to be taught a lesson. So, an urgent message goes out. Get the bastard. Use the heavy squad, if available. And because the moron's got his phone switched on, it turns out to be child's play to track him down. Surprise, surprise – he's out running in and around Victoria Park in Hackney.

Except.

The penny drops the moment the brickie gets out his phone. Despite the growing darkness, he's seen my legs. He wasn't expecting what he sees and does a double-take. A disabled guy. How does that work? A double amputee, no less. How can this be the person Tanya told them about? He's minus two legs and has these blade things on his feet. It's not a million miles from the dilemma I've been grappling with as I've been running. If Tarik had been a woman, would I have still punched her in the face, tied her up and poured boiling water over her? For the African and the brickie, are they going to beat up a disabled guy just to teach him a lesson? Assuming they've even got the right guy which, on the face of it, doesn't look likely.

There's one way to find out.

'Listen, fellas. I need to get going. You've got the wrong guy.'

I say this whilst bobbing from one leg to another, like a boxer ready to land the first punch. I have little option when standing still on these blades. It's like being on tip-toe the whole time, made worse by the springy nature of the material they are made of. I know from experience this constant twitching combined with the weird blade shape can intimidate. Sure enough, the brickie looks at the African and the African looks at the brickie. This is not the territory they were expecting to be in.

Thinking this would be an opportune moment to make myself scarce, I am about to set off when the brickie steps forward, holding his hand out against my chest to prevent me from moving.

'Where do you think you're going, sunshine?'

His face is up close to mine. The temptation to headbutt him there and then is almost overwhelming. Instead, I say nothing.

'I think we need to check this guy Rich Somers's phone, don't you?' He leers at me, hitting the dial button on his phone. A muted ringtone buzzes from the trash bin several yards behind me. The Nigerian, Samuel, steps around us both and runs to the bin, fumbling around inside before locating the ringing burner.

'Did you put this there?' he says, his white teeth gleaming as he stands in front of me, holding the phone close to my face.

'Honestly?' I say in my most bemused voice. 'Why would I do that, Samuel? Just face the facts. You've got the wrong guy.'

'I tell what we're going to do,' the brickie says, confidence returning and wanting to re-establish control. 'I'm going to text your photo to Tanya. She'll tell us whether we've got the man she thinks is Rich Somers or not.'

He holds up his phone in front of my face, but I'm having none of this. With a swipe of my left hand, I send his phone flying, at the same time springing forward and landing a headbutt to his face. Samuel, surprised, lunges to grab me, but I am already on the move, hearing a satisfying crack of glass as one of my blades steps on the brickie's phone.

When I need to be fast out of the blocks, these new legs of mine can fly. The brickie will take valuable seconds to get off the deck. Even Samuel will struggle to catch me as I get into my stride. I tear along the park's now deserted asphalt path, pounding the surface as if I am sprinting the eight hundred metres for Paralympic glory. I glance fleetingly over my shoulder and smile. The other two are a long way behind. I am conscious of my stumps in the sockets as I run, the intensity of my pace causing more discomfort than usual. Up ahead is a low-level steel fence edging a road that cuts across the park. I leap over the fence, cross the road and over another fence on the other side, spotting thick shrubs near a deserted children's playground close to the roadside. I want to see what the other two will do, so I squat down in amongst the shrubs. The light has almost gone, which makes my hiding place even safer.

I peer across the road and see Samuel arrive first, followed a while later by the other guy. They stop by the roadside, looking left, right, all over the place. I can't hear what they are saying, but they look really pissed off. Samuel pulls out his phone, the glare from the screen lighting his face as he holds the device to his ear. The call over, they remain where they are, waiting for something or somebody. Sure enough, in next to no time, a Mercedes saloon pulls up alongside.

What's interesting is the man who gets out the passenger seat. I know this man. Over two-fifty pounds, toned body, thick neck, and arms like tree trunks. Someone to stay on the right side of. Yesterday, this Mister Muscle was in my office, together with the puny bouncer-in-training from Alisa's nightclub.

From across the street, there are a lot of arms waving. Probably a lot of swearing, too. I can't see, but the brickie guy's face looks mashed up to me. Too bad. The gesticulating continues before, eventually, being replaced by resigned shoulder-shrugging, the signal for everyone to get inside the Mercedes. Once the car has driven away, it's my cue to emerge from the shadows. I take a moment to reflect on what has just gone down.

A piece of shit called Gregor, a man involved in trafficking and abusing girls at various skin joints around the country, uses Mister Muscle as one of his heavies. Mister Muscle, it now appears, is connected to Tanya, a woman running a business hiring out cheap migrant workers to farmers in the Fens. He's either affiliated to Tanya or – and here's the good news – possibly part of the same gang. Tanya, or her predecessor, worked with migrant traffickers across Europe to bring Baz, his sister and many others like them to the UK. Tanya is up to her neck in the human trafficking business. Just like Gregor. The hired muscle links the pair of them. If they're part of the same gang, then the million-dollar question is this: who's pulling the strings? The head honcho. The ultimate gangmaster. By my logic, assuming it's not too premature to contemplate, this is the one person who might be able to tell us what happened to Baz's sister. Assuming she's still alive, that is.

Samira's Story

Part 3

Miraculously, painfully, we crossed into Bulgaria, exactly as our newfound farmer friends had predicted. The border crossing turned out to be so uneventful we almost didn't believe we'd made it. We had lain side by side on an old mattress, tucked inside the main body of the machine and hidden from the sky above. It had been a rough journey, the combine bouncing along many miles of poorly made-up roads: first Turkish, and then Bulgarian. My brother had indeed suffered, given his injuries and bruises. What I remember the most was the dust. It was everywhere, forcing us to cover our noses and mouths. Breathing was a struggle, made worse by the stifling heat. However, we made it.

By the time we arrived at our destination, it was nightfall. There to meet us, as promised, were our new helpers: another farmer and his wife, this time Bulgarian. Neither spoke English, but the woman had cooked a vegetarian moussaka for us to share with them. As we sat in silence in their simple kitchen, eating simple but delicious cooked food for the first time in a while, Baz and I realised how hungry we were. We devoured every scrap, instantly feeling exhausted.

We slept that night on the same mattress we had lain on earlier, nestled in amongst hay bales in a cattle barn beside the house. Everything was basic, but we didn't care, even when using an old bucket as a latrine. When we woke the next morning, the farmer's wife had placed a bowl of apples, bread rolls, a small carafe of fruit juice and some yoghurt and honey on a tray nearby. Equally welcome were the two well-worn hand towels and a square of soap she'd left next to a standpipe at the far end of the barn. Washed, fed and refreshed, we had almost begun to feel human again when we heard a car stopping on the road outside. The peace and calm of our small idyll was about to be shattered.

'Congratulations. You make it to Bulgaria!'

Hearing this voice sent a chill through us both. The dark brown hair, those piercing blue eyes and that sneering look: it was the woman from the previous night. Worse, the two unshaven men who had abused me so severely were standing next to her.

'You should be happy to see us.' She then glanced at Baz and spat on the ground. My stomach was doing somersaults. I felt nauseous, my entire body began shaking. Baz stepped closer, grabbing hold of my hand to reassure me. If the woman saw the panic and confusion on my face, she ignored it.

'I told you, crossing borders is dangerous. Also, very expensive. Bribes have to be paid; farmers compensated. So far, each of you owes two thousand euros.' I let out a gasp. This sum was incomprehensible.

'Relax. You can pay for everything later. When you get to the UK. First, you need to make investments. Transport across Europe is not cheap. For you, maybe another fifteen-hundred euros. Each. Petrol, drivers, the costs of the car: they all add up. Finally, the crossing into the UK. Very dangerous and very complicated. Today, our price is seven thousand euros. Per person – and that's a good price, believe me. One hundred per cent guaranteed. Plus, we promise we won't take you to Calais. The Jungle is gone, but there are still many, many migrants there. People selling paddleboards or places in dinghies for five hundred pounds. Across the English Channel! This is madness. No, we use different methods. We take a lot of risks. There are also many, many costs to be taken care of.' She smiled fleetingly.

'For the pair of you, both young and able to work, it will be no problem. In the UK, we find you work, we find you a place to live. You are lucky – you will earn lots of money. If you want a European passport, we can organise. You can afford the price. However, if you don't work hard or don't do what you're told; if you ever try to run away without paying back the money you owe; trust me, there will be consequences.' She glanced once more at the two men beside her. 'You both know what I mean when I say consequences.'

She dug out her phone and played with it before handing it across for Baz and me to see what was on the screen.

'To make things clear. I wouldn't want there to be any uncertainty.'

On the screen was a picture of our parents, their faces red, swollen and terrified. They were sitting, hands tied behind their backs, staring blankly at the camera. Tears were rolling down their cheeks, a machine gun pointing at them held by someone standing to one side. In an instant, my entire body gave way. I ran to the bucket in the corner and vomited up my breakfast.

'It would be sad if anything happened to either of these two lovely people,' was what I remember her saying from across the room.

For the long drive across Europe, they squashed us into yet another battered old van. Baz and I were wedged side by side, two rows back in the rear: for a time, the woman had the next row to herself; and in the front, one man drove whilst the other slept in the passenger seat. Talking was forbidden. It was still too hot for me to be covered. Although it was just my brother next to me, this inability to cover my face compounded my shame. I felt unclean and uncomfortable the whole time. Every few hours we would stop, the two men switching positions. We headed into Romania, and I remember little other than mile after mile of bland, flat nothingness. Close to Bucharest, we pulled off the motorway and stopped at a nondescript house in the middle of nowhere. Briefly, we were allowed out of the car to stretch our legs. I remember drinking cold water out of paper cups poured from a jug and eating simple pastries and cabbage rolls someone had prepared.

Two men, older than Baz, were waiting to join our little group: one was from Georgia and the other Armenian. They, too, were seeking a new life in the UK. Back in the car, the new arrivals joined the woman in the row in front of us. She was engrossed in taking calls on her phone. Baz and I leant against each other in the rear, our eyes mostly closed. My brain and body were in such a numbed state of shock that sleep was impossible. The flat, monotonous landscape seemed never-ending. First Hungary and then Slovakia, both countries that came and went with little passing interest along the way. The exception was Bratislava. Shortly before reaching the outskirts of the city, the woman announced she would be leaving us.

'I need to visit my mother. She is sick,' she said. 'We will meet again when you get to the UK. If you cause trouble or misbehave, then you will be punished.' She then looked at Baz and me. 'You two are well-placed to remember the punishment your two drivers specialise in.'

We dropped her off somewhere in the city centre. I remember Baz pointing to some steps leading to an old castle as she climbed out of the van, but then she was gone and we were on the move. In no time, we were back on the motorway. Day became night as we drove first into Austria, and then Germany. An unspoken air of malevolence pervaded this next stage of the journey. At one stop, soon after Vienna, the man from Georgia asked for extra time to finish a cigarette. The driver refused, saying he was impatient to get going. There was an argument, a bit of shouting, then both drivers laid into the poor man with fists and boots. After that, no one spoke, not even during the rest stops. As I knew from bitter experience, the two men sharing the driving were amongst life's very worst. At every opportunity, one or the other would make an excuse to bump into me and rub my breasts or fondle me. Baz and the others could only watch, shocked and numbed by the controlling influence these two held over us. The unpleasant atmosphere was palpable. It made me feel like a piece of meat, prodded and poked as if by potential buyers at a cattle market.

Mostly, everyone tried to sleep. I stared into the blank nothingness of the night, watching the hypnotic effect of car headlights as they came and went. Sometimes, Baz and I would whisper words of comfort to each other, but these were snatched moments. The whole time, we had one eye on the driver's rear-view mirror. No one wanted to be caught breaking the rules.

It was the morning of the following day by the time we entered Belgium. Our speed slowed to a crawl in heavy traffic the nearer we got to Brussels. One man upfront became busy with calls and texts on his phone. Baz and I had long since lost our sense of direction. However, we knew Belgium to be near the coast and wondered how they planned for us to get across the infamous English Channel. Back in Iraq, there had been endless stories about people attempting to cross the narrow waters in rubber dinghies, either getting caught and being sent home or, worse, drowning. It was a thought always lurking when we'd first set out on this journey. With this illegal and risky crossing fast approaching, our anxiety levels were rising.

Outside Ghent, our driver pulled off the motorway and into yet another service station, this time stopping beside a small group of people milling on the pavement. It became clear this group had been waiting for us: we were the last remaining few to arrive. We numbered twenty in total, and Baz and I identified a few fellow Kurds. In hushed tones, they explained the plan. We were expecting to make the crossing by ferry, concealed inside a container lorry. This news was helpful and made us feel more at ease. The thought of riding a dinghy across the English Channel, most likely in the dark, had been terrifying.

We were given money for a hot snack and drink, told to make ourselves comfortable, and then instructed to head to the HGV park at the rear of the service station. There, standing next to one of the many refrigerated container lorries, was a man we didn't recognise beckoning us towards him. The container he was standing next to had its rear doors open. On first inspection, it looked full. However, in between neatly stacked cardboard boxes piled high on pallets and wrapped in plastic film, a small passageway to the front was just navigable. They had lashed the pallets to the floor in such a way as to hide the far end from the rear door when it was open. I found climbing inside a struggle, but Baz and the others were there to help. What hit me was the cold. Once everyone had scrambled aboard, the man jumped inside with us and started giving simple instructions in English.

The lorry was heading to Zeebrugge where it would board a ferry across the Channel to a place called Purfleet. I had never heard of Purfleet. I now know it to be in the east of London. When the lorry approached the docks at Zeebrugge, the driver would turn on the refrigeration unit. We would need to do our utmost to keep warm inside the container. Tucked away at the far end was a pile of old, much-used blankets, anoraks, woollen gloves and mittens. The refrigeration was an attempt to fool body scanners designed to spot heat signatures given out by stowaways. Not just those hiding inside the containers either. Often, they picked up lone migrants clinging to the lorry chassis or lying on the roof. By making it super-cold, we were told, it was possible to conceal bodies from some scanners. We had to lie flat on the floor at the far end, cover ourselves in coats and blankets, and not move or make any sound. Finally, it was vital to switch off all mobile phones, and not reconnect them until we had arrived in England.

The man waited for us to take up our positions at the far end of the container. He watched and waited as we sorted out blankets and coats between us and wrapped ourselves up as best we could. Satisfied we were ready, he shuffled his way towards the rear door and jumped to the ground. Finally, as if a gun was being fired, the thick outer door was slammed shut. With a sense of dread, we all heard it being locked, bolted and sealed from the outside.

Then, and only then, did it hit us. Trapped in our human coffin. Buried alive and in complete darkness. Despite the rape and repeated abuse I'd suffered, this somehow felt equally as scary. One of the single most terrifying experiences of my entire life. The jolting thunderclap as the door slammed tight shut. The instantaneous shift from the safety of daylight to complete, total, terrifying blackness. The pervasive stench of soiled coats and old blankets that were now wrapped around our bodies. The constant vibration caused by the tractor unit, made worse by the swaying motion of the trailer on the road. Finally, perhaps most frightening of all, the moment when the refrigeration equipment was switched on: the intense, seeping, bitter, all-pervasive silent cold, arriving from nowhere and trying its level best to turn our blood to ice.

Twenty modern-day slaves were beginning their own special journey to hell.

17

'He sounds Nigerian.' Grace is giving her verdict on the nationality of my would-be attacker, Samuel. 'Most Ghanaians would not be like that. The man's probably from Lagos. They can be the very worst.'

I love Grace's pronouncements. I never knew there was so much rivalry between the two former British colonies. Perhaps there isn't, and I am just hearing Grace's personal bias. She has form. She married a Nigerian. Look how badly that turned out.

'The thing is, the muscle who came here Monday with the puny bouncer from the nightclub – he's an associate of the people in the park yesterday. Whilst he didn't see me yesterday, I saw him. He was in charge. By now, he'll have learned about the man out running with blades on his feet. The same person who headbutted one of his associates. In a rhythm not a million miles from the moves that went down at the club on Friday. Okay, the man he saw in this office on Monday was in a wheelchair, speaking in a Zimbabwean accent. The man in the park yesterday was out running and sounding one hundred per cent British. The muscle guy won't be fooled, though. He'll be putting two and two together. Probably ending up with a number larger than four. This will sound to him like the same guy. So, I figured the muscle is going to come back here. Looking for me. Which explains the extra hired help out front this morning.' I give her my best smile. 'To protect you, in the event I may not always be around when the man next makes a social call.'

Grace is feeling put out. When I got home last night, I called a buddy from the gym. A decent man named Vince O'Leary. Vince is a former boxer, tough as old boots and, currently, down on his luck. For some time, I've been on the lookout for work I could put his way. Seeing the muscle guy on pickup duty in the park yesterday, I figured Grace might appreciate an extra pair of hands over the coming days. Not so much to babysit, but in case they turned the heat up, and the office needed more protection. Vince was happy to help. He's always spoiling for a fight. Grace, however, requires more convincing.

'No one's about to cause trouble on my watch, trust me, Mister Rick.'

'I know that, Grace. You're the very best, no question. Think of Vince as someone here to lend a hand. Just in case you're ever outnumbered.'

Grace, bless her, grunts indignantly.

'I don't think Kels is going to be happy about someone taking up lounging rights on her sofa. What about Freds?'

'Vince can feed Freds a few biscuits. They'll soon become best friends.'

It turns out Vince and Kels get on like a house on fire, much to Grace's chagrin. Talk about opposites attracting. On the one hand, there's Vince, over two hundred and twenty pounds, five foot eleven and arms and thighs like tree trunks; and on the other, there's Kels, stick-thin, light enough to lift in one hand and someone whose idea of a workout is tapping out source code on a keyboard at one-twenty words a minute. Deep down, Vince is a softy. He seems beguiled by Kels's vulnerability. As for Freds, he might just as well be Vince's therapy dog, given the attention my new office security guard is giving this overfed Alsatian.

'What have you got?' Kels is sitting across from me. A pair of worn trainers are perched on the edge of the cheap office furniture. Her hair is still the same messy green and red colour. Today she's chewing gum and has a pair of mirror sunglasses perched on her forehead.

'Sorry, but I can't hack phone records. Telecom companies have systems like Fort Knox. We'd need an insider.'

‘I’m surprised you haven’t got one, Kels.’

‘I never said I hadn’t.’

‘What have you found?’

‘So far? Not a lot.’ She’s got something, I can tell. With Kels, it’s like you have to play this game of Blink. She stares at me, giving her gum a good workout; I continue staring back at her, also saying nothing.

‘One thing.’ There’s a smile on both our faces, now. She may have blinked first, but she has something up her sleeve. ‘This man, Gregor.’

‘Go on.’

‘GPS says he’s currently in the Kilburn area.’

Why does that not surprise me? Kilburn is about as multicultural London as you can get. Seedy nightclub owners living cheek by jowl with wealthy foreign businesspeople.

‘What else?’

‘The phone you gave me yesterday. From this woman’s driver.’

‘Tanya, you mean?’

‘Exactly. It has Gregor on speed dial.’

‘Seriously?’

‘One hundred per cent.’

‘Well, that’s a lucky strike.’ Understatement of the year, more like. It confirms a clear link between the gang trafficking sex workers and the gang who brought Baz and his sister into this country. More to the point, it connects Tanya and Gregor.

‘Pity I didn’t grab Tanya’s phone while I was about it.’

'Maybe you were distracted.' I look up and find her giving me one of her cheeky, coy looks.

'It wasn't like that.'

Kels, economical with words as ever, bats back a disbelieving shrug.

'I'd be interested in what her driver's top ten recent call list looked like, though.'

'Thought you'd ask,' Kels replies and hands me a single sheet of paper. 'Some were in his address book. For those, we have a name. Others are just random numbers at the moment.'

I peer at the list. Tanya, Gordy Lennox, Gregor, then a list of unspecified numbers, including two incoming international calls: one from a country code I recognise as being French and one other.

'Which country has code 421?'

'Slovakia.' Now that I think of it, Tanya had said she was from Slovakia.

'I guess it's too much to hope one of these other numbers might be someone further up the gangland tree.'

'You tell me.'

'How do we find out?'

Another shrug from Kels.

'Maybe we just call them.'

'Pretending to sell double-glazing, you mean? Be serious, Kels.'

'I am serious. You of all people should be able to think up an excuse. Or get Grace. She's good at the charm.'

Kels might have a point. Grace is usually excellent at this sort of thing. As if on cue, there's a knock on the open door to my office.

'I've been talking to Inés,' Grace proclaims loudly, as if addressing a wider audience. 'She wanted me to remind you she's working at home today.' She pauses and peers at me over the rim of her reading glasses. 'Having the boiler fixed, whatever that means. Is this making any sense to you, Mister Rick, because it seems too cryptic for me?'

She leans her bulky frame on the back of a chair for support, giving me the full, beady-eyed treatment. I hold her gaze for a while, then laugh. This is the moment to come clean about the hidden meaning of Inés's message.

'You mean, you're planning a sneaky look at her confidential files?' Grace asks. 'Why, you wily old devil, Mister Rick.'

'Maybe her lot knows about Gregor?' Kels says.

'The same thought had already gone through my mind. It's why I suggested she work from home one day. You know, the new boiler idea.'

'I don't know about you, Kels,' Grace says as if I was no longer in the room, 'but I don't know what on earth Mister Rick is still doing in the office?' She then turns to look me in the eye. 'Go on, go and see Inés. Right now. Be a nice man and take her some flowers. That always works – well, it did for me, not that it happened often. Then, come back later and tell us what you've found.'

I never make it to the car. I get as far as the private car park around the back of our offices, down a short side alley, when I realise my journey to see Inés is about to be disrupted. A black Mercedes saloon is blocking the entrance. Standing in front are two people I recognise. One is Samuel, the man Grace is convinced is from Lagos. The second is the muscle guy who visited here Monday. Both are big, stocky fellas. Well, too bad: so am I. Help and support from Vince might have swung the odds more clearly in my favour. However, seeing these two once again is making me pissed. They are both going down because, make no mistake, these two are not here on a social visit.

‘I thought you were disabled?’ It’s Mister Muscle himself in his deep voice.

‘Your point being?’ I say and hitch the leg of my chinos up a fraction so he can see the reality for himself. Just in time, I remember to use the accent my father taught me all those years ago.

‘I thought you were in a wheelchair.’

‘Sometimes I am, sometimes I’m not. Does it matter?’

He ignores me and turns to the man Grace thinks must be from Lagos.

‘Is this the man you saw in the park yesterday?’

‘I think so, apart from what he has on his feet.’

‘What are you on about?’ I say, my voice indignant. ‘You,’ I say to the muscle guy, stepping forward and pointing, ‘come around here Monday, frightening the hell out of my staff and clients, with some bullshit about me visiting a nightclub. Now you’re back again, with more make-believe stories. You’re doing your level best to intimidate me. I have a good mind to call the police.’

‘Sounds like the same guy,’ Samuel says to the muscle. ‘Only, yesterday he had these blade things on his feet.’

‘In that case,’ the muscle guy says, flexing his biceps and rubbing the knuckles of one hand in another, ‘maybe it’s time to set the score straight.’

With more thought and some cool-headed deliberation, I might have walked away from this. However, the sun is hot, and I am fast becoming pissed off. Worse, these two are keeping me from my private get-together with Inés and her fictitious new boiler. They both start inching towards me, one tentative step at a time. I’m not necessarily the world’s best hand-to-hand combat fighter, but when I’m pumped and ready for a fight, I feel able to give as good as I get. I’m certainly not afraid of being outnumbered.

'What's wrong with you guys?' I say, rooted to the spot. 'You're so weak and puny it needs two of you to take down one disabled person, is that how this works?' They glance at each other, nonplussed. Then the muscle guy gives Samuel an imperceptible nod of the head. It's a 'you go first' signal. The black African now has a clear run at me, confident he has all the backup he's ever going to need.

I watch him approach, holding both hands half-raised up like a boxer. He bobs and weaves, his actions tentative. I remain rooted to the spot, a bemused smile on my face. It's my best *I can't believe you are going to do anything this stupid* look. He's sweating as he inches nearer, his eyes darting, looking for the opportunity to land the opening punch to my face. All the while, he's looking puzzled. By all rights, I should be showing signs of fear or at least some readiness to fight. In me he sees neither. Plus, I'm this disabled guy. I'm guessing he's uncomfortable beating up someone like me. Which, of course, works to my advantage. It'll be taking the edge off his aggression. I let him stew as he inches closer, doing nothing until he's about three metres away.

'We haven't got all day,' the muscle guy calls out. This provokes a reaction, although not the one he or his buddy is expecting. It's the cue for the previously impassive Ricky Baxter to spring into action. The result is some two hundred and twenty pounds of muscle and sinew charging directly at the African. This unexpected onslaught from close quarters causes Samuel to close his eyes, his brain telling him to prepare for a massive collision. Which, sad to say, is not in my game plan. At the last moment, darting deftly to the right, I thrust an elbow up under the man's chin, causing his head to snap back, ready for my follow-through: a back-handed knuckle punch to the nose and face.

With one eye on the muscle, ten metres away and still static, I swivel and deliver a follow-through left-right-left combination punch to the African's solar plexus. His knees buckle and he sinks to the pavement. I turn to face his colleague. Somewhat to my surprise, he is not rushing to help.

'Are you joining in? Or is your buddy the only one getting a workout today?'

Which is when, out of the corner of one eye, I notice Vince emerging from the side alley, hastening towards where Samuel is struggling to his feet.

‘How come you get all the fun, boss?’

‘I was wondering whether you might make an appearance.’ I turn to face the muscle guy. ‘My friend and I are game for a few rounds if you are?’

The man doesn’t reply. Humiliated and angry, he’s smouldering. Coming to terms with the realisation he’s already lost this fight.

‘Any time you want a rematch, we’re happy to meet at the gym. Meanwhile, let’s do each other a favour and call it quits.’ The muscle grunts and beckons for the other guy to come back to the car. I turn to Vince. ‘How come you knew to come and find me?’

‘The dog was going berserk.’

‘Who, Freds?’

‘The same.’

‘One helluva smart Alsatian, that one.’

‘Should’ve brought him out here with me. He would have sorted those two out.’

‘It might have saved my knuckles some aggro.’ I watch Samuel mopping blood from his nose and face with a handkerchief. Faint police sirens are suddenly audible.

Vince gives an apologetic shrug.

‘Sorry, boss, but Grace was insistent. She made the call.’

I turn to our two visitors.

‘Time to get going. We’ll say this was a misunderstanding. Next time, if you come looking for trouble, I promise: one or more of you are going to end up looking like me.’ I raise both trouser hems so they can see my prosthetic legs.

18

'What do you reckon that was all about, Sarge?'

'I'm not sure. There was an altercation in the car park. One neighbour saw the whole thing, start to finish.'

'A gangland bust-up?'

'Not sure. The guy who runs the charity, Ricky Baxter. He told the officer at the scene that one of the two men had turned up at the same place earlier in the week.'

'Did he say why?'

'No, other than it had been a case of mistaken identity.'

'Which, as subsequent events now show, may not have been true. Baxter seems to keep himself in good shape. For someone in his condition, I mean.'

'Yes, the eyewitness says the African never stood a chance. One minute he was approaching Baxter, intending to rain body blows. Next thing: he's lying flat on his back.'

'Baxter was that good?'

'Apparently, boss.'

'You say there was another bruiser at the scene, also working for the charity?'

'A man by the name of O'Leary. A former boxer, now their head of security.'

'Odd. I mean, why does a small charity warrant a head of security, for God's sake?'

'They give support to abused women. I'm guessing here, but it wouldn't be impossible to imagine some of their more vulnerable clients needing protection.'

'You believe that?'

'It's not unreasonable.'

'I'm not convinced. What else did Baxter say?'

'Not a lot. Well, apart from one passing comment the officer noted in his write-up.'

'Go on.'

'The mistaken identity thing earlier in the week. The man turned up convinced Baxter might have visited a certain nightclub recently.'

'Now that is interesting. I don't suppose he mentioned which one?'

'Not according to the report. Baxter said it was a load of hogwash and dismissed the idea point-blank.'

'Could Baxter be our mysterious assailant with the cable ties and hot water torture treatment, I wonder?'

'The thought went through my mind.'

'Well, he'd fit the mould. Apart from the prosthetic legs bit.'

'Didn't stop him winning the fight today, though, now did it?'

'Point well made. Question is, why did they walk away Monday yet today they're back spoiling for a fight?'

'Maybe we'll never know.'

'I'm tempted to say leave it there, Sarge. However, the nightclub business is twitching my radar. We've got Blacksmith simmering at the moment. I'm wondering if this could all be connected.'

'With Blacksmith?'

'Sure. It fits the pattern.'

'Wow. That could bugger things up.'

'Precisely. Why not do a little digging on Baxter and his charity? I'd like to find more about the man and his methods. Don't ask me why. I've got an uncomfortable feeling about where this one might be heading.'

19

It's later than planned when I'm finally sitting down in Inés's kitchen nursing a cold beer. She has pushed the boat out for my arrival, arranging for her daughter to be on a two-day stay over with a friend. Leaving just the two of us alone in her spacious, second-floor apartment. By the time I turn up, sporting yet another set of grazed knuckles, hot and steamy from my encounters in the office car park, Inés is looking radiant. Her naturally frizzy hair is all gleaming from the shower. She's wearing this sexy top and short pants combo, which I'm finding hard to keep my eyes off. There's even beer and pizza laid on for what now is going to be a late lunch for us both.

We've just started to relax when work intervenes and she's busy with yet another call. To keep me occupied as I tuck into still-warm segments of pepperoni and cheese, she nudges one of her work files across the kitchen counter. Before I even lay a finger on it, she gets up, blows a provocative air kiss, winks, then heads to a comfy chair across the room. Ample opportunity for me to nosey around the file without her, in theory, being any the wiser. Grace would be proud of me.

The file proves interesting. It contains confidential papers and internal reports looking at the surge in trafficking in the UK. In particular, the rise of gangs originating in Eastern Europe, now building a footprint here. I don't find it surprising to read about gangland competition. Witness Tanya and me: if I had the cash to splash, she claimed she could find me whatever people I needed. At short notice, too. Implied was the unspoken assertion: why bother looking elsewhere when I can get you everything you need with minimum hassle? The report documents how people trafficking is permeating other areas of illegal economic activity such as prostitution and the county lines drug scene. I don't find this altogether surprising either, given what turns up on Grace's and my doorstep all too often. It's a sad reflection on society. By turning a blind eye to most of it, we're almost condoning this form of modern-day slavery.

One police report near the front catches my eye. The subject is a gang linked to the Serbian mafia with a growing footprint in London, Manchester, Liverpool and East Anglia. According to the report, the gang has been ruthlessly successful in smuggling people across Europe and into the UK. There are also rumours about its unenviable reputation for mistreating workers. Not for no reason is the Serbian mafia renowned for being brutal and unforgiving. The report mentions an undercover police operation underway, codenamed Blacksmith. Blacksmith has been investigating this gang for a few months now. I make a mental note of this and read on.

There is little information about gang members apart from a few blurry surveillance photographs and one or two names. One picture stands out from the others, and not only because it's a woman. It is someone with shoulder-length hair. In the photo, her hair looks dark. In my most recent memory, it was blonde. I also remember the piercing blue eyes. Not to mention the distracting way she occasionally licked that bottom lip.

According to the report, her name is Irina Moravková.

Otherwise known as Tanya. Plus, I know her to be a Kocianová, not a Moravková. In all other respects, it's the same woman. Unless she has an identical twin.

According to the report, this is the woman responsible for smuggling migrants across the Turkish border into Europe. More recently, she's moved to the UK. Nothing I didn't already know, to be fair, other than the different name. Yet, there's more. Moravková / Kocianová is thought to be associated with a wide spectrum of illegal activities: prostitution rings and pop-up brothels; county lines drug gangs in the east of England; various skin joints around the country; and the supply of illegal seasonal workers in the agricultural sector. There's even speculation in one email that she might recently have become the gang leader. The file is sketchy on her whereabouts. On that front, I may yet be one step ahead. I, at least, have a mobile number and an email address.

Next to her picture is a grainy photograph. Someone by the name of Gregory. Bald, puffy-faced and with a scar down one pockmarked cheek. Could this be our man, Gregor? I don't recognise the face but there again, I don't think Gregor or I have yet had the pleasure. There's more. He is rumoured to be the owner of a string of London-based nightclubs and massage parlours. Rumoured because the actual owners lie hidden behind impenetrable layers of limited liability partnerships and offshore companies. I scan through the list of clubs and one catches my eye. A place called the Pink Geranium, its address listed as just off the High Road in Kilburn. Where Kels had said Gregor's phone was located.

Across the room, Inés is trying to wind up her call. Furtively, I take out my phone and snap photos of both people. The file refers to an undercover police operation already underway. If the police are involved undercover, that's probably good news. Except undercover operations usually take time to come to fruition. Ducks invariably need to be lined up before anyone's usually prepared to take action. Rather different to the Ricky Baxter no-nonsense approach. I want to save the Alisas and Samiras of this world before time runs out. Always presuming that for Baz's sister, it's not already too late.

20

'How's the new boiler?' I am trying to keep a straight face as I say this, but I lose it. 'Those fitters didn't hang about. They'd been and gone before you or I knew anything about it. Shame, though.'

'What is?'

'That's one excuse you won't be able to use again in a hurry.'

'I'm sure we can think of others. Anyway, who's saying there won't be other boiler issues that need fixing?'

'I guess.'

'Did I catch you reading through my work papers by any chance, Mr Baxter?'

'Perish the thought.'

'Just as long as you didn't leave greasy pepperoni and cheesy fingerprints everywhere.'

'I was careful.'

'Find anything interesting?'

'The gang connected to the Serbian mafia caught my eye.'

'What about them?'

'One woman in the report. I met her. Yesterday, when Baz and I went for our Fenland day out together.'

'Seriously?'

'One hundred per cent. Only she went by a different name. Plus, she's dyed her hair a different colour. I prefer blondes, I hope you realise?'

I duck as Inés attempts to throw a playful punch.

'Chestnut-brown isn't bad.'

'Be very careful, Ricky Baxter. You met her?'

'I have her business card, along with a mobile phone number and email address.'

'That could be useful.'

'What, you mean you want me to share this?'

'You scratch my back, I'll scratch yours. What else caught your eye?'

'Another mugshot in the file. Someone called Gregory. I was wondering whether this could be Gregor, the man I'm looking for.'

'That's what crossed my mind. It's why I brought that file home.'

'It says he's involved with a club in Kilburn called the Pink Geranium. I had someone track his mobile phone for me. It, too, was in the Kilburn area.'

'You could just be clutching at straws.'

'Or I could be on the right track. There's one way to find out.'

'You're going to visit the club, aren't you?'

'An evening in a girly club might be fun.'

'Can I come?'

'Seriously?'

'Sure. I've never been to such a place. I'm curious.'

'They're not exactly women-friendly places. You might get propositioned.'

'Listen, Ricky. I can handle myself. Besides, a night out at a strip joint is going to be an education.'

'Just don't get in the way if things take a turn for the worse.'

I catch Inés wincing at my battered old VW parked on the pavement outside her house.

'This thing is diesel, right?'

'Correct.'

'I'd have thought something a little greener would have been more appropriate.'

'You didn't complain the other day when we went to Newmarket and back.'

'I criticise no one on a first date.'

'But you are now?'

'If it were me, I'd be driving an electric car. Especially around

London.'

Grace has been nagging me to change cars for the same reasons.

'I'll put it on my to-do list.'

'Why not ask Grace to take care of it? She'd have it sorted in a heartbeat.'

'Have you two been colluding?'

Inés says nothing, climbing in the passenger seat with a grin on her face. I start the engine. It's after seven-thirty in the evening and the rush-hour traffic is easing. In the close confines of the car, I get a strong waft of Inés's scent. I've no idea of the brand, but it smells nice. Whilst negotiating the traffic, we talk about this and that. I say stupid things to make her laugh. From time to time, I catch her playful glances out of the corner of my eye. This is fun and I'm enjoying her company.

Perhaps it's because my mood is up, or my guard is down – but it's only when we are waiting at some lights near Tower Bridge that I notice the motorbikes. Two of them. Hovering five cars behind us in the queue. Both look the same make, model and colour. Both riders are decked out in identical black helmets with opaque visors. There's nothing unusual in that. Most likely couriers. Except I'd seen them both in my rear-view a few miles back. As we'd been crawling through heavy traffic in and around Whitechapel. Whilst I had been distracted by Inés's charms, subconsciously my brain had been sending warning signals. Messages reminding me that bikers rarely hang on cars' tails in heavy traffic. Despite all the speed cameras everywhere, bikers usually overtake vehicles at every opportunity. Especially at moments such as this, when we're stuck in a queue, the traffic lights ahead set to red. That's when I'd expect to see them meandering their way to the front. Particularly couriers. These two behind are not couriers. They are sitting waiting, one foot on the ground to steady the bike, five cars back. It's probably nothing. I try to ignore them, continuing to regale Inés with a story about Grace as the lights turn to green.

We continue around the Tower of London and into Upper Thames Street, a road running parallel with the River Thames along its northern bank. The traffic is flowing, and Inés is busy with a text from her daughter. Another set of lights up ahead turns to amber and I brake to a halt. I am now the first car in the queue. I check the mirror. The bikers are still there, still five cars behind. Surrounding us on both sides are office buildings. This is the edge of the City's business district.

'Everything okay?'

'Marta wants to know whether she can stay over an extra day.'

'That's good, isn't it?'

'I guess.'

'You don't sound convinced.'

'Is it that obvious?'

'It would give us more time together.'

'I'm just not too sure about this other girl she's with. Her parents give her too much freedom.'

'Then say no.'

We are on the move again. This area of London is quiet. No shops, few pedestrians and speed cameras everywhere. The bikes are still on my tail. Another set of lights looms, and, as I approach, they turn to amber. I hit the accelerator, crossing the junction as the lights turn red.

'Practicing for Silverstone?' Inés quips as I check the mirror. 'Lucky there's no red-light camera.'

'I'd have been fine,' I respond, still staring at the rear-view. 'However, the two on my tail wouldn't.'

'What do you mean?' Inés says, swivelling in her seat.

'We've got company. They've been following us for the last ten minutes. Two bikers. They both jumped the red light.'

'Are you sure?'

'Pretty much.'

'Who is it, any ideas?'

'I can take an educated guess.'

'You do have this habit of annoying the wrong people.'

'Welcome to my world.'

I toy with trying to lose them around the back streets of the City, but then have another idea as we pass underneath London Bridge. I make an abrupt left turn into a side street, then curse. I've made a mistake. It's a dead-end. Out of options, I swing into an office loading bay a few metres down the deserted street, catching sight of the bikes making the turn behind me as I disappear from view.

'What's happening?' I don't answer, rapidly making a three-point turn in the cramped confines of the empty loading bay before switching off the engine and climbing out.

'Stay here. Don't leave the car,' I shout, with as much authority and urgency as I can muster.

'What are you doing?' she asks, but I am already heading into the fading light outside.

The bikes have come to a halt a few metres away from the loading bay entrance. Both riders are off their machines and removing their helmets. One is a man I don't recognise. North African, six-two, one-ninety pounds at a guess, bald with a tattoo of a scorpion on his shaved head. The other is a woman. There is something about her that's strangely familiar.

'Why are you following me?' I walk to within a few metres of where they are standing.

'We want to give you a message. Something unambiguous.' It is the woman who speaks, and suddenly I get it. This is the person from Inés's files. Not Tanya. This is Irina. Today, her dark hair is cropped short, like a man's. Not shoulder length, as in the photograph. Or shoulder length as her lookalike, Tanya, wears her blonde locks.

'Irina Moravková – I presume that's your name? What message?'

'You're remarkably well informed for someone close to losing their life, Ricky Baxter.' I notice the steely blue eyes: cold, confident and penetrating.

'What makes you think that? The losing the life bit.' I am watching them both, but it is Scorpion-Head who's bristling. He alternately clenches his fists and then splays his fingers wide.

'You seem determined to poke your nose into our business. Assaulting our people. Treating them like shit, for want of a better phrase.'

'Perhaps that's because you seem determined to treat migrant workers under your control like shit too.' I smile at her glibly. 'For want of a better phrase.'

'Welcome to life in the real world, Ricky. These are people desperate for work. We look after them.'

'Treat them like animals and abuse them along the way. Is that how real life works?' We stare at each other for several seconds. She's quite good-looking, in an unhelpful way. 'You'd better tell me the message. This modern slavery shit makes me sick.'

'Ah yes, the poor disabled brother who's on a personal crusade to atone for what happened to his sister. You're not the only one who's been doing their homework.'

'Can we get to the point?'

'We wouldn't want to keep your date in the car waiting. Her name is Inés, right?'

My natural disposition against hitting women is disappearing rapidly.

'So, here's the message. If you cause any more trouble with our people –' she pauses and smiles '– then I can no longer guarantee the safety of those you seem so committed to care about. The girls who work at some of our clubs, for example. Oh …' She pauses for dramatic effect. 'And I think there's someone called Samira you seem desperate to find. The message, Ricky, is simple. Stop poking your nose into what doesn't concern you. Leave us alone.'

'And if I don't?'

'Then you will not only endanger your own life but also the lives of those nearest and dearest to you. Not just Inés and her lovely daughter, either. It would be sad if anything were to happen to those working at your charity, for instance.'

'I never negotiate.'

'Too bad. I thought you might say that.' She picks up her helmet and puts it back on, at the same time swinging her leg over the saddle to sit astride the bike once more.

'One more thing,' she says, raising her visor.

'Humour me.'

'I'm a businesswoman. Money can solve a lot of life's problems.'

'In what way?'

'Well, one million sterling might bring a halt to certain misunderstandings between the two of us. Two million might secure Samira's freedom.'

'Bullshit.'

'You think?' She switches on the ignition and Scorpion-Head follows her lead.

'I doubt she's even alive.'

'Oh, she's alive. Just a bit fucked up.'

My blood is turning icy cold.

'It's what happens sometimes. A young, pretty migrant with too many debts and not enough money coming in each month.'

I've had enough of this. I charge at her, determined to throw her off her bike, female or not – I'm beyond caring. However, she's one step ahead, having kicked the bike off its stand. The moment she sees me coming, she twists the throttle and accelerates several metres away before stopping once again.

'Think about it, Ricky. A simple business transaction. It's only money. A fact I'm sure your mother is only too well aware of.'

'My mother has got nothing to do with this.'

'Our mothers are an integral part of all our lives.'

'If you say. How do I contact you?'

'You don't. No one does.'

'What, no follow-up conversation after all this bullshit?'

'You're a smart man, Ricky Baxter,' she says, revving the throttle. 'I'm sure you'll find a way.' She flips the visor down and the two bikes tear away.

Inés and I never make it to the Pink Geranium. We spend the evening back at her place licking our wounds, nursing a bottle of red wine and a bowl of spaghetti. It was bad enough finding a woman such as Tanya involved in running a gang. To find another who could pass for her twin also in the mix is more unsettling. Perhaps this really is the person running the show? As of right now, anything seems plausible.

'She knew so much about everything. Not just me. She knew about my mother's money. Not to mention Baz's sister.' I don't have the stomach to tell Inés about Irina knowing about her daughter. I suddenly remember I need to check my bank account. I use my smartphone to log on. Thank the Lord all the money is still there.

'What happens now?'

'We sleep on it. Tomorrow we regroup and think up a plan.'

'You're not about to fork out the money?'

'Are you kidding? As the Americans would say, I'm offence, not defence. I'm not going to be shaken down.' I almost add 'especially not by a woman', but think better of it.

'What about her threats?'

'If they want to play rough, then we'll be ready to respond. How can we find out more about her? Her name and picture were in that file of yours today. Would any of your work colleagues know anything? Where she lives, friends and associates, that sort of thing.'

'You've already met the person you think is her sister. Perhaps that's the place to start.'

'Maybe. However, if you – or the police – had anything more to go on, that would be super helpful.'

'I'll do what I can. Which reminds me. I took a photo earlier. While you and the woman were having your little chat.'

'This was when I told you not to leave the car?'

'Like you, I'm not very good at obeying instructions. Here,' she says, scrolling through her photos. 'I only just remembered to turn off the flash. Look.'

There are a few blurry images, one of which shows the bike's number plate.

'Can you send it to me?'

'Sure,' she says, and a few seconds later I hear the familiar *ping* of a message arriving.

'Got it. Look, I can't have you or Marta caught up in this. This is not your fight.'

'Why should it be?'

'The woman knew all about you. She mentioned your name.'

'What?' This gets her attention. 'How the hell did she know?'

'You tell me. If her threat is serious, it makes you more vulnerable than I'm happy with.'

'Shit, Ricky! Why didn't you tell me earlier?'

'I'm telling you now. She even knew about my mother's money problems.'

'You've got me worried.'

'Don't be. I'll take care of this, I promise. What have you got on over the next few days?'

'Marta goes back to school in ten days. We were planning to take one final mini-break somewhere next week.'

'That might be perfect timing. Could I send Baz to come and keep an eye on you both until then?'

'Baz? He's not going to hurt a fly.'

'Normally, you'd be right. However, on this issue, I think you're wrong. Physically, the man's stronger than he's ever been. He's always down at the gym, pulling weights. If he thinks this is connected to finding his sister, nothing in this world is going to stop him. Believe you me.'

'Okay, if you're sure. I like Baz, he won't get in the way. I'd rather have you here.'

'Me too, but I need to take care of Gregor and his cronies before it's too late.'

'Shouldn't we tell the police?'

I shake my head.

'What will they do? Waste our time, file and ignore. Unless you can find a way to feed the information back into the undercover police investigation the file said was underway.'

'There might be a way. I'll ask around at work in the morning.'

21

'How does this woman know so much?' Grace has this strident manner of speaking when she's indignant. It's after nine in the morning, and everyone is not yet at their best. I didn't sleep that well, plus I had to leave Inés's place early and head back home for a change of clothing.

'I don't know. She knew about Inés and her daughter too.'

'No big deal.' Kels yawns, speaking with a quiet authority. This is early for her. At least she responded to my text asking for an urgent staff get-together. We are milling around the front entrance, waiting for Baz. Freds has taken up his usual position on the sofa. Kels is nursing one of Grace's coffees in her special mug.

'Why's that, Kels?'

'You've been out together. It's public domain stuff.'

I try to shrug this thought off by heading back to my office. To my surprise, I find Vince following me.

'Have you considered having the office swept for bugs?'

'You think someone might be listening?'

'How else did that woman know so much?'

'It's an interesting idea. To be honest, it hadn't crossed my mind. It would explain a lot. How do we check?'

'Let me give someone I know a call. Probably wise in the interim to delay the staff meeting until you know the place is clean. Either that or go someplace else to talk.'

'Okay.'

I need to speak to my mother. Given what Vince has just said, I wander outside to make the call.

'Hi Mum,' I say as soon as she picks up. 'How're things?' She launches into a long diatribe, in the middle of which I am surprised to learn that Howard, or Murray as I now know him, has written a letter of apology.

'He told me he was always going to repay the money. How sorry he was for all the pain and grief he had caused.'

'Bullshit.'

'I know. However, whatever you said to him must have worked.'

'You're not about to kiss and make up?'

'I may have been stupid once, but believe me, I have learned my lesson.'

'Good. I want to send you your money back before I'm tempted to spend any.'

'I don't want most of it, Ricky. Why don't you look after it? Put it in the charity you're involved in.'

'I can't take it all.'

'Send me a million, you keep the rest. If I want any extra, I'll ask you for it in due course.'

'That's super generous, I'm not sure what to say.'

'Your sister would be proud, Ricky.'

'I hope so. Where do you want me to send the money?' She reads out the details, and I jot them down on my phone as we're talking.

'Call me and come and visit soon.'

'I'd like that,' I say, and ring off.

Back at my desk, I log in to my bank and wire the money across to her. With three and a half million left in my account, I transfer another two million to the charity's account and put the rest on deposit.

Back in reception, I tell Grace and Kels the news about the delayed start.

'I got up early for nothing?' Kels stretches and Freds growls at the unwelcome movement.

'I did bring you a coffee,' Vince says, and I notice the two of them exchanging a smile.

I retreat to my office and Grace shuffles after me, holding another of those manila folders of hers.

'Anything turn up yesterday?'

'That Jamaican girl I told you about came back in, wanting more advice.'

'Anything you need to tell me about?'

'Not at the moment. I think things are under control.'

'Nice work. Nothing from Renata?'

'Not a whisper. I guess that son-of-a-bitch banker got his comeuppance.'

'I doubt we'll be hearing from him again. Anyone else drop by?'

'Not particularly. However, I've something I need to show you, Mister Rick.'

'What's that?'

'Best not say out loud.' She's in her usual chair opposite my apology of a desk, looking around to check no one is in earshot. 'Just in case.' She passes the file across the desk. I open it. Inside is a handwritten letter. It's from Alisa. When I read it, my heart sinks.

'We should head outside.' On the way, we bump into Baz who is just arriving. I ask him to join us. We head in silence through the side alley to the car park out the back. It is not so hot today, a welcome breeze in the air.

'Sorry I was late,' Baz smiles. 'Had to see doctor.'

'Everything okay?'

Baz winces and shakes his head. 'My leg. In the heat, not so good. Rubbing.'

'Is it infected?'

'Not yet. Doctor gives me pills. It'll be okay.' It's what all of us amputees fear most: an infected leg stump. If left untreated, it can be deadly.

We stop to let Grace catch up. I tell Baz Vince's thought about the office being bugged. His eyes widen in amazement.

'Really? Like in the films?' He is enthusiastic about the prospect, which I find laughable.

'Grace has shown me a letter from Alisa,' I say to him. 'She's apologised. They have forced her back to work. They were threatening her family back in Latvia.'

'These people are animals, Mister Rick. Is that how they treated you,

Baz?'

'Honestly, yes. All the time. They very bad people.'

'We have to help that girl,' Grace says, shaking her head.

I turn to Baz.

'Listen. On a different matter, Inés and I were in the car yesterday evening. I tell him about being followed and my conversation with the woman, Irina.

Baz listens hard, making sure he's understanding. It's not always easy for him, so I speak with care.

'She also mentioned Samira.' At this, Baz's eyes widen. 'She said her name to test my reaction. She claimed to know we were looking for her. I asked whether Samira was alive and she said yes. We only have her word to go on, but it seems positive.'

'Amazing!' Baz's broad, beaming grin is infectious. Grace steps forward and the two of them embrace. Whether it's the news or because of being squeezed hard, there isn't a dry eye anywhere.

'Anything else?' he asks, wiping his eye with the back of a hand.

So, I tell them the rest.

'Two million, Mister Rick? That's outrageous.'

'You mustn't pay.' Baz's words weren't intended as a question.

'We won't pay. We'll get her back, though, I promise.'

'No paying money,' Baz insists.

'You'd better work on this plan of yours, Mister Rick. If you are not sorting these people out quickly, I just might need to do it myself.'

Bethnal Green is a cosmopolitan neighbourhood with many interesting characters. None more than Vince's friend, Floyd. Floyd arrives within the hour dressed in a navy singlet and scarlet sweatpants, sporting dreadlocks and a knitted black Rasta hat set at a jaunty angle. Like Kels, Floyd is a man of few words but many skills, one of which is operating a handheld gadget he's brought with him. Within five minutes, he is calling Vince and me into our meeting room, more commonly referred to by Grace as 'the conference suite'. Floyd is on the floor, pointing at something under the table, a chipped, second-hand pine piece dominating the room. I hitch up my trouser legs to show off my prostheses.

'Sorry. I don't do a lot of kneeling these days.'

'It's okay,' he says and peels something off the underside of the table, placing it on top for us to look at. It's the size of a matchbox, but about a quarter of the thickness, attached by a strip of double-sided sticky tape. The tough variety that doesn't lose its adhesive qualities.

Floyd puts his fingers to his lips and beckons Vince and me outside.

'You have the choice,' he says in a whisper. 'Either you make a big fuss and the world and his neighbour knows you know about this little beauty. Or –' and he looks at Vince and winks '– you could always hide it away and bring it out when you want to have a little fun.'

After a thorough search, Floyd finds one other identical device behind the sofa in Grace's waiting area. This one, it would appear, is no longer active.

'Voice activated. Too much chatting going on out here,' Vince says, winking, his comment directed at Kels. 'You lot have worn the battery down.' Kels makes a face but says nothing. Floyd announces the office is clean, and I hand over forty pounds in cash for his time and trouble. Vince heads out the door with him. He tells me later he took the active device to the betting shop next door and stuck it underneath one of the counters.

It's midday by the time we regroup in the 'conference suite'. Usually, just saying those words brings a smile to my face. Not this morning. Whether it's a shabby meeting room or a plush conference facility today seems irrelevant: all of us have serious business to attend to. Grace has made everyone yet more coffees, Vince gaining a mug of his own that looks identical to Kels's. Talking of which, Kels's hair is looking unusually tidy, swept to one side and held in place with a grip. An extensive array of hitherto unseen metal piercings has been exposed. I've never seen her like this before. I look across at the two of them as they exchange a private glance, smiling at each other unaware that I'm watching. It's a small gesture that twitches my radar. Even Freds has taken up residence beneath the table by Vince's feet. Every so often, I see his head appear in Vince's lap, another of Grace's biscuits disappearing below the table. Maybe there's more than just some nice chemistry in the air between them both?

The room is abuzz with talk about the bugging devices.

'How did they even get in here?' Grace is saying to no one in particular. 'No one's been in this room all week.'

'Not true,' I remind her. 'On Monday, we had Sofia and Lisandra, remember?'

'I'd forgotten. It wouldn't have been them, though?'

'Seems unlikely.'

I check my watch and call for quiet.

'We've stirred a wasps' nest,' I begin and then give a brief recap.

'Gregor, the woman in Boston, and now the woman you saw yesterday. You think they're connected?' Vince is straight in with the first question, itching to get involved.

'It looks that way.' I glance at Baz to check he's following. He seems unusually spaced out, but he smiles thinly, giving me another half-shrug. Today, it could mean one of so many things: happiness that Samira may be alive; a simple 'thank you' for being there for him; or else the same polite smile he gives everybody. I've known Baz for many months. I still find him hard to fathom.

'Are there any photos?' Kels stares at the table in front of her as she speaks. Although amongst friends, she finds group meetings difficult. Her hair is looking unusually tidy, swept to one side and held in place with a grip. An extensive array of hitherto unseen metal piercings has been exposed.

'The blonde-haired woman in Boston, no. The one I met yesterday, yes. I have a picture on my phone.' It takes a moment to locate the photo snapped from Inés's file. I pass this to Grace, who takes a long, disapproving look before handing it to Baz.

'They're not the same person? Tanya and Irina?' Kels persists.

'No. When I saw the dark-haired woman's picture in the file, I thought Tanya must have dyed her hair and changed her name. Now that I've met her in the flesh, she's not the same person. I'm certain.'

'Twins?'

'Maybe. Similar enough to be family. Might even be sisters, despite the different surnames.' I am about to add something when I notice Baz's face. He's staring at my phone, looking as if he's just seen a ghost.

'What's the matter, Baz?'

'I know this woman.' He mutters as if talking to himself. The room has gone silent, all of us willing him to continue. When he looks up, he has tears in his eyes.

'This woman,' he says, his voice stronger, angrier and more confident with each breath. 'This woman is not good. This woman very, very bad. My sister raped because of her.' His eyes plead with me. 'I was beaten because of her. We take lorry to England and nearly die because of her.' He spits out the words with both passion and venom. The room is on tenterhooks. 'You meet her, Ricky? Yesterday, you meet this woman?' He stares, eyes wide, his emotions barely in check.

'I did.'

'Very, very bad woman. She is evil.' He places undue emphasis on the last syllable, the sound echoing around the room.

'She mentioned Samira. We're getting closer, my friend, we really are.' I glance at Grace, and she gives an approving nod. 'We need a plan. Something clever. Something they won't be expecting. Let's not forget, she's now threatening us. All of us, just to be clear. I am not prepared to take these threats lightly. We need to do our homework. Hence this get-together.' I turn towards Kels. 'Time for some of your magic, Kels. Any bright ideas?'

Kels stares at the table, shaking her head and saying nothing.

'If you let me have my phone back a moment,' I continue, 'I might have something that could help.' I search for the photos of the two bikes and their number plates and pass the phone to Kels. 'See if you can trace these number plates. One belongs to the woman. The other was being ridden by her bodyguard. A man with a shaven head and a scorpion tattoo on top. You can see part of his face at the edge of the picture.'

'Interesting.' Kels looks intrigued. 'I'll see what I can do.'

'I've another idea.'

'What's that, Vince?'

'Let's go after the pimp. You and I should visit the club in Kilburn. I'd happily beat the crap out of Gregor and anyone else who gets in our way. Then we use him as leverage to get to the woman. Lean on the bastard. Let's make their lives uncomfortable, for a change.'

'I think we've already done that. But I like the plan. What do you think, Baz?'

Baz, however, is only half with us. It takes a few moments before he realises I am talking to him.

'Sorry, Ricky.' He smiles then reverts to his serious face. 'This woman. Her mother is in Bratislava.'

'How can you possibly know that?'

'We drive from Turkey to Belgium in minivan. This woman is in minivan until Bratislava. She has sick mother there.'

'In Bratislava?'

'Yes!'

'Interesting.' Tanya had told me she was Slovakian. Maybe they were indeed family, after all. 'Can you remember where, exactly?' I suddenly remember something that Irina had said yesterday. *'Our mothers are an integral part of all our lives.'*

'Bratislava big city. I don't remember. Wait, we stop near castle. On small hill. I remember lots of steps after she leaves minivan.'

'Did you see a house or apartment block?'

'No, we quickly moving again.'

'If you went back, would you remember?'

'Sorry,' he says, this time with a shrug. 'No passport.'

I'd forgotten this crucial bit of information.

'I could go,' Kels announces to the table. 'I have a gaming friend who lives there. She and I could find this woman, no sweat.'

'Seriously?'

'If Grace looks after Freds, sure.' She looks at Baz. 'Come back to my place. We can use Google Maps on the big screen, see if it jogs your memory.'

'Sure,' he says with a croaky voice, visibly in shock.

'Could you get a flight later today?' I say to Kels. 'This might be urgent. Check into a hotel if need be. Grace, would you mind looking after Freds?'

'I'd be delighted,' Grace beams.

'Baz, when you're finished with Kels, I need you to babysit Inés and her daughter, Marta.'

'What is babysitting?'

'Look after them. Protect them, in case someone shows up with bad intentions.'

'Of course.'

I turn to Vince.

'Vince, your idea about visiting the nightclub. I like it.'

'About time. I've been looking forward to a punch-up.'

Samira's Story

Part 4

This time, it felt different. Yes, it was yet another period of extended inactivity, but no longer were there extraneous sounds or movements. No deckhands lashing down lorry wheels. No more lurching from side to side caused by ramps or bends in the road. Nor any swaying motion caused by choppy seas, either. The container was stationary. There wasn't even another engine that could be heard. In the pitch darkness, numbed to the bone by the ever-pervasive cold, our battered bodies were struggling with yet another chilling thought. What if they had abandoned us?

Some considerable while later, when we had almost given up hope, we heard a metal chain at the far end of the container. Next, there was a rattle of bolts. Finally, the rear doors were flung open, the light so intense that none of us could see. For a moment, I thought I might even be dead. Were Allah's two angels, Munkar and Nakir, about to appear, ready to test our Muslim faith? Then it dawned. Against all odds, we might have made it. In that brief, euphoric moment, everyone began wailing and rejoicing.

Our moment of jubilation was short-lived. After staggering out, clutching our meagre possessions, we found ourselves in a lorry loading bay. Two minibuses were parked nearby. Otherwise, it was deserted. As we huddled around, dazed and confused, they sorted us into groups: the fourteen men into one minibus and six women into the other. Baz tried to protest. A man we had never seen before grabbed his arm, yelled at him to shut up, threatening to beat us all if he uttered another word. We were so exhausted from the trauma in the container that this verbal barrage sapped what little remaining energy we had. Neither Baz nor I said anything further. Which is to my eternal regret, since these were to be our last few precious moments together. Once aboard our minibus, I tried peering through the window to see if I could wave at him in the other vehicle. It was not to be. No sooner than I thought I'd spotted his face than the vehicle he was in set off, never to be seen again.

We drove for a long time, stopping only once for petrol and to allow each of us to use the basic facilities on offer. I used copious amounts of liquid soap from a plastic dispenser to wash my hands and face. Try as I might, I couldn't get rid of the stench of soiled coats and blankets from my nostrils. The whole journey, the nightmare at the Turkish border, had left me feeling unclean. It is a feeling that has never left me, even to this day. Back on the minibus, I tried sleeping but was worried about Baz and where he was being sent to. Whenever I convinced myself he might be fine and able to cope, my thoughts turned to my parents and my nightmares took on a different form altogether.

It was late in the day by the time we arrived at our destination. Everything was unfamiliar – the buildings, the shops, the people, the way they all dressed, the cars, the amount of traffic, even the place names and street signs. I had no comprehension about whether the house we were about to enter was someone's home – or what it was. Or how typical it was of the way people lived here compared to what I had been used to in Iraq. We were soon to find out. Any hopes our nightmare of a journey might be over were dispelled the moment all six were inside and the door closed behind us. Our driver turned out to be our guide.

The place was hot, airless and musty. They took us into one room, about four metres by three. There were six grubby mattresses on the floor piled on top of each other and several sweat-stained pillows. This was to be our bedroom. Opposite was a larger room, with two old sofas and a few bean bags scattered. Down the hall was a filthy toilet, looking as if it had never been cleaned. Out the back was a kitchen, equally dirty. On the upper floor, up a set of rickety stairs, were more rooms: a bath and shower room, which had cheap lino flooring and walls with several tiles chipped or missing; another disgusting toilet; and a bedroom, similar in size to the one downstairs but partitioned into three small cubicles. Each cubicle contained a simple cast iron bed and a thick curtain on an overhead rail, acting as a door. We were forbidden from using this room since, we were told, more guests would be arriving. The driver collected two plastic bin liners from the back of the minivan. One contained basic cleaning products plus sheets and towels that looked clean but hadn't been folded with any care. Inside the other were a few food items and some toiletries. Our job for the evening was to get the house neat and tidy, ready for first thing in the morning when we would be taken to start our first day's work. The driver showed us an old vacuum cleaner, mop and bucket in a small cupboard under the stairs and then left us to it.

We all mucked in, trying our best to remove years of dirt and filth. It took forever before we had made a discernible difference. Well beyond midnight, we halted, all of us too tired to contemplate food. I lay down on a mattress and fell into a troubled sleep.

Next morning, we were awoken by the sound of people at the front door. There were two of them. One, our new driver, stood like a sentry until it was time to depart. The other was a young female doctor, there to give each of us a thorough examination. One by one we headed upstairs, where we were told to strip naked, lie on one of the cast iron beds and allow ourselves to be subjected to the most thorough medical review any of us had ever experienced. I particularly remember her hands. They were rough and uncaring, the woman oblivious to the shame such an intrusive and brutal examination was causing. Various swabs and blood samples were taken before we were dismissed and told to dress and finish eating breakfast. By nine, we were back in another minivan, this time heading to a large industrial complex. Our job for the next few days was the same for us all. Cleaning.

The first day, we cleaned until eight at night. Over the coming days, some of us worked during daylight hours, and some worked the night shift. During this first week, we were too exhausted, physically and mentally, to complain. We were working, and work was the reason we had left our troubled homelands. It never dawned on us things might be about to get worse.

The evening of the seventh day was when reality struck. The blow, when it came, was cruel. Three of us were returning in the minibus from a long day cleaning at a chemical factory. The other four were at the house, getting ready to work the night shift. Tired and hungry from our exertions, we found the front door open and a woman standing outside waiting. With her shoulder-length blonde hair, I didn't recognise her at first. Then she began speaking, and I realised she had to be the twin of the woman from my nightmares. Standing beside her was a bald man. Someone with pockmarked cheeks and a scar down one side.

'Welcome to England, the land of your dreams.' All of us were sitting, perched on the sofas or bean bags in the room next to our bedroom. 'I come bearing news,' said the woman. The bald-headed man stood beside her, saying nothing, his eyes roaming like a farmer appraising his flock. 'The tests are back and the doctor says everyone is fit and healthy.' She paused, looking at each of us, one by one. 'Which is good. However, you get little for free in life. The fact you've made it to the UK and are working means you owe a lot of money. Many thousands of pounds. It is the investment you chose to make to reach this country. Sadly, you are not yet earning enough to pay for rent, food and the modest repayment plan we are compelled to charge. Your debts continue to grow. Cleaning jobs these days don't pay enough. There is, however, a solution. One that doesn't bring shame or harm to you or your families back home. You are young, healthy, good-looking women. Tonight, you'll be learning how you can make serious money.' She turned to the man next to her. 'Let me introduce Gregor. He's going to tell you what will happen next.'

'It's very straightforward,' the man began, his face serious. 'This evening, you'll be learning how to use your bodies to help pay off your debts.' There was a gasp from several in the room.

'Oh, grow up, the lot of you,' the woman hissed, her change of tone cold and harsh.

'From now on, you work for me,' the man growled. 'You are all good-looking young women. Do as you're told, and you'll come to no harm. If you don't, there'll be consequences. Do we understand each other?' He studied our frightened faces one by one.

'What's going to happen? What are we going to be doing?' It was a young Armenian girl, her voice quivering.

'You'll see,' the man replied, just as there was a loud knocking on the front door. The woman disappeared before returning with four middle-aged men by her side. Two of them I instantly recognised. Even now, I remember feeling sick to my stomach. My entire body began to tremble, I had no control over it.

'Tonight, you get your first lesson. Pay attention and learn well. Do not resist. The more you fight, the more difficult you'll make things.' The blonde-haired women stepped aside, and the four entered the room. In unison, they began loosening their belt buckles.

22

The Pink Geranium is more of a gentleman's cabaret than a pole dancing venue. Punters sit at tables, eating and drinking, eyes glued to the stage show upfront whilst being served by waitresses wearing too few clothes.

At two in the afternoon, business is slack. The bouncer at the door is not someone I recognise. If he's been told to be on the lookout for two men of our description, he gives no indication. He swings the door wide, and we step inside under his watchful gaze. Not a complete fail, unlike the puny guy last Friday. Still a B-minus. It would have been more impressive if he'd asked a few questions. An A-plus would have checked our ID, perhaps logging our names in a register. The B-minus guy does none of that.

Vince's eyes are on stalks as we grab a seat at an empty table. A blonde server in tights and a figure-hugging leotard is quick off the mark. We both order bottles of beer, she blowing us an air kiss before wandering off.

'You never mentioned the perks that went with the job.' Vince watches her as she heads back to the bar, black fishnets in high heels on full display. 'What's the plan?'

'Sit back, watch and soak up the atmosphere. I'm keen to see who comes and goes, whether we recognise anybody.' Today, I'm Ricky Baxter, not Rich Somers, and therefore as British as they come. The beers arrive, our waitress leaning forward as she sets the bottles down. Ample views of a generous cleavage are on full display.

'That'll be thirty pounds, gents.' I can't guess the accent, but it doesn't sound English.

'Bloody hell,' Vince splutters.

'I've got these.' I place two notes on the tray. When she doesn't move, I realise she's waiting for a tip. I fish out an extra five-pound note and hand it over.

'Thank you,' she says, wiggling her boobs in our direction. 'Tips are best kept somewhere secure, wouldn't you agree?' She winks at me and flashes Vince an enormous smile.

'Where are you from?' I ask as Vince obliges with the tip money.

'Romania,' she says, securing the fiver inside her halter. 'Talk to you both later.' We receive another air kiss before she flounces back to the bar.

There are about twenty customers in the place. A number have the remnants of finger food at their tables.

'Interesting place for a working lunch,' I say, watching one naked girl on stage doing weirdly implausible things with a rocking chair to music.

'Eye-wateringly expensive.'

'More upmarket than the place last Friday.'

I'm seventy pounds down and well into our second Beck's when I nudge Vince.

'It's Lisandra.' We watch a platinum blonde woman enter the club and wander over to talk to the barman. 'Do me a favour, Vince. Tell her Ricky Baxter would like a quiet word, would you?'

Vince walks confidently up to the bar area and whispers something in Lisandra's ear. The Latvian spins around, eyes scanning the room. To her credit, she doesn't blank me. Instead, she makes a beeline for our table.

'Lisandra, I'm surprised.'

'What the hell are you doing here? You can't be seen talking to me. You have to leave at once.'

'Where's Alisa?'

'I don't know. I've not heard from her all week.'

'What about the Estonian girl, Sofia?'

'She's also working here now.'

'I thought you were going to leave all this crap and put it behind you. I even gave you money, remember?'

'Sure, and we were all very grateful.' Even in the dim light, her cheeks are blushing. 'But it's not as easy as you think. These people are not nice. They threaten my family. They send me photos and force me to work. Look, please go.'

'Who runs the club?'

'I don't know his name. This place is even worse than the other. The bouncers are always trying to screw the girls. Especially on payday.'

'Are you serious?'

'It's how it is.'

I look at Vince and he looks at me. I suddenly remember something.

'Lisandra, wait. Let me show you this.' I dig in my pocket and find my phone. I hunt for the picture of Gregor from Inés's files. 'Do you recognise this man?'

She peers at the image and then glances around the room.

'That's him,' she says, a mixture of surprise and fear etched on her face. 'He owns the place. I hate him.'

'Is he out the back?'

'Not yet. Maybe later. Now, please, get out of here. Before there's any trouble.'

'One last thing. Was it you who placed those two bugs in our offices? The one in the meeting room and the other in reception?'

This gets a reaction. Without a word, she storms off angrily.

'Well, I guess that settles it then,' I say to Vince.

'Why would she have done that?'

'They would have put the squeeze on her. Her and Sofia. Threatening to beat up friends and family back home if she doesn't co-operate. These bastards own these girls. There's nothing they feel they can't do and get away with it.'

'Like screwing the girls before payday?'

'You ready for that fight you've been hankering after?'

'Don't look now, but the fight may be coming our way.'

I glance up and see a familiar face heading towards our table. It's Mister Muscle himself, flanked by two others I don't recognise.

'You need to come with us. Both of you. It's time we had a little talk.'

They lead us in and around the tables, towards the back of the club. Mister Muscle is in front, Vince and I go next, with the other two bringing up the rear. We pass our waitress, standing by the bar, loading drinks on a tray. Her eyes are on stalks as she sees us being frogmarched out like this. With the head of security, no less. I wink at her, blowing an air kiss as we pass. For the moment, all's fine. Nothing's about to happen on the main floor of the club, a fact that is proven moments later when we go out the rear fire exit.

Outside, in a private back alley, is another heavy I've never seen. He's holding a baseball bat. This isn't Gregor. From the way he's behaving, he's in charge, though. When the door behind us closes, the two in our wake have fallen into position behind us once again. Which makes us six in total. Four against two. Nice odds, in normal circumstances.

'You're an annoying piece of work, Ricky Baxter.' It's the heavy speaking. The accent is Slavic. Possibly Russian, it's hard to tell.

'Is this how you try to woo new customers? Fifteen pounds a beer, plus tips, followed by a session with the baseball bat? If so, it isn't working.'

'You've been causing everyone a lot of problems,' he says, ignoring my taunt.

My brain is working overtime. Four against two. I don't usually mind those kinds of odds, even with a baseball bat thrown in. Four against one would have been worse, but not impossible. Four against two, with Vince pumped and spoiling for action. This may not turn out the way they're hoping.

'Why isn't Gregor here?'

'Gregor leaves trash like you to people like me.'

'You're garbage collectors, is that it?'

'We don't collect. We dispose.'

'Pity. Gregor and I need to set the record straight.'

'Your attitude is unacceptable.'

‘Bullshit. People who demand sexual favours from female staff. That’s unacceptable.’

Baseball Bat stares back, saying nothing. All that’s audible is the rhythmic tapping of the baseball bat against the palm of his left hand. Tap, tap, tap.

‘Too bad you don’t listen to warnings,’ he says, giving the tiniest nod of his head. Sensing movement behind, Vince and I move back and to one side, creating a small circle between all six of us. On my left, I have one of the two who was standing behind us. On my right is the man with the baseball bat.

Without waiting for the shadow boxing to begin, I pounce, deciding to attack first the man on my left. The one who probably believes he’s only going to be a spectator in this contest. I lunge straight at him, aiming an elbow directly at his neck, catching him by surprise since he’s had no time to put up any defences. On contact, I snap my elbow upwards. This causes his head to whip backwards. In the same breath, I deliver a powerful, right-handed follow-through punch directly below his ribcage. The neck doesn’t know whether it’s coming or going. One moment it’s snapping skywards, the next it’s falling forwards. Directly into the path of my fist, now on an upward trajectory to connect with the man’s nose. The coup de grâce is a knee powering directly into his nuts.

As the defeated man’s body slides to the floor, I sense the man with the baseball bat is fast approaching, preparing to lash out. The moment my knee has connected with the other man’s gonads, I pull his body across mine to act as a shield. The procedure half works, half doesn’t. The bit that half works is that most of the force from the bat hits my human shield on one of his arms, rather than mine. There is a sickening sound of splintering bone and a scream of pain from the already-wounded man. The half that doesn’t is that the bat continues its powerful downward swing and connects with the metal on my prosthesis. There is an almighty metallic clanging sound. I fall to the floor and find my prosthetic leg has detached.

In the middle of a fight, this is a bit of a bummer. I glance across at Vince and see that he, like me, has felled one opponent, but is now locked in a serious one-on-one with Mister Muscle. On my side, it’s just Baseball Bat and me for the moment, and I’m one leg down.

Down, but not out.

Baseball Bat dropped the bat when it connected with my leg, the unexpected resistance from the metal in my prosthesis bouncing the handle out of his hand. Its momentary loss provides a precious second or two of respite while he reaches to retrieve it.

I can be nifty on my hands, knees and bum. I've said before, in the middle of the night, you'll find me half crawling, half monkey-grabbing my way at speed to the bathroom rather than using the wheelchair. That, plus my gym work, and I'm a tough guy to beat on a one-hundred-metre crab crawl. Even with one leg attached and the other with just a metal spike sticking out the end. Which gives me an idea. I half-roll, half-crawl to within touching distance. When he stoops to pick up the bat, I am ready to put my whacky idea to the test. A spring-loaded leap off the floor, using power from my arms and shoulders, combined with a bit of leverage from the knee with the one prosthetic still attached. It's akin to a karate kick whilst still lying on the deck. The Ricky Baxter variant is to snap-thrust the exposed metal spike directly into Baseball Bat's thigh. The tip rips through the man's cargo pants like a knife through butter, ramming hard against his thighbone. With blood gushing, I withdraw the spike and roll away without getting soaked. The man falls to the ground, writhing from the puncture wound.

Nifty prosthetic legwork, Baxter.

Across the courtyard, Vince has Mister Muscle in a headlock. Both are on the ground, their faces covered in sweat. Despite Vince's strength, the muscle guy is good at wriggling his way out of trouble. I grab the baseball bat and crab crawl over towards Vince.

'Need some help?'

'Only if it hurts.'

'Happily,' I say, swinging the bat so it hits Vince's opponent directly on the leg. The man screams and goes limp in Vince's arms.

'There we go,' Vince says, more to himself than me. 'What happened to your leg?'

'I'll tell you in a moment. Make sure the others won't cause more problems while I sort it out.'

Both the prosthetic and my stub liner seem fine. I have to wipe a little blood off the spike, but then it clicks back in without a fuss.

'You having problems?' Vince asks as I struggle to get to my feet.

'Getting off the deck is not as easy for me as it is for you.'

'Need a hand?'

I shake my head.

'What next?' Vince asks.

'I think we should head back inside. I'm betting security is thin at the moment.'

'You planning on having a nosey around?'

'I'd like another word with Lisandra. Maybe even Gregor, if he ever turns up.'

With the fire escape door closed, the only way back is around the side and through the front entrance. If it surprises the man on duty to see us, he doesn't show it. Doesn't even register we've met earlier. Or work out that here we are, back again, and he never saw us leave. In my book that earns him a downgrade, from a B-minus to a C. A fail, no question.

Inside, we scan the floor for signs of Gregor but can't see him. It's possible he might have been watching the action out the back on one of the security cameras. My guess is he hasn't turned up. Otherwise, we'd be seeing all sorts of commotion. The only sign of anything untoward is out the back near the fire escape. There's a management type in a waistcoat and tie doing a fair amount of to-ing and fro-ing, barking instructions into a hidden microphone. Periodically he opens the fire escape door and then comes back inside. Our waitress from earlier is quick to spot us and flounces back in our direction.

'Why, back again? That didn't take long.' She leans towards us, boobs working overtime. 'You boys look like you need another drink.'

'We're looking for Lisandra. The platinum blonde.'

'The new girl? I suspect she's getting changed.'

'Can you take us?'

She looks me up and down as if debating whether to hustle some extra cash for her cleavage.

'Sure,' she says, then spots the management type and her tone changes. 'As soon as he's out the way.'

'Who's he?'

'Works for the guy who runs the place.'

'The boss not in yet?'

'Not that I've seen. There seems to be some kind of problem. Anyway, they don't like customers talking to the girls out the back.'

'Tell you what,' I say, pulling a wad of cash from my pocket and peeling a twenty from the bundle. 'Why don't you find her and bring her to me?' I lodge the folded note in the same place Vince had earlier and head back to our old table. As she walks away, I notice the management type disappearing out the front. He returns a short while later with two paramedics in green scrubs, with first-aid kits slung over shoulders. They hurry with him through the club.

'Someone must have called for an ambulance.'

'That spike of yours was wicked.'

Two more paramedics appear, this time led by my newly downgraded bouncer. Most punters are oblivious, the floorshow continuing without interruption. Then our waitress is back, with Lisandra close behind, dressed in a long silk dressing-gown.

'Look, I told you both to go. Leave me alone.' It's not the most welcoming she could have been, but it's enough to send our waitress scurrying. I pull out a chair.

'Sit.'

'I can't be seen talking with you.'

'This won't take long.' Tentatively she sits, and I launch right in. 'Let's start by getting a few things straight. I don't give a shit about bugging our offices, if it was you. It's history. We've all moved on. Understood?'

She smoulders, but eventually nods.

'The people who run this place. They may think they own you, putting pressure on the family back home, that sort of stuff. We need to put a stop to all that. It's why I run the charity. To keep shit like that from happening. I need your help in trying to track down Alisa. I'd like to know what's happened to her, where she's being forced to work and so on. You and the others who know her can help, I know you can. Here,' I say, and search in my pocket for a business card. 'Take this. You've no idea where she is?'

She shakes her head, taking the card and slipping it in the pocket of her gown.

'Find her, for your sakes and the sake of maybe hundreds like her. I need to find her. Before it's too late. The moment you hear, call me. Any time of day or night works for me. The number is on the card.'

'Okay,' she says, this time with tears in her eyes. 'They threaten my family. How will you stop them?'

'I'll find a way. That's what I do. Someone's got to sort these people out, once and for all.'

'I'm sorry about earlier. About the other stuff.'

'It's over. Forget it. Get back to work. Before you go, where do I find Gregor's office? The man who owns this place?'

'See those stairs in the corner?' She points to a recess beyond the fire escape I hadn't noticed before. 'Up one floor, second door on the left. He could very well be here soon.'

'Thanks. We're on your side. Don't leave it too long to find your friend. Call me, do you hear?'

As she heads off, Vince and I look at each other.

'You're going to check out Gregor's office?'

'Seems churlish to waste the opportunity. Here,' I say, rolling two twenties from my cash bundle. 'Get some more beers lined up. I won't be long.'

'I'll text if I see anything,' Vince calls out, but I'm already slipping into the shadows. I make my way to the back, narrowly avoiding the management type. He's too preoccupied with the medical emergency to bother about a stray punter apparently searching for the gents.

I dart up the stairs and find myself in a plush carpeted area, with soft sofas and dim lighting. There are several doors, but only one with 'Manager, Private' on it. The second on the left. The door isn't locked and I barge straight in. I'm half-expecting to come face to face with Gregor, only to find the room empty. I even have to switch on the light.

It turns out to be an upscale version of Tariq's office in the other club. This one has two comfy sofas, an enormous coffee table and even a window. The desk and chair are also more luxurious. However, there are similarities. The metal filing cabinet, for one. Plus, the same make and model of wall safe. I have no idea what I'm looking for. On a whim, I try the combination I used with Tariq's safe, but it doesn't work. I sit at the desk and open the drawers, finding nothing interesting. Next, I search the filing cabinet, twisting the handle and opening both doors. Inside are bottles of booze and some glass tumblers. Also, a few items of stationery; a large box of condoms; a cigar humidor; and several boxes of cigars, their cellophane wrappers unopened. Nothing of much interest to me here. I'm pondering the wall safe, wondering how to find Gregor's code, when my phone buzzes. It's a text from Vince telling me a uniformed police officer has arrived at the club. I need to get my skates on.

I return to the desk, an idea forming. Gregor changes the safe codes each week. What if he keeps the codes in the same place at each of his clubs? I open the top left drawer of his desk and reach inside to check. As I'm fumbling around, my hand brushes another piece of card clipped to the underside. Like before, it's a card with a list of six-figure codes written on it, with one code not yet crossed off.

I enter the digits and the safe opens. It's less full than the first. No bundles of cash, not even a weapon. What I do discover, hidden under a pile of papers, is a black notebook. Smaller than a paperback but the same thickness, it is a well-thumbed tome. A flick through the pages reveals it is what an accountant would call a ledger. Only the assets it records are not cash but people. A double-page for each woman, records entered month by month: opening debt; interest and other charges; wages earned; cash paid; and the balance outstanding. By my quick calculations, there are thirty or forty different names in the book. Most have entries crossed out and updated to show where each person is currently working.

I put the book in my pocket and recheck the safe. Tucked at the back, in a neat stack and held together by an elastic band, are several bank debit cards. I put these in my pocket too, closing the safe just as my phone buzzes. It's Vince: two more police have arrived. I hit the lights and hurry out, back down the stairs.

'I hope you didn't tip the waitress too much,' I mutter, taking a long pull from the bottle awaiting my return. 'This beer is lukewarm.'

'She only has eyes for you, mate. Lucky you turned up when you did. I was about to help myself. Did you find anything?'

'I'll tell you later. We should make ourselves scarce.' There are now three police officers milling near the front entrance, along with the management type.

'Front or back?'

'Front, I guess. If we go out the back, we'll be recognised.'

Just when I think we've escaped unnoticed, one of the police officers puts an arm out to stop us.

'Excuse me, sir. No one's allowed to leave. There's been an incident. We need statements from everyone.'

'We've got to get back to work. Could we do this another time?'

'I'm sorry. You'll have to wait until we've taken statements from everybody.'

'How long will that take?'

'As long as it takes, sir.'

'What kind of incident?'

'We'll explain all that when we take your statement. For now, take a seat, both of you. We'll be with you as soon as we can. I'm just waiting for two more colleagues to arrive, then we can get started.'

We come to a grinding halt at the first question.

'Name?'

'Ricky Baxter.' As he's writing this down in his small, black notebook, he stops, mid-flow, and looks up. A penny has dropped.

'You run the charity down at Bethnal Green.' It is a statement, not a question.

'How do you know that?'

'I recognised the name. There was an altercation in the car park at your place yesterday.'

'Several hundred crimes a day across Metropolitan London and you remember the one linked to me. Why's that, officer?'

‘It’s sergeant. Sergeant Matt Wellby.’

‘Very good, Sergeant Matt Wellby. The question’s still the same.’

‘There’s an investigation underway. Gangs and gang-related crimes. Me and the boss, DI Saunderson, we’ve had clubs like this on our radar for a while.’ He turns to look at Vince. ‘Your name is?’

Vince tells him, and another look of recognition dawns.

‘You were also involved yesterday.’ Another statement, not a question.

‘No, I arrived after it had all kicked off.’

‘Really.’

‘Look, two guys jump Ricky in the car park. He fends off one of them, I turn up and the pair scarper. End of.’

‘You seem to know a lot about Vince and me, Sergeant Wellby. We’re not involved in running any clubs. Would you like to explain why you’re here? What’s going on?’

‘Earlier this afternoon, four guys working here were assaulted. We’re trying to find out who was involved, and why.’

‘You’re linking our presence here today to an assault on the other side of town yesterday? Making the automatic assumption we must have somehow been involved, is that it?’

‘What brought you both here today? To a club which, in your own words, is indeed on the other side of town.’

‘Vince recently joined the charity. We can’t afford to pay a great deal, so this is my treat to him. Welcoming him aboard and to say thank you for joining. A boys’ outing. The place came recommended, so here we are.’

‘Shame they didn’t mention the beer prices,’ Vince chips in. ‘Fifteen quid for a bottle of beer, tips on top.’

'Ah, look, here's the boss.'

A tall, thin man approaches our table and sits down, offering a handshake to us both.

'DI Saunderson,' he says, by way of introduction. 'Tell me what you've got, Sarge.'

'Remind me, what exactly does your charity do, Baxter?' It's Saunderson speaking, his face gaunt. It's a face belonging to the perpetually tired.

'Supports women who've been abused. Testosterone-induced unpleasantness. Often sexual, frequently violent.'

'Would your clients typically be migrant workers?'

'A fair number.'

'What about people who work in clubs like this?'

'What about them?'

'Is that why you're here?'

'What, to see one of my clients?'

'Maybe. Or the alleged perpetrators of certain crimes against one of your clients. It's a thought.'

'I never discuss my clients with anybody. Not even the police.'

'Last Friday, two male security guards at a club in your neck of the woods found themselves at the wrong end of some vigilante-type rough justice. One was severely beaten; the other had boiling water poured over his privates. Today, out the back of this very club, at or around the time the pair of you were enjoying your supposed celebratory beers, four grown men suffered a similar fate. No boiling water treatment this time, but some nasty injuries, nonetheless. There was a baseball bat involved. Plus, one of the injured has a severe puncture wound to his femur. He's lucky not to have bled to death. The other three won't be coming back to work for a long time either. That's grievous bodily harm in our book. Carries stiff penalties in a court of law.'

'Sounds like a bit inter-gang warfare.'

'Can't be ruled out.'

'If those four were anything like the two who assaulted me yesterday, it sounds like they got what they deserved.'

'It wasn't you then?'

'What wasn't me?'

'The four out the back. You and your friend here, enjoying a little knockabout. You were a boxer once, isn't that right, O'Leary?'

'I also enjoy pretty women,' Vince retorts.

'It might also have escaped your notice, Saunderson, but I am a double amputee.'

DI Saunderson clears his throat, pausing for a moment to fiddle with the cuffs on his shirt. 'The thing is, gents, we might unwittingly all be batting for the same team. Sergeant Wellby and I, we work in a specialist unit. We investigate gangs, in particular those involved in trafficking. It doesn't take a vast amount of intelligence to figure the people we might be interested in might also be connected to the sorts of clients you see in the charity.'

'I suppose it's possible. What about it?'

'I'd like us to have an off-the-record, hypothetical conversation. You happy with that?'

'Try me.'

'Imagine there are certain people involved in running a lucrative but completely illegal people trafficking business. I call it a business advisedly. Make no mistake, this is a slickly run affair: well-organised and adept at keeping its nose clean. Word on the street is that some in the gang are doing bad, perhaps unspeakable, things to various migrant workers. Surprise, surprise, no one's prepared to come forward and give evidence. So, let us suppose the police, in their wisdom, begin an investigation. Undercover, mind, all very hush-hush. The aim being to gather information and evidence about the leaders of the gang before rushing in to make arrests. This takes time. Let's even assume they plant one or two people on the inside. Hoping to uncover as much information as possible about what is going on. Waiting to judge the optimum moment to pounce. Which might take a little time and effort since any arrests will require co-ordination with officers in other countries. To avoid members of the wider gang in different parts of Europe escaping and being lost, perhaps forever.' He looks up to check he's still got our attention before continuing.

'Now, suppose one or two members of the public were to learn about a few isolated incidents involving people from these gangs. Perhaps from a whistle-blower. Perhaps, even, from the efforts of a charitable organisation set up to help victims of abuse. Hypothetically, you understand. These might well be good, honest, public-spirited people. People like you and I, believing they know their right from wrong. They might be so appalled about what they hear, they become tempted to take matters into their own hands. Administer the odd bit of their own justice. Which a few on the Force might, privately, even feel was warranted. If not long overdue. Arguably, even fun to observe, always assuming it didn't risk buggering up the entire undercover police operation running in parallel.'

'Your point being?'

'My point is this. We might be tempted to overlook one or two infringements by such public-spirited people. In particular, if some less pleasant members of the gang found themselves unable to turn up for work for a few days. However – and hear me out on this – not at the expense of wrecking the entire operation.'

'Are we done?' I say, looking at Vince and shrugging. 'It's just that in your hypothetical example you might be forgetting one crucial fact.'

‘Which is?’

‘Every day that passes while covert police investigations continue with nothing happening, more and more people are being abused and made to suffer. The scale is horrific. Come and work in my charity and see for yourself, if you don’t believe me.’

‘We’re asking you to back off, Baxter. Walk away from here today, and we’ll forget all this happened. That’s a promise. What occurred earlier might even have brought a smile to one or two faces. Unofficially, you understand, but still a smile. Any more interference, though, and I can’t make any such promises. If it looks like you’re about to threaten the entire operation, be under no illusion. We’ll throw the book at you.’

‘Well, that’s nice to know. Can we get going?’

‘Sarge, see them out, will you? Baxter, remember what I said. We’re on the same team, you and I. Don’t screw it all up just for a few localised victories. This thing is bigger than you can possibly imagine.’

23

Grace is alone in reception when we return., with Freds on the couch opposite. Grace suspects the Alsatian capable of sleeping with one eye half-open. Watching for food, rather than intruders.

'How did you get on?'

'We kicked a hornets' nest.' Vince tells her, taking up her place on reception duty while Grace follows me back to my office.

'Come on, Mister Rick, what happened?'

I tell her everything, including the encounter with the police.

'They warned you off?'

'In not so many words. Have we used up our supply of spare burner phones?'

'There are two or three left, I think. Do you want one?'

'I think it's almost time for me to give Gregor a call.'

'How many do you need?' Grace is already hauling herself to her feet.

'I'll take a couple. I need to replace the one in the car.'

She returns with two phones, their packaging removed.

'What was in the safe?'

I tell her and watch her jaw hit the floor.

'Gregor will not be happy.'

I pull the pile of debit cards and the black notebook out of my pocket.

'Whose cards are those?'

'Pick a name at random from any card. I'll see if there's an entry for that person in the notebook.' Grace picks up the pile and looks at the card on top.

'How about "M Petrovs".'

I check the book and find a match on the fifth page.

'Here we go. Mariss Petrovs. Works at the Pink Geranium. Current balance owed is £7,530.'

'That's a lot of money for a young woman to be owing. Why does this man have their bank cards?'

'Leverage. Many don't speak English on arrival. Gregor's minions open up bank accounts and sort out the paperwork as part of a packaged deal. Everything is sent care of the club. Gregor pays monthly wages into their bank accounts to give an appearance of legitimacy to the taxman. That's after deducting debt repayments and taxes, naturally. He'll then use the debit cards to withdraw enough money for each girl to live off each week. The cards are kept in his safe to prevent the girls from accessing their money. From time to time, I suspect he'll raid various accounts and steal their money. Especially if they misbehave. That's quite some leverage.'

'It's disgusting. It shouldn't be allowed.'

'Can you make a photocopy of every page in this book? Plus all the cards. We need to keep the originals somewhere secure for the time being.'

'What about the strongbox I use for the petty cash in reception?'

'For the moment, that'll have to do.' I check my watch. It's already five in the evening and I'm nowhere near ready for the gym. 'Where's Baz?'

'On his way to babysit Inés's daughter.'

'Marta's going to love that. How did Baz and Kels get on?'

'Fine, I think. Kels is on a flight out of City airport leaving shortly.'

'Did Inés call?'

'Not since I rang her earlier to say Baz was on his way to pick up Marta.'

I grab my mobile, on the point of dialling her number when it vibrates in my hand. It's Inés calling me.

'Ricky?' Immediately, I sense something is not right.

'I was about to call. What's up?'

'Come quick.' She rattles off an address, which I commit to memory. 'Meet me there as fast as you can.'

'Hold on, what's the matter?'

'Marta's missing.'

'Shit! Are you sure?'

'The police are at her friend's house now. The two girls went for a walk this afternoon. Her friend went to a shop whilst Marta was on her phone. When she came out, Marta had vanished. They found her phone on the pavement. You've got to help me find her, Ricky, this is desperate.'

'I'll be ten minutes max, depending on traffic.'

'Trouble?' Grace asks.

'Marta's missing.'

'Oh, Lordy. It's happening. This is Gregor, isn't it?'

I'm already by the front reception, Grace struggling to keep pace.

'Vince, Inés's daughter's gone missing. Sounds like Gregor. I've got to go. Guard the fort when I'm gone and keep your eyes peeled.'

'Sure. Shout if you need any help. I'm always happy to lend a hand.'

Several police cars are parked on the roadside by the time I arrive. Traffic is snarling to a crawl as drivers slow down to stare. The first person I recognise is Baz.

'I'm sorry,' he says as I clamber out the car, desperately looking to see if I can spot Inés. 'If I was quicker with Kels, maybe this not happening. This is my fault.'

I swivel on my feet to look at him.

'Baz. This cannot be your fault. Stop blaming yourself. We have to focus on finding Marta, not blaming each other. Where's Inés?'

'Inside house.' He nods towards a property which has two shirt-sleeved police officers wearing fluorescent vests standing by the door. At that moment, my phone buzzes. I don't recognise the number.

'You're very annoying bastard, Ricky Baxter.' The voice is rough, the accent east-European, the sound gravelly. 'You make a huge mistake with my people today.'

'Oh yeah?' I say with as much disinterest as I can muster.

'You're a thief. You stole from me. So, now I've stolen from you. Marta is pretty girl. My customers will be thrilled to see one so young and innocent now available.'

'She's a minor. Kidnapping and assault of an underaged teenage girl is a big thing in this country.'

'You want the girl, I want what you stole back. All of it. Bank cards, the lot.'

'The police have them, not me.'

'Bullshit.'

'They're onto you, Gregor. They're watching the clubs, not to mention your other seedy operations. If you've got Marta, they'll already know about it, trust me. You get seven years for abduction. With other charges stacked up, waiting in the wings, most likely they'll throw the book at you.'

'I'm not frightened of anybody, Ricky Baxter.'

'Knowing about some of the informants in your operation, in your position, I'd be shitting myself.'

'You're talking bullshit. There are no informants in my business.'

'You think?'

'Listen. You want the girl; we're going to trade. You, plus the shit you stole from my safe. Only then the girl goes free.'

'You expect me to walk back into the Pink Geranium and hand myself over?'

'That would work.'

'Gregor, you need a change of medication. I told Irina, and I'm telling you. I. Do. Not. Negotiate. End of. One more thing, just so you can never say you weren't warned. If I discover you or one of your people have laid a finger on that girl, I am personally going to come and rip you a new arsehole.' Which is when I stab my finger on the 'end call' button and go in search of Inés.

'What the hell do you mean, you know where she is?'

'Gregor just called.'

'My God, Ricky. What are we mixed up in?'

We're standing in the hallway. Marta's friend, Jess, and her mother are sitting in the kitchen with a community support officer. Inés's initial enthusiasm at my arrival is dissipating fast.

'Let's step outside.'

'How the fuck are we going to get Marta back?' she screams at me, once we are out of earshot of the uniformed officers by the door.

'I'm sorting it!

'You're sorting it? You're the fucking reason she's gone missing.'

'Not directly. It's linked to yesterday evening. To what that woman said.'

'Tell me you've got a plan, Ricky. Otherwise, I'm minded to find this Gregor myself and sod the consequences.' She spits out these words, eyes flaring and bottom lip trembling. I've not seen this side of Inés before.

'Vince and I visited the Pink Geranium earlier. A few of Gregor's men got hurt. He's now pissed and wants an exchange. Marta for myself.' It's a shortened version of the truth, but sufficient.

'Will you do that?' It sounds like a question but comes out more like an order.

'If I trusted his word.'

'What if he's lying?'

'Then he might not live to regret it.'

It's almost dark. I am sitting in the car, about fifty metres from the club's entrance. Baz is in the passenger seat. We both have an unobstructed view of who's coming and going. About twenty metres behind us is the turning that leads to the cul-de-sac at the rear of the Pink Geranium. The area where Vince and I had our earlier workout, four against two. Baz has shifted the wing mirror on his side. Like me, he's keeping one eye on our rear. The game plan is to watch and wait. So far, the club appears to be having a quiet night.

The doorman is yet another I've not seen before. Gregor must have a limitless supply. This one looks like he'll make the grade. Smartly turned out, attentive and polite. He's stopping punters on the way in, asking questions. Plus, being friendly to punters on the way out. Making them feel looked after. Probably an A-minus. If he was checking proof of ID, he'd be scoring better marks. Writing details down would be outstanding.

I check my watch. Time to give Gregor a call. Using one of the two burners Grace gave me, I dial the number. It rings several times before the call is answered. There's only silence from the other end.

'One hour from now, the girl walks through the front entrance of the Pink Geranium. Uninjured and unrestrained. If that happens, I'll come in.'

'You take me for a fucking imbecile? The police will be crawling all over the place. I have a counter-offer. Rumour has it you've got something of a sweet spot for one of my girls. A girl by the name of Alisa. The deal is this, Baxter. I agree to your suggestion. With one variation. Any police, you can kiss goodbye to Alisa. Understood?'

He takes my silence for assent.

'I thought you never negotiated?'

'Don't misunderstand me, Gregor. This is not a negotiation,' and I stab the button to end the call.

'You think he has Samira?' Baz asks a little later. I shake my head, staring through the front windscreen rather than making eye contact. Candidly, I don't have a clue where Samira might be. It seems unlikely she'll be working the clubs, from everything Baz has told me about her.

'Alisa, yes. Samira, no,' is what I end up saying, and place a reassuring hand on Baz's arm. 'We'll find her, I promise. I have a plan.'

'Really?' Baz's face lights up, his expression full of hope. I don't want to overcook the notion of my plan too much. There are too many unknowns, not least the complication of Marta's kidnapping.

'First, we get Marta back.' I look at Baz and shrug.

Earlier, Inés had not been happy. About me charging off to find her daughter without telling the police all I knew. I told her the police were conflicted. It was going to jeopardise their operation against Gregor, Irina and everyone. The police would drag their feet and go cautiously. I, on the other hand, was going to confront Gregor and do what I usually do. The two of us had argued, and there'd been tears. She, understandably, feared for Marta's life. She also didn't want me hurt, either. I told her to trust me and promised to call later.

'We never make gym today.'

'No, my friend. That's twice this week, I'm sorry.'

'Maybe we get workout here, at the club?' He smiles. Bless Baz, he thinks he's John Wayne now he's developed his physique. 'Is Gregor coming tonight?'

It's the one question I'm not sure about. If the situation was in reverse, would I be turning up at the club tonight? I think it unlikely. Gregor will want others to bring me to him. Once he's sure I've got all the missing items with me. Which, of course, I haven't. As he most probably had feared. Thus making it unlikely he is going to risk making an appearance.

'On balance, I doubt it.'

I call Inés and give a potted version of my conversation with Gregor. She has a friend with her and seems to be holding up, all things considered.

'Where are you now?'

'Near the club. Baz and I are watching and waiting.'

'Do you think she'll show?'

'There's a good possibility.'

'God, I hope you're right, Ricky. I want to come and join you. I'd like to be there when she arrives.'

'I don't think that's wise. For your sake and hers.'

We argue back and forth, but eventually she resigns herself to take my advice. I end the call and look across at Baz.

'How much time remaining?'

'About thirty minutes.'

'Not long now.'

24

Baz notices the other car first. He nudges me and we stare in our respective mirrors. The vehicle parks up a few metres behind. My first thought is that it's a resident arriving home. Either that or one of the club's punters. It is now dark, and the street is not well lit. Once the car's headlights are off, it takes a few moments for our eyes to readjust. I want to see who gets out. The minutes tick past slowly. Either I've missed something, or the driver has stayed put in the car.

'See anything your side?'

Baz shakes his head.

'The guy must be on a call.'

'Maybe he's watching too.'

'Us, you mean?' It's an interesting thought. Gregor gets a call, sends out a few scouts before the girl turns up. I curse myself for not having thought this through. 'You know, you could be right.'

I consider getting out and checking. In hindsight, not doing this proves a mistake. Too late, we discover a second car approaching from the rear. It, also, slows as it approaches, but then rolls forward until it is alongside us. Which is when it stops. So close, in fact, I'm unable to open my door.

'Move!' I shout to Baz, but we've been too slow. Whilst distracted by the second car, someone, presumably the driver of the first car, is now leaning against Baz's door. The passenger window of the stationary vehicle buzzes down and my heart sinks. It's Saunderson, the detective inspector Vince and I met earlier. Doubtless his sidekick, Wellby, is nearby. Come to think of it, it might even be his backside leaning against the door. I buzz my window down.

'Ricky Baxter.'

'What's up, Saunderson?'

'Have you forgotten our conversation of earlier this afternoon? The one where I said I might forget certain infringements as long as you stopped interfering with live police operations.'

'What about it?'

'Your presence this evening suggests you have chosen, deliberately, to ignore my advice.'

'It might have escaped your notice, Saunderson, but a fifteen-year-old girl has been kidnapped.'

'I wonder why, Baxter? It might have escaped *your* notice, but the police are not ignorant. Yes, we know about Marta's abduction. We also know in about twenty minutes, she's expected here. Again, I wonder why?'

'Because Gregor wants to trade. Me for her.'

'You really think Gregor's going to show his hand? He's too smart to make himself associated with a minor's abduction.'

'I know that.'

'Do you? I tell you what I think. I think if we left matters up to you, you'd be blundering your way into the Pink Geranium hoping to find Gregor. Only, you'd soon discover he wasn't there, which is when you'd get angry and risk screwing everything up. Any chances we might then have had of rescuing that poor girl would be scuppered.'

'They're only meant to be bringing her here because they think I'm going to show.'

'Correct. However, they also believe you'll only make an appearance once you've satisfied yourself she's here. Either way, we, the police, are going to be ready to grab her.'

'You mustn't do that,' I blurt out, then regret it.

'Now you've lost me.'

'There's another girl, working at the club. A Latvian called Alisa. She's a client. Gregor's threatening to kill her if the police show up.'

'Too bad, Baxter. Our priority's the young girl. The good news is we're going to get her back. The bad is that you and your friend are going to be spending the night in a police cell. Under arrest.'

'What the hell for?' I look across at Baz, rolling my eyes in disbelief.

'Many reasons I can think of off the top of my head. Violent assault against four men this afternoon, for starters. Then, there's obstruction of justice during an ongoing police operation. You knew when you spoke with your friend, Inés, earlier where the girl was. However, you deliberately withheld information from the police at the scene. I warned you, Baxter. About not poking your nose into this case anymore.' He looks up at the man with his backside welded against Baz's door. 'Sarge, read Baxter his rights, can you? Then, get him cuffed, in the back of your car and off to the police cells for the night. I'll deal with him once we're finished here.'

'What about the other one?' Wellby says, pointing to Baz.

'Take him along for good measure. I don't want any of Baxter's crew getting in the way. We've got a fifteen-year-old kidnap victim whose life is on the line. This is now a police matter. Do I make myself clear, Baxter?'

'You realise you've just passed the death sentence on an innocent Latvian?'

'I doubt it. Besides, I've only got your word she even exists. On recent form, the chances of you telling me the truth are slender.'

God knows where Wellby takes us. The small holding cell Baz and I find ourselves in smells of stale bodies with a heavy undertone of disinfectant. There are two rock-hard plastic beds: each has an apology of a pillow and blanket. In one corner, a stainless-steel toilet without a seat. All phones, watches and other possessions have been confiscated on arrival, along with wallets and money. Oddly, we are both allowed to keep our prosthetics. My stump is sore, not altogether surprising after the antics earlier in the day. I ask Baz about his rumbling infection. He shrugs and smiles, as ever.

'Earlier, not so good. Now, better.'

'You'll be out in no time. They've nothing to charge you with.'

'What about you?'

'Me too,' I say with more confidence than I feel. Saunderson sounded keen to find excuses to keep me off the streets. I lie on the bed and stare at the ceiling. The lights are harsh and permanently on. I think about Marta and how Inés will be feeling. I seem to have screwed this one up. I close my eyes and let my mind drift. In time, I must have fallen asleep because I'm jolted awake by the sound of someone arriving.

'Baxter, you've got a visitor.'

Baz stays behind as I am led by this burly night owl to a small, windowless detention room. The visitor turns out to be Saunderson. He is pacing the room when I arrive. For someone as tall as him, he looks uncomfortably thin. Perhaps it's the time of night.

'Did you get Marta?'

He turns to look at me and beckons to a small square table with two chairs. Spotlights from above cast shadows, accentuating the bags under his eyes. A clock on the wall shows the time: one-thirty in the morning.

'She's safe.'

'Thank God. Where is she?'

'Back with her mother. We made some arrests.'

'Gregor?'

'Heavens, no. Just some underlings. The driver who brought her and one other. No one with any proven links, other than they seem to be on the club's payroll.'

'Are you going to pull him in?'

'Perhaps. Depends on what the others tell us.'

'Did you bring them here?'

'They've gone to another station. We didn't want them sharing a cell with you two.' He smiles weakly. 'We want them talking to us, not beaten to a pulp.'

'You think I'm like that?'

'Baxter, I'm not here to lecture. Some might reflect that skewering someone's thigh with a prosthetic leg spike or mashing a kneecap with a baseball bat puts you in the same category of wanton thuggery as those who go about abusing women.'

'I don't get it.'

'I think you do, Ricky Baxter.'

'What are you suggesting?'

'If you're not careful, your actions will make ordinary, decent people think you're no better than one of the bad guys.'

'Is that so?' I find his words weirdly unsettling. 'What happens now?'

For a time, he doesn't answer. Instead, the two of us eyeball each other. I can play this game if I need to.

'Your friend, Shabaz. He's an Iraqi, isn't he?'

'Who, Baz? Yes. He would tell you he's a Kurd. From northern Iraq.'

'I'm guessing he's a migrant.'

I shrug but say nothing.

'Probably an illegal. A man with no passport.'

'Your point being?'

'We don't particularly want to throw the book at you or your friend. Trust me on this, Baxter. We'd rather have you on our side. I'm a convert to pragmatic policing. Some things we push hard on; others we turn a blind eye. Unless we feel compelled to do otherwise.'

'What do you feel at the moment?'

'That we're teetering on a knife-edge. This could go either way. I'd like to give you the benefit of the doubt. However, you're a tenacious son-of-a-bitch. I'm not sure you're prepared to let this thing go.' He stares hard at me, and I reciprocate. 'We could always take your prints. You know, check them against our records. We lifted some dabs from a nightclub last Friday evening. Some unspecified male, about your height and build, did unpleasant things to two nightclub bouncers using cable ties and boiling water from a kettle. Who knows, if we're lucky, we might even find a match?'

'Who knows?' I answer, keen to change the subject. 'How far off are you from nailing the leaders of this gang you described earlier?'

'Higher-ups than Gregor, you mean?' He contemplates this question. 'A fair way.'

'We're likely talking months, not weeks, right?'

‘That order of magnitude.’

‘I want to wrap this up in days.’

‘You think?’

‘I know.’

‘That statement alone makes me want to keep you locked up for the duration.’

‘Talk to me about Irina Moravková.’

‘How the fuck do you know about her?’

‘She and her bodyguard accosted me yesterday.’

‘Holy shit!’ He clasps his head in both hands and stares at the table. ‘Why didn’t you tell me this earlier?’ he says, eventually looking up.

‘You never asked. You never mentioned her.’

‘How the hell have you become mixed up with Moravková? She’s right up there, I hope you realise? Right at the very top table. Slippery little bugger. No one seems to know how to find her.’

‘I haven’t been mixing with her,’ I say in all truthfulness. ‘Before yesterday, I’d never even met her. I did, however, meet her body double.’

‘You did what?’

I tell him about meeting Tanya and then about the incident with Irina and the two motorbikes. Not the entire story in either case, but enough to give a flavour. It is the middle of the night, after all.

‘We had no idea Moravková was even in the country. We’ve been watching all the ports and airports specifically.’

‘Listen, if they can smuggle migrants in and out undetected, I’m sure they have a way to get the big cheeses into the country when they want. We're not talking about flimsy rubber dinghies or clinging to the undersides of lorries either.'

'Fast boats or private planes are what we think she uses. We've tried to cover all the bases.'

'Clearly not enough of them.'

'You think this other woman might be a sister? We've not had that on our radar at all.'

'Could even be her twin.'

'That's unhelpful.'

'No disrespect, I think this is a perfect illustration of the fundamental differences between our two approaches. You lot are going by the book, step by step. Me, I yank one or two chains here and there and, suddenly, I have this Irina breaking cover to give me my first and final warning. Marta's kidnapping was a direct consequence. What do you know about Moravková?'

'I'm not sure I have the authority to tell you.'

'I thought you said we were on the same side?' He studies me for a long time before answering. I could swear the bags under his eyes have got bigger.

'She's one of the gang leaders,' he says eventually. 'She might even be top dog. In these types of organisation, hierarchy and position are less important. She's been working the migrant routes through the Balkans and into Europe for some time. Tough cookie. What was your impression?'

'Bit of a monster. Cold and calculating. Lacking emotional engagement with her fellow human beings, is what I thought.' I pause, staring at Saunderson. 'Sadly, she was also quite good-looking.' I give a wincing smile. In return, I receive an amused shake of the head.

'I believe you. Did she leave a calling card? Tell you how to reconnect and discuss the natural chemistry between you both?'

'I did ask. She told me if I wanted to make contact, she was sure I'd find a way.'

'How?'

'Depends on whether you and I are on the same team or not, doesn't it? The slow route or the fast-track method.'

'By rights, Baxter, I should press all charges and have you taken out of the picture for the duration.'

'I have a good lawyer.' Not strictly true, but I know Grace could find me one. 'We'd post bail. Do you really want to fight, or do you want to beat these buggers?'

'What do you think, Baxter?'

'To use your own words, we're teetering on a knife-edge. Actions speak louder than words. The longer you keep me locked up, the more I'll be convinced we're not on the same side.'

25

The next morning, sore and stiff from a restless night on an uncomfortable bed, we're woken early. With his shift soon to end, the burly custody officer escorts Baz and me from the holding cell and hands back our possessions. We are, we're told, free to leave.

My first task is to call Inés. It's gone six in the morning and she should be awake. Having thought a lot about this overnight, I am still not sure how she's going to react. In the event, I needn't have worried. Far from blaming me, she's made the mental leap to conclude that if I hadn't been willing to trade myself for Marta, with or without the police's intervention, then she wouldn't have her daughter back. Her anger of yesterday gone, not only is she keen to see me, but also she's happy to continue having Baz babysit them both. I ring off and find a text from Grace and several missed calls. Ominously, the text was sent at four-forty in the morning, the calls every half an hour since. I dial her mobile. She answers almost immediately.

'Mister Rick, where have you been? There's been a disaster.'

'I've been in a police cell all night. What's happened?'

'My Lordy, a police cell? This gets worse. Someone's set fire to our offices.'

'What?' Baz turns to look at me. I am simultaneously shaking my head and rolling my eyes.

‘Around three in the morning. They broke the conference suite window and threw in a petrol bomb.’

‘How bad is it?’

‘Freds and I are here at the moment. The room is pretty messed up. Elsewhere, it’s not so bad. The alarm went off real quick, and the fire brigade wasn’t far behind. There’s water everywhere.’

‘Have the police been?’

‘I think so. In the confusion, there have been so many comings and goings.’

‘I’m going to collect my car. I’ll be with you as soon as I can.’

The damage, when I lay eyes on it later, is more extensive than Grace had intimated. Mercifully, most of it is superficial. The walls and ceilings in the conference suite are blackened, the second-hand wooden table that once dominated the space now a charred ruin. The cheap grey carpet tiles covering the concrete floor are sodden underfoot. My own office has survived relatively unscathed. There’s water in places on the floor, but the furniture, what little there ever was, remains intact. The smell of smoke is everywhere. Grace is checking the filing cabinets in the corner of my office when I enter.

‘Oh, you’re here. Thank the Lord.’

She rushes to give me a spontaneous hug. This, in her book, is one occasion that evidently warrants human contact.

‘What have you and Baz been doing in a police cell, Mister Rick?’ She steps back, peering at me like a judge over the rim of her glasses. As if my demeanour was going to tell her all she needed to know.

‘It’s a long story.’ I look around the office. ‘Do we have the power back on?’

‘Not yet. The electrician is on his way.’

‘I saw Freds out the front. Has he been okay?’

‘He’s fine. He loves all the commotion, everyone back and forth, giving him attention.’

‘Any news from Kels?’

‘Not a peep.’

I go for a wander and end up back in the former conference suite. The glass in most of the windows has been destroyed, the fresh air doing its best to clear the stench of smoke and damp.

‘Have you contacted the insurers?’ Grace has meandered into the room after me.

‘They’re sending a loss adjuster around later this morning.’

‘That’s quick.’

‘Business is slow. It’s still the summer holidays.’

‘We’ll need the carpet tiles put in a skip and dehumidifiers everywhere. It should soon dry, especially in this weather.’

My phone buzzes. It’s a text from Kels, asking me to send her a copy of the picture I have of Moravková. I find the shot snapped from Inés’s files and ping it straight back. I decide not to mention the fire.

‘What time is Vince due?’

‘He’s normally here around now.’ With that, I hear Freds barking and look up to find the man himself peering around the door frame.

‘What the bloody hell’s happened?’

Grace fills him in. He looks at me and shrugs.

'Seems we didn't make any friends yesterday. How did you get on, Ricky?'

It's the moment to tell Grace and him the whole story. When I get to the bit about Baz and my night in the cells, Vince laughs out loud.

'Rather you than me, mate.'

'We do have Marta back, but I'm worried about Alisa. I feel responsible.'

'What do you want to do, Mister Rick?'

'Can you deal with the loss adjusters and start getting the place cleaned up?' I ask Grace. 'If so, Vince and I need to find Alisa before it's too late.'

'It's already in hand.'

I turn to go and then remember. 'What about that notebook and the debit cards?'

'I made copies like you asked. They're in my strongbox, along with the originals.'

'They survived the fire?'

'Good as new.'

Which is when the office phone rings. Grace steps to one side to pick up the call.

'What are you thinking?' Vince asks me as we head out the door.

'The time has come to confront Gregor in person. The longer we leave it ...'

'Mister Rick!' Vince and I are outside when I hear Grace shouting from behind. 'Mister Rick, there's a police officer on the line. Says it's very urgent. His name is Saunderson.'

'Tell him I'll call back in a while,' I say, already turning towards the side alley leading to the car park.

'He says it's about Alisa.'

I stop dead in my tracks and turn to face Grace. Vince and I exchange glances. I let out a heavy sigh and begin walking back to the office.

'I think I need to take this call,' I say, as much to myself as to Vince or Grace. My heart feels heavy with a sense of foreboding.

26

'What time did you and Baxter finish up last night, boss?'

'About two in the morning.'

'He must have been pleased we got the girl back.'

'Relieved, more like it, Sarge. Though he was anxious about another woman.'

'Who?'

'A client of his. Someone working at one of the clubs. Baxter claimed Gregor was threatening retaliation if the police showed up.'

'Bloody gangsters, the lot of them. Baxter's no better.'

'Funny you should say that. I told him the same thing myself.'

'I bet he enjoyed hearing that.'

'I doubt he'll lose any sleep over it. I've got to hand it to him, though.'

'What?'

‘He’s got further in two or three days than we have in the last few months. Guess who he said he bumped into?’

‘You tell me.’

‘Only Irina bloody Moravková!’

‘In London?’

‘That’s what he said. Accosted him and his girlfriend on the streets.’

‘Bloody hell! The rest of the team aren’t going to enjoy hearing that. How the hell does she come and go so easily? She’s been on everyone’s red-hot ‘must stop’ list.’

‘Baxter reckons Moravková’s got a body double with blonde hair, goes by the name of Tanya. Tanya Kocianová. Ring any bells?’

‘News to me, boss. Let me check the system. Not heard of her at all. How did Baxter meet this Tania?’

‘Went on a fishing expedition in the Fenland farming community with his sidekick, Shabaz. The Iraqi Kurd he calls Baz. Claims to have run into her up there.’

‘Nope. There’s no record of anyone by that name in our database. Perhaps Irina wears a blonde wig occasionally.’

‘Same thought crossed my mind. However, Baxter was adamant they were two different people. I guess he should know.’

‘Well, it’s another lead to work on.’

‘I thought it was quite helpful.’

‘You let Baxter go, though, didn’t you? You had ample grounds to detain him, but you let him off the hook. Why?’

‘Fair question. It’s one I’ve been wrestling with a lot these last few hours. Basically, I concluded we’re more or less on the same side. Even if he does charge in like a bull in a china shop, stamping on everything and everybody with his oversized feet.'

'You referring to his prosthetics?'

'Very droll, Sarge.'

'Hang on a moment. Oh, shit. Come and look what's just flashed up on the screen.'

'What?'

'A body's been found on a residential street near Mile End. Close to Victoria Park. A woman in her twenties, found dead on the pavement. That's near where Baxter lives, isn't it?'

'I guess, along with several thousand others. What about it?'

'Says here she was a hostess in a nightclub near Stratford.'

'Please don't tell me her name's Alisa.'

'It doesn't give a name. At least I can't see one in this report. Let me check another system.'

'I've got a bad feeling about this. Does it say how she died?'

'Overdose. Forensics thought it might be fentanyl. Shit, it has to be the same woman. A Latvian by the name of Pakalnina. Alisa Pakalnina.'

'Baxter's going to go mental.'

'What do we do now?'

'I'd better call him. He'll be out of custody and won't want to hear this at all.'

27

I remember once hearing an American talking about addiction. This was a good, honest middle-class man who had led a blemish-free existence for most of his life, apart from one brief spell in his late teens when he'd been arrested for possession of what the DEA calls a Schedule II drug. He received a fine and a suspended sentence. It was a wake-up call. From that moment onwards, he declared himself clean. He went to college, graduated and joined the Marines. He proved to be a fine recruit. Three years after he passed out from the Marine Corps Recruit Depot in South Carolina, out of the blue, his CO summoned him and told him he was being dishonourably discharged. He had failed to declare the drug infringement on his Marine application form. The reporter asked him how he'd coped with this setback.

'Not well,' had been his candid reply. 'At first, with alcohol. The drugs came later. It began with the booze.'

I know how he felt. I'd felt the same way when Cath died. I made an almost identical resolution. I kept away from drugs, but my bender lasted the best part of several weeks. It began that very night, and my drinking didn't stop until the day I tried my luck on the Swiss Wall above Champéry in Switzerland a few weeks later. The fact I'd probably had several beers before that fateful ski run was most likely a contributing factor to the loss of both limbs. The accident proved a vital wake-up call.

They say a memory learned is rarely forgotten. The trick is knowing the triggers that allow your brain to unlock a forgotten recollection or behaviour. The moment the call with Saunderson is over, I already know how I am going to cope with Alisa's death. Or rather, my failure to keep her alive. The same way I responded to Cath's sudden departure. Alcohol. It's not rational, but it's going to happen. Where's my fighting spirit, some might ask? In a glass. Doesn't Gregor warrant the Besim and Tariq treatment? He might. In time, he most likely will. My brain, however, is telling me I need a drink. As I walk out the door, past a bewildered-looking Grace and a confused Vince, I am heading for the pub. It's only ten in the morning. The place around the corner will just be opening.

'What's happened?' Vince calls after me, even though they can already guess from my demeanour.

'Mind the shop for me,' I shout back at him, already striding out. 'And check that Baz has got Inés and her daughter covered.'

The first beer hardly touches the sides. With the second, the voice in my head starts talking to me.

Failure. Once is unfortunate. Twice unforgivable.

If you go throwing your weight around, Ricky, you've only got yourself to blame for the consequences. Do you understand?

If Besim and Tarik had been women, would you still be punching them in the face and pouring boiling water over their boobs and bits?

Then, from out of nowhere, I remember Saunderson's words.

Some might reflect, Ricky Baxter, that skewering someone's thigh with a prosthetic leg spike or mashing a kneecap with a baseball bat puts you in the same category of wanton thuggery as those who go about abusing young women.

This last one hurts. I buy another beer. Only halfway through this third pint do I feel my sorrows begin, slowly, to drown.

'Mister Rick. Mister Rick. I am needing you awake, not sleeping.'

Someone is shaking my arm. I look up and see Grace's face coming into focus.

'Look at you, Mister Rick. You should know better. Drinking at this time of the day. It's not even lunchtime.'

'Go away.' Even I don't like the sound of my voice. However, as Grace comes into focus, sitting next to me at the pub table with her arms crossed, I know I'm in trouble.

'What is it with you men and alcohol? Are you finished with your drinking now, Mister Rick? Because if so, we have a business to run.'

'Alisa's dead,' I mumble.

'So, the world's problems are on your shoulders now, is that it? I've never heard anything so ridiculous in all my life.' I notice she has moved my beer glass to a different table.

'I need more beer.'

'You, Mister Rick, need strong, black coffee. What would Inés be saying?'

'She'd be joining me.'

'No she wouldn't, and you know it. I've even had Kels on the phone.'

'Kels?'

'Yes. But I'm not letting you speak to her while you're like this. It wouldn't be right.'

'Grace, I've let everyone down.' It's when I turn to stare at her I realise I am about to get a lecture.

'Whenever my husband appeared in the house as drunk as you are, I would run for cover.' Grace's sing-song cadence is soothing and melodic. 'When he was drunk, he was so violent. I used to ask him why he'd been drinking. He never told me. I suspect his subconscious mind was already trying to run away. Instead, he would hit me, beat me with his belt and do things – if I told you about them now, I, too, might hit the bottle. Thank the Lord, those memories are behind me. I don't need the booze to drown my sorrows. Can you guess why, Mister Rick?'

I am receiving this monologue whilst staring at the table. I look up fleetingly and see the stern look. Arms crossed, Grace is giving me both barrels.

'The reason I don't need booze, Mister Rick, is because of you. The reason Baz has not broken down and drowned in his grief for his sister and family back home is also because of you. Same with the Renatas of this world – why do you think they sleep at night? Why do you think Inés has so much goddamned respect for you? Is it because at the first sign of a disappointment you run for the booze and drown your sorrows? No, it's because you put yourself before others and you sort stuff out. You charge off to find her daughter with no fear for your personal safety. That's the Mister Rick we all need in our lives. Are you listening to me? It's time you sorted yourself out and gave yourself a damned good talking to. There are far too many people in this world who depend on the Ricky Baxter they know and love. They don't need him sitting in the boozer at eleven-thirty in the morning. You have work to do, Mister Rick. Who gave you permission to get pissed just because they find some poor Latvian girl dead? You need to be out finding these horrible people and sorting them out fast.'

I look into those impenetrable brown eyes of hers. To my surprise, I don't see anger or disappointment. I see compassion. In that instant, tears well and I look away to hide my embarrassment.

'I'm sorry,' I mumble. 'We're a good team, Grace, you know that.' When she sees my eyes, she cries out.

'Oh my Lord, now you stop that, Mister Rick. Otherwise, you'll have us all going.'

Because Grace is intelligent, she doesn't send me home to fend for myself but takes me back to the office. Vince has been minding the fort, supervising four men who have turned up with a skip. Currently, they are removing sodden carpet tiles and the charred remains of the conference suite table.

'The men helped me move the sofa into your room,' Vince announces. He's too polite to make any comment about my state of inebriation. 'After a night in the cells with Baz, I reckoned you might need a kip. I'm sure Freds will be happy to share some sofa space.'

Grace, thoughtful as ever, has left a large mug of lukewarm black coffee and some paracetamol. I down these, shuffling an unusually grumpy Freds to the other end of the sofa, and lie down. Instantly, I'm asleep.

Some time later, I feel Freds stirring. As I come to the surface, I find Inés at the door alongside Grace.

'Is this what happens when you share a police cell with Baz? You're forced to sneak back to the office to sleep things off.'

I smile thinly and raise my head. The room moves a little before settling down to something like normal.

'I gather you might be a little delicate.'

'How's Marta?'

'Fine. At home with Baz, talking to a Community Support person when I left. I thought I'd come and find you.'

'We lost Alisa.'

'These are not nice people, Rick.'

'I should have done more.'

'That's a crazy thing to say. You're going to find Gregor and the other two women, aren't you?'

'I hope.'

'And Samira?'

'Who knows?'

‘Now you’re being ridiculous. Stop beating yourself up.’

‘I think I need the bathroom.’ I rush past Inés, just making it in time. When I return, Grace is holding out a glass of water.

‘I could make more coffee if you like?’

‘Don’t worry,’ Inés interrupts. ‘I’ll take him home and look after him.’

‘Just make sure he rests. I need him fit and well for the morning.’

‘What’s happening in the morning?’ I ask, leaning against Inés for support.

‘You are heading to Paris.’

‘Ooh, can I come?’ Inés pipes up.

‘If Mister Rick says.’

‘What’s happening in Paris?’

‘Kels needs you to meet someone.’

‘Kels? But she’s in Bratislava. Why am I heading to Paris? It’s Saturday tomorrow.’

‘She said she’d call later today once she had more to tell. She sounded excited. When she and I spoke, I hadn’t reckoned on you conducting your own private beer tasting.’ Once again, she peers at me over the top of her glasses. ‘Are you well enough to be taking all this in?’

‘Sure,’ I say with more confidence than I feel. ‘If Kels says I need to go, I think I should go.’

‘Good. You’re booked on the first Eurostar. It leaves at twenty to six in the morning. It should get there by nine.’

‘I should probably try to find Gregor first.’

'I really don't think that's wise,' Grace says firmly. 'Let him feel he's won a minor victory. Leave it twenty-four hours. There's no point charging straight back in like an angry elephant.'

Grace's words make Inés laugh.

'I like that. Ricky Baxter as an angry elephant. On second thoughts, I can't go to Paris. I have too much on. Marta and I were planning to go away for a few days next week.'

'Too bad. I was rather hoping you might keep an eye on Mister Rick.'

'Don't worry,' I say to them both. 'I feel well and truly admonished. I won't be wandering off the reservation in a hurry, I promise.'

28

'I don't believe it!'

'What's up, Sarge?'

'It's weird. We've just had a tip-off from UK Border Force. Your man, Ricky Baxter. He's on his way to Paris, on the early morning Eurostar.'

'Paris? What on earth's taking him there, for God's sake?'

'Your guess is as good as mine.'

'Is he on his own?'

'As far as we know.'

'Off on a romantic liaison on the banks of the Seine, do we think?'

'With someone else, you mean? He seems to be getting on quite nicely with the Keller woman.'

'That never stops some people. What's Gregor or Irina got business-wise in Paris?'

'Nothing we're aware of.'

'So, a client gets murdered, Baxter is rightly pissed, he'll assume Gregor was behind her death, yet what does he do? He heads to Paris. Despite my warnings, I'd rather expected him to be thumping down Gregor's door and pouring boiling water over his privates.'

'Maybe he's heeded your advice.'

'Who, Baxter? Don't make me laugh.'

'SWhy Paris?'

'Precisely. Who do we know over there?'

'What about Diday?'

'The woman who helped on the O'Grady operation? That's not a bad idea. She was reliable. What time does the Eurostar arrive in Paris?'

'In about thirty minutes.'

'See if you can make contact and call in a few favours. I'd love to know what the hell Baxter's up to.'

Samira's Story

Part 5

I still screw my eyes tight shut, even now. These days, I'm finding it more and more difficult to transport my conscious self to my special place. Everything has become foggier, my recollections less coherent. I think I am losing my mind. Every day I pray to whatever God put me in this hellhole: please take me to a new life somewhere else. Somewhere better. Surely that is not too much to hope for?

I have lost track of time, let alone my senses. Days have become weeks. Weeks have merged into months. Some days, I am so drained, so exhausted, I wonder whether I am still alive. I hear no news about anything. They tell me my dear brother is dead, that my family back home in Iraq are safe, but only because my work here keeps them alive. I no longer believe them or anybody. What is truth? What is life? What, especially, is its purpose?

Countless times we have moved locations. Pop-ups, they call them. Often different cities. They put us up in Airbnb's or rented accommodation, often for no more than five days at a time. Sometimes they drive us, but more often than not we take the train or the bus. They control us through our debts. We are not about to wander off and escape. What awaits our arrival is always the same. After all this time, I feel more like an animal than a human being, fatted for the bedroom rather than the slaughter. As part of our diet, they feed us drugs. At first, we hated it. Now we crave our nightly fix, transporting our minds to this foggy space. For a few hours each night, our cares no longer torment us. In this manner, we drift from customer to customer. At the weekends, there can be six or seven clients in one evening. I am beyond caring. I do what they ask. It allows me to pay my bills, reduce my debts, and to help ease the suffering my parents would otherwise be enduring. That is what I believe. That is what the other girls believe. None of us feels strong enough any more to challenge what we are told. The work is endless. At those times of the month when our bodies force us to take a break, we are taken to Gregor's nightclubs instead. I dread these days more than any. There, in sordid back rooms, we use our bodies in different ways to what God intended in order to keep earning money.

One evening, out of the blue, something strange happens. The woman from my nightmares appears. Not the blonde-haired version I met one week into our life in England. Well, it is her, but also it is someone different. My mind is playing tricks. This is the woman from my Turkish border nightmare. The same dark brown hair, now cropped shorter, like a man's. The same piercing blue eyes. She even recognises me – and laughs. She calls out my name. See, there are two of them after all. This one and the blonde – the one I thought at the beginning was the same woman but wasn't. Side by side. I think I'm seeing double, apart from the hair. They are talking about me. Not in a language I understand. They keep looking at me and smiling. In a leering, rather than happy, way. As if I was the subject of one of their jokes. Then the one with the dark brown hair comes and sits opposite.

'It's been a long journey, Samira. They tell me you're a hard worker. Your brother would be proud.'

'My brother is dead.' When I have eaten and the drugs are kicking in, my voice is always flat. Sometimes, I can't believe it is me who is speaking.

'Let me tell you a secret,' she continues. 'Your brother is not dead.'

Despite the drugs, these words shock me, though don't start imagining me jumping up and down for joy. My reactions these days are always muted by the chemicals in my blood. 'Is this true?' I say, my tone matter-of-fact. I struggle to process words at the best of times. I feel confused. Confused because I do not understand how he could have been dead before and now alive. I do, I confess, feel a faint glimmer of hope, the first in a very long time.

'He suffered an accident at work. For a while, we thought he had died. Recently, we learned he's alive. That might seem good news. The bad news is he's not been repaying any of the money he owes. With interest, his debts have become substantial.'

'Why are you telling me this?'

'Because, Samira, within a family there are obligations. When one member doesn't pay –' she pauses, studying her fingernails '– there have to be consequences.' She looks up and smiles. 'Sometimes, the price is necessarily high.'

The woman stands up. Without another word, she and her lookalike twin with the blonde hair walk away, leaving me alone to contemplate her words. Could it be true that Baz is alive?

Another person then enters the room. Someone else I recognise. The female doctor with the rough hands.

'Hello, Samira,' she says, taking an elasticated strap from her medical bag and tightening it around the bicep on my left arm. 'We meet again.'

'What are you doing?' I ask as she begins probing the inside of my elbow joint with two fingers.

'Feeling for a pulse. I need to conduct more blood tests.' She takes a needle from a sterilised pack and inserts it into a vein.

'Why?' I watch, transfixed, as she fills several empty plastic vials with my crimson blood. When she finishes, I hold a piece of cotton wool over the puncture wound and wait for her to fix a piece of sticky tape on top, as she did the last time.

'Because we want to check you're okay.' It is a pointless answer, but as much as I expected.

The examination proves less intrusive than before, although, strangely, in some ways it is more thorough. She peers into my eyes at great length and takes swabs of saliva from my throat. I'm told to piss into a plastic jug, which I refuse to do in front of her, so she has to leave the room. Next, a load of measurements: my height, and the dimensions of my arms, hands, legs and feet. Finally, taking the slimmest set of electronic scales from her bag, she records my weight. Forty-four kilos. Like a child. I am not tall and have not been eating well.

She departs as quietly as she arrived. It leaves me wondering about many things. My brother, and the hope he might be alive. The two women who I had thought were the same, but now I know differently. The surprise blood test and medical. And finally, the woman's cryptic comment before she left. 'Sometimes, the price is necessarily high'. What was that supposed to mean?

Two days later, without explanation, I am on the move again. The few meagre clothes and possessions I own have been bundled into my bag. Once more, I am sitting in another vehicle, travelling to another nameless town or city. This constant changing of locations has become routine. This occasion, however, feels different. For starters, the vehicle is not an old, battered minivan but a smart new car. Unusually, I am the only one on the move. Typically, there might be five or six of us crammed in together, being shuffled to a new pop-up. This time, it is just the driver and me. He isn't the usual sort, either. This one is smartly dressed and has a weird scorpion tattoo on his bald scalp. He doesn't utter one word the entire journey, and it is almost dark by the time the car turns in through a gated entranceway in the middle of the open countryside. The house we arrive at looks immense and old, set in large grounds. It is like nothing I have ever seen before.

The driver escorts me inside, makes me sit in an ornate library, and tells me to wait. And wait. After ages of being still, when I am tempted to wonder if anyone is ever going to appear, I hear a voice calling to me. The one I now dread more than almost any on this planet.

'Samira.' I turn to stare at the advancing figure. Once more, my mind is transported back to that hideous night in Turkey. 'Welcome to my home.' She is standing in front of me, looking from all angles, appraising me like one would a stallion. 'Aren't you going to ask why you're here?'

I shake my head and stare at the floor, my breathing shallow. I don't know whether to be terrified or relieved. Perhaps this is the end of the road. Maybe I am to be given one last meal before being taken into the fields and shot through the back of the head.

'Don't look so terrified. There's nothing to be frightened of. I want you to relax. Think of this as a mini-holiday. I want you eating well and sleeping well. Most importantly, I want you to rest. My sister and I have a special task we want you to perform. Something generous: very humane, but also courageous. Do this, and we will wipe the slate clean. Forgive all your debts. And those of your brother. It will be life-changing. How does that sound?'

'Why?' I don't trust anything she says. Especially given the way she spoke about Baz the other day.

'Because you are a special person, Samira.' I say nothing. 'Unique.'

'What is it you want?'

'Nothing dangerous. Nothing illegal. We require you to be generous with your body one last time. In a different way, but many times more important.'

A sudden thought pops into my head.

'You want me to have someone's child?' To my horror, she laughs.

'Don't be so foolish. Nothing so dramatic.'

'Will I be staying here?'

'For a couple of days. After that, you will be with Gregor in London. Until the time comes for you to perform the task I mentioned.' My alarm must have shown on my face. 'Don't look so worried. He and his men are under strict instructions. No one is to lay a finger on you anymore, I promise. One of his girls will look after you.' She can see I am still frightened. 'Come, let's have some food. I will then show you to your room. I think you'll find it very comfortable.'

29

Even before the Eurostar is pulling out of St Pancras station, I am asleep, woken only by the change in pressure as the train enters the tunnel under the English Channel. I reflect on the conversation with Kels the previous evening. I was sober by that stage, if not at my best.

Grace had been right. Kels had been pumped up. Her electronic snooping had kicked off even before her plane had left the tarmac at London's City airport. Armed with the Slovakian number she had unearthed from Tanya's driver's call list, she had used a piece of GPS tracking software to trace the caller's location to the University Hospital in Bratislava. She then dialled the number and discovered the person at the other end was a consultant nephrologist at the hospital by the name of Tomas Horváth. Kels had felt it necessary to explain that meant Horváth was a kidney specialist. Like many medics, he apparently spoke good English. I imagine the conversation between the two of them having gone something like this:

'Doctor Horváth? I am Tanya Kocianová's new assistant. You rang Tanya recently.'

'Tanya Kocianová? I don't believe I recognise the name.'

'My apologies. You probably know her by her maiden name, Moravková.'

'Ah yes, now I remember.' An educated but lucky guess on Kels's part. 'Yes, it was about her mother's transfer to Paris, I recall. I had to contact her driver to make the arrangements.'

'That's the reason for my call. I've recently started working for Tanya. I'm ringing to find out what further arrangements might be required.' Kels speaking on the phone would be like putting a shy person behind the wheel of a car. As long as there was no need for eye contact, she would sound more or less normal.

'About the Paris transfer, you mean?'

'That and beyond.'

'It depends on the test results. She's seeing Doctor Joubert when she arrives in Paris next week. We should know the results within a day or two at most.'

'Did Tanya's driver resolve everything? Or does anything else need sorting?'

'No, I think it's all in hand. Tanya's pilot is bringing her to Paris. The dialysis arrangements at the clinic she's staying at are all confirmed.'

Early the next morning, settled in her friend's apartment in Bratislava, Kels had her second lucky break. Her gaming friend, the one whose apartment floor she was camped out on, had another friend who was an administrator at the University Hospital. After a brief telephone exchange, favours were called in, the friend agreeing to do some quiet digging into Moravková on the hospital's patient records system. By ten in the morning, Kels had received Elena Moravková's home address together with a summary of her medical condition. The prognosis did not sound good. Aged only fifty-nine, she had one kidney that had ceased to function, and the other operating at only around thirty per cent. Without a transplant, she was unlikely to see the year out. Finding a suitable donor was proving problematic since she had an unusual leukocyte antigen type. Kels had explained these were tissue proteins. If money was no object, the medical team in Bratislava had said, she should consider going abroad, where the research and testing facilities were much more extensive than they were in Slovakia.

Most people might have stopped there, thinking they'd already uncovered enough. Kels, newly emboldened by her discoveries, decided she needed to see Moravková for herself. Posing as a market researcher seeking feedback on the local hospital's nephrology department, Kels found a clipboard and went knocking on Elena Moravková's door. As Baz had suggested, the apartment was close to the castle, although not somewhere, Kels admitted to me, she would likely have found on her own. To her surprise, Moravková not only answered the door but also invited her in. Kels described her as being unkempt and mildly eccentric, which, given Kels's own extreme style, left me wondering how bad it might have been.

They sat in Moravková's kitchen. She explained to Kels she had taught English in a school for many years and was happy to speak the language. Kels began asking several pre-scripted questions relating to her condition and the treatment she'd been receiving. As Moravková began talking, elements of her story tumbled out. She'd had two daughters who now lived abroad. Their tissue types were such that the proteins they'd inherited from Moravková and her late husband made them unsuitable donors. Already, she had waited two years to find a donor in Slovakia, but to no avail. Now on full-time dialysis – the kind allowing her to lead mostly a normal life but still requiring her to be wired up to a machine at night – she knew that without a transplant, she would die in months. Her daughters had offered to pay for her to get treatment abroad. Specifically Paris, where researchers at the Paris Transplant Group had made considerable strides in helping patients to get as near-perfect a donor match as possible. The good news, she announced to Kels, almost in a whisper, was that her daughters believed they might have found a donor. She was soon to travel to Paris for tests. If all went to plan and the donor proved suitable, she would have the operation within days.

The final nugget came when Kels was saying her goodbyes. She asked when Moravková was flying to Paris. First thing on Sunday had been her reply, to which Kels had asked whether there were many direct flights.

'I'm lucky. My daughters are successful business people. They use private planes all the time. They are letting me use one to fly direct from here to Paris-Beauvais airport. It's where many of the private charters go, apparently.'

Waiting for a taxi at the Gare du Nord, I have the distinct sensation I am being watched. There is no one I recognise, but my hackles are raised. I am about to dismiss it as paranoia when I spot a man turning abruptly away from my backward glance. I had seen this same person on the station platform when I'd left the train. I remember walking past him and thinking he had an angular, beak-like nose.

Moments before it's my turn for the next taxi, I peel away from the queue, pretending to take a call on my phone. I meander this way and that, looking as if I'm deep in conversation, eventually ducking behind a set of pillars and disappearing. Thus hidden, I watch in amusement as first beaky nose, then a female colleague come rushing past, searching but failing to spot me. Waiting until they have disappeared in the opposite direction, I hurry back to the front of the taxi line, make my apologies to a few angry people, and take the next taxi.

Unsure who might be interested in my visit to Paris, I sit back and try to relax. The taxi crawls its way through the morning rush-hour traffic to the hospital in Clichy, where Christian Joubert has his clinic.

'*Bonjour*,' I say in my best sing-song French to the young receptionist. '*Parlez-vous Anglais*?' I deploy my best Rich Somers with added Zimbabwean charm.

'Naturally. How may I help?' She flicks a blonde fringe to one side and returns my smile. She has lovely eyes.

'I am looking for Doctor Joubert's assistant. Am I in the right place?'

'Today, that's me. My name is Claudette.' She offers her hand, which

I shake.

'Working the weekends?'

'In this place, we work every day.'

'Join the club. Let me introduce myself. I'm Rich Somers, general sorter-out of things to the Moravková family. I believe you have Mrs Elena Moravková booked in to see Doctor Joubert on Monday, is that correct?'

'Let me check, Monsieur Somers. Yes, here we are, she will see Doctor Joubert at nine in the morning. Staying at a private apartment for three nights. Arriving Sunday. We have arranged for the dialysis equipment and fluids to be ready for her arrival for the duration of her stay.'

'Excellent, thank you. It matches what I have here too,' I say, staring at imaginary calendar entries on my cell phone.

'Very good. Was there something in particular you wanted my help with? Otherwise, I believe we are under control with all the arrangements from our side.'

'There was one small … thing.' I wince as if it's a matter of some embarrassment. 'Madame Moravková is anxious about the transplant, assuming it happens. She appreciates the enormous support her daughters have given in helping her find a suitable donor, so is keen not to trouble them with this request. Part of next week's assessment is verifying the suitability of one particular donor, I understand?'

Claudette stares at the screen and scrolls down before nodding in the affirmative.

'Since I was coming to Paris today, she asked if I could find out just a little more about the donor. She's a little worried about everything. I'm sure you see this a lot.'

'We do, and it's perfectly normal. Let me see what I can tell you. Yes, here we are. The donor, she is a woman, younger than Madame Moravková, same height and body mass. That's almost all the information I have.'

'A European?'

'I don't think so. No, she is not European, I can see now.'

'Do you know what nationality?'

'She is from Iraq.' There's an ominous feeling in the pit of my stomach.

'When you say younger, how much younger?' I ask.

'It says she's eighteen.' Alarm bells are now ringing loudly.

'Is such an age difference unusual?'

'A little perhaps, but not especially.'

'Will she be paid? The donor, I mean.'

'My goodness, no. Although you are right: some people,' she says, reducing her voice to a whisper, '*les migrants, peut-être* –' she raises her eyebrows '– are desperate. We never approve of selling organs for money. However, it's difficult to police. Naturally, we demand that the donors sign declarations. Honestly, though, we can never be totally sure.' She looks at me and shrugs.

'I don't suppose you know the name?'

Claudette shakes her head.

'Until it is confirmed we have a strong match, we never know, I'm sorry.'

'However, she's in the UK right now?'

'That is correct.'

'The transplant, if it happens, will be performed here?'

'Not perhaps this hospital, but in Paris, *bien sûr*. The team here are world-famous. Our diagnostics are amongst the best in the world. She can have confidence in a successful outcome after an assessment at Doctor Joubert's clinic. Besides,' she shrugs, 'the UK health system is so unpredictable. Transplantation is never straightforward. Madame Moravková's condition is complicated. That is why we are happy to welcome her to Paris.'

I leave the hospital and search for a taxi. In this part of Paris, that proves easier said than done. Here, there are almost no shops, the tree-lined streets flanked by badly parked cars, apartment blocks and faceless buildings. I have been walking for ten minutes, searching in vain for the familiar green light of an empty taxi, when a grey Renault pulls to the curb. A man in the passenger seat buzzes the window down. Immediately I recognise him. Beaky nose. In the driver's seat, the women from the station I'd seen earlier.

'Get in,' he says and reaches behind to flip the door. There's no menace in his tone, and so I get in. I reckon I have the advantage in the back, sitting behind them both, him in particular. I have, after all, some cable ties in my pocket.

'Why are you following me?' I ask.

'Making sure you are not causing problems.'

'I saw you at the station. You weren't very good.'

'That's what you think. We found you, didn't we?'

'Who are you?'

'Shall we say DI Saunderson sends his compliments? He hopes you are not disobeying his orders.' All is suddenly much clearer.

'Well, I'm in Paris, not London, so I must be.'

'Perhaps. What were you doing at the hospital?'

'Client-patient confidentiality. My lips are sealed.'

'No matter, we'll find out. Where to next?'

'Are you offering to play taxi driver?'

'We have two options. You get out of the car, wait for a taxi, and we follow. Or else we agree to help each other and make life more agreeable. You choose.'

'If I get out of the car, I'm quite good at playing cat and mouse.'

'Maybe, but don't forget: Paris is our city. We'll find you.'

'Beauvais Airport then, please.'

'Not Roissy?'

'Thanks, but no. Beauvais will do fine.'

'Any particular reason?'

'Sorry, client confidentiality again. My lips are sealed. Doubtless, in time, you'll find out.'

30

Not everything works out the way we plan. With my Eurostar return still nestling in my pocket, I was expecting to return to Gare du Nord station by train from Beauvais. But that was before I wander into the Private Aviation terminal at Paris-Beauvais and, out of the blue, bump into none other than one of my oldest friends, Kit Myers.

Myers and I have history. In the way adolescents growing up together and misbehaving always have history. Most of it was stuff these days we'd rather was kept under wraps. We weren't at the same school but in the same farming community. Kit's father used to be a bush pilot in and around Bulawayo. He and his wife were good friends with my parents and must have fled to the UK about the same time we did, since I have known Kit almost forever. As young boys, we were always larking around and misbehaving. Doing things we weren't meant to be doing. Then, in our teens, we began discovering women, and our partying took us in different directions. Eventually, we lost touch – until now.

'Ricky Baxter! Is it really you, mate?'

'Kit Myers, I'll be damned! My God, how long's it been? Twelve years at least.'

'Probably more.' In this unexpected manner, our catch-up begins. Not least because he's staring at me.

‘Good Lord, Ricky, what happened to your legs?’

Slowly we exchange stories. Myers is a full-time pilot, working for a business hiring chartered jets to wealthy executives and their families. Which is how I get to be offered a free ride with him back to London’s City airport. As I say, not everything works out the way you expect it.

‘When are you leaving?’

‘I have a take-off slot in just over an hour.’

‘Will you be flying the plane?’

‘Is the Pope a Catholic? Of course, I’ll be flying the bloody plane – a Cessna Citation. You’ll be very comfortable. Come on, we’ve time for a quick coffee before I need to do my pre-flight checks.’

‘Okay,’ I say, before adding: ‘There is a reason I’m here today. I’m looking for some help in tracking details about an inbound charter. It’s a private plane, arriving from Bratislava on Sunday.’

Which is how Myers introduces me to a friend of his. Antoine Laroche works for a rival operator and is of a similar age to Kit and me. He joins us both in the pilots’ lounge.

‘Irina Moravková? I know the name. Her pilot, he is a friend. Operates a Cessna 172. What we call a Skyhawk. Rubber band aircraft, not a jet. It’s nice. Not so fast as the Citation, but ...’ He gives a suitably Gallic shrug.

When I mention Bratislava, however, Laroche shakes his head.

‘The Skyhawk, it won’t have the range. It can refuel, naturally, but my guess is she’ll be chartering something bigger. The M2 or an Embraer 450, probably.’

‘Does Moravková use her plane a lot?’

‘The Skyhawk? According to her pilot, yes. He and I had a drink a few months ago. They say she’s a wealthy lady. He did tell me something interesting, though. Apparently –’ he lowers his voice ‘– she prefers to sneak in and out of the UK through the back door.'

'How does she do that?'

'Touch and go landings is my guess. That's the normal way. Especially with a small turboprop like the Skyhawk.'

'You've lost me.'

'It's simple, Ricky,' Myers intervenes. 'It's like my old man used to do all the time as a bush pilot. You fly from A to B, but on the way do a quick stop-off at point C. Perhaps you're dropping off a parcel. Or a passenger. A couple of minutes on the deck, then you're off again.'

'Would that be possible in the UK?'

'With a 172? Sure. All over the south of England, there are plenty of small airfields, many of them grass strips used by crop-dusting farmers, in theory. In reality, they're barely used. The airstrips are still maintained, however.'

'How would it work in practice?'

'I'm guessing there'd be a flight plan filed from Beauvais to Cambridge or Norwich airport. Possibly Southend, or Biggin Hill. They'd then pick a small grass strip somewhere nearby. The Skyhawk wouldn't be flying high. Besides, that thing can land on a sixpence. So, in it comes, wheels down on the grass or whatever and grinds to a halt. Passenger jumps out, the pilot slams on the power and away it goes. If the strip's long enough, he probably doesn't even need to turn the plane around.'

'Just like in the films,' Laroche chips in.

'Is this possible?'

'*Mais oui*!' Laroche continues. 'It's harder when you use a big destination airport because the manifest procedures are more robust. However, choose a smaller destination, somewhere just for light aircraft and limited radar. The pilot happily could do a touch and go at a nearby strip before landing at the intended airfield. No one would have a clue.'

‘Not about to become a smuggler, are you, Ricky?’ Myers quips.

‘I never realised it was so easy.’

‘Come on, time to go. Thanks, Antoine.’

We get to our feet. Whilst shaking hands with Laroche, I ask one last question.

‘Tell me, is there a way to look up some of Moravková’s recent flights to the UK? I’d be interested in finding out where she’s been flying to.’

‘Sure. Easy. Give me your mobile and I’ll text you with whatever I find.’

I hand him my card before following Myers out towards our plane.

31

It's four in the afternoon when the taxi drops me back at my house. I'm keen to make my gym slot today. I've already spoken to Grace. The office is slowly getting back to normal, she tells me, though the constant hum from dehumidifiers is testing her patience. I promise to fill her in about my trip in the morning. Usually, she doesn't let me get away so easily with delaying the gossip. However, after my moment of madness yesterday, I sense she's cutting me some slack. Especially since I told her I was hoping to spend the evening with Inés.

I have my key ready to unlock the door when I stop in my tracks. The wood around the frame is splintered. Someone has forced the lock with a crowbar. Bracing myself, I step inside and am confronted by mayhem. Everything has been trashed, all my possessions strewn everywhere. Each drawer, every cupboard. It's as if a bomb has gone off. I call Grace.

'Sounds like Gregor wants his stuff back,' she says.

'It's why I called. Can you and Vince move the originals out of the office and put them somewhere safe?'

'Sure. What about the copies I made?'

'I think it's time to share them with Saunderson.'

'What if he wants the originals?'

‘Tell him you don’t know where they are. Say I’ve got them.’

‘Do you need me to come and help clear up, Mister Rick?’

It’s a tempting offer, but I can’t ask this of Grace. Not given all she’s done. Not on a Saturday.

‘I’m fine at the moment. Thanks anyway.’

‘You calling the police?’

‘No. The time has come for Gregor and me to meet face to face.’

That time is approaching faster than I expect. I am clearing bits of detritus when my phone goes. Surprise, surprise, it’s Gregor.

‘Thieves keep messy houses, so I’m told.’ This is followed by a roar of laughter. I breathe carefully and say nothing. ‘Listen, you piece of shit. You have something I want. I have something you want.’

‘I have nothing you want. The police have it all.’

‘I’m talking about you.’

‘What about me?’

‘I have the Iraqi girl. The one you’re so desperate to find.’

‘Consider yourself dead, Gregor.’

‘Check the window, if you don’t believe me. There’s a black panel van with its side door open.’ The line goes dead. I move to peer out the front. There is indeed a black van double-parked outside my house. As I watch, the door slides open. Kneeling on the floor, hands and feet bound and a gun pointing at her head, is a young woman I have never met. Even from this distance, she looks like Baz. She also looks frightened and vulnerable.

Too late, I sense movement behind me. I swivel around. It is Irina's fellow biker. The North African. The one with the scorpion tattoo on his head. He must have come in through the back. There's a gun pointing directly at me. Suddenly, I seem to have lost the advantage.

Rough hands truss me like a chicken. For once, I'm not the one using cable ties. Scorpion-Head points the gun, whilst another minion works the nylon strap into the locking mechanism. One pair for my wrists, now behind my back. They then hustle me into the van, before placing another tie around my prosthetic feet. More or less where the ankles should be.

The girl and I lean against each other, back to back. For good measure, Scorpion-Head cuffs me hard across the face with his gun before leaping in the front with the other guy. The pistol-whipping sounds worse than it is but still creates a gash on one cheek.

'Samira?' I whisper, tentatively.

'Yes,' comes an equally hesitant reply. I breathe out a huge sigh of relief.

'Baz is safe. I thought you'd like to know.'

We don't speak again. Instead, I feel her sobbing, her body trembling gently against mine. In my pocket, my phone buzzes with an incoming text. Probably Saunderson checking up on me.

In time, the van comes to a halt in an underground garage somewhere. When the side door slides open, a small reception committee is waiting. It would seem I am the guest of honour. A man in a black T-shirt steps forward to cut the cable tie holding my prosthetic ankles together. I shuffle my way out of the van and onto my feet, my hands still tied behind me. Samira for the moment remains in the van.

One by one, five bouncer-types take it in turns to step forward. Two of them I recognise, three I don't. As the first one comes to a stop, tattoos on both forearms, he smiles thinly, then rains a right-left-right power punch combo directly at my abdomen. I brace in anticipation, but the force of the delivery still winds me. Definitely not a fail. He then steps aside and a second man advances, ready to go through a similar drill. It's Black T-shirt. Same thin smile, same combination punch. Also not a fail, though marginally not as strong. The third person waiting his turn is the puny guy. The one from the club that first Friday night. He doesn't smile but gives a cocky leer. It's his *I knew you were lying the other day* self-righteous expression. I've had enough of this playground bullshit. The moment he's about to imitate his betters, I deliver a massive headbutt directly to his nose and face. Strike one, and sod the consequences. As an afterthought, as his head sags downwards, I deliver a driving knee hard into his crutch for good measure.

The fourth man is quick to respond. Agile on his feet from the moment he steps forward, I soon have him marked as likely to be my most dangerous opponent. As the puny guy staggers to one side, this next one uses feet, not hands. First dancing a little jig in front of me, he quickly lashes out with his right foot. A bent-knee snap-kick targets my ribcage; the follow-through goes for the head. The first is on target, the second missing narrowly as I swerve away. Immediately, I feel an explosion of pain in one of my ribs.

As the fourth guy steps back, satisfied, the last remaining attacker is Scorpion-Head. He has a bike chain in his hand. Folded over, so it's two strands together. In the wrong hands, this could be a very nasty weapon.

'What kind of fight do you call this?' I am struggling to catch my breath, shooting pains from my angry and battered ribcage sending out alarm signals. 'Five fit and healthy against one disabled guy. The one, by the way, with his hands tied. If you want a fight, at least cut me loose so we can do this fairly.'

Scorpion-Head considers this for a moment.

'Sure,' he eventually says, to my surprise. 'One less thing for us to do later. With your dead body, that is.' He nods at Black T-Shirt, who steps forward with the pliers.

'Turn around.'

I do as he asks, one eye watching over my left shoulder. The moment I hear the nylon being cut, feel the release of pressure on my wrists, I pounce. Pivoting to my left, I deliver a right hook directly into the side of Black T-Shirt's face. Which has three consequences, the most immediate being an acute stabbing pain courtesy of my injured chest. Then Black T-Shirt falls in a satisfying heap to the floor. Finally, Scorpion-Head strides directly toward me like an angry bear, his right hand raised. My brain registers what's happening only as the chain is arcing downwards towards me. I try ducking sideways, but it still connects with my left arm. If not for my jacket, it might have been game over. As it is, the end of the chain wraps around my bicep with such force it rips the material to shreds and tears into the muscle.

Common sense should tell me to step back and reappraise options. The fighter in me wants to attack. With the bike chain still around my upper arm and not yet ready to unravel, I tug hard and draw Scorpion-Head in slightly closer. He's distracted by the chain not releasing, providing an opportunity for me to drive a massive, clenched fist to his face. You know when you hit a target well, and this one is on the money. Scorpion-Head now out for the count, that leaves just two remaining.

The moment my luck runs out.

From one side of the garage, a door opens. It's Gregor, flanked by two men. Both with guns. Both pointing directly at me.

'Tie him up.' The two remaining men, still on their feet, are happy to oblige. The guy with the tattoos on his forearms takes pleasure in yanking my hands hard behind my back. His karate-kicking colleague works the cable tie around my wrist, tugging sharply to tighten it. Given the open wound on my upper arm, I'm close to passing out from the pain. Scorpion-Head, staggering back on his feet, moves to stand beside Gregor. I can feel him eyeing me with deep loathing.

'Bring Baxter and the girl inside. Put them both in the basement lock-up.'

As Samira and I are frogmarched at gunpoint past Gregor, he puts out an arm to stop me.

'One more thing before you go.' I turn to look him in the eye. He's bigger than expected. Almost my height, well-built, pudgy around the gills with a scar on one cheek. 'You know, I think I'm going to have to teach you a lesson.'

I am tempted, there and then, to jump right in and have a go myself. This is the man responsible for so much abuse. Uncharacteristically, I do nothing – primarily because of Samira.

'You two,' he says to Tattoo Man and his colleague behind me. 'Hold him steady.' The pair forcibly grab my forearms. I am not in good shape, I realise. The area where the bike chain mauled me feels on fire. My ribcage, too, is ready to burst into an angry chorus at the slightest provocation.

Which is when Gregor throws his first punch. Not a weak amateur's feeble effort. This comes from a man my size and weight, and I am on the receiving end of the full sledgehammer treatment. I tense my abdominals in readiness when I see his arm swing, but it doesn't soften the blow.

'That one's for Besim.' Almost immediately, he strikes a second time, on this occasion with a double punch, right then left. 'Those two are for Tariq.' He keeps going like this. Punch after punch after punch. I lose count. I try to retch, but the pain in my arm, ribs and stomach is becoming intolerable. 'Come on, Baxter,' he taunts. 'Where's your fighting spirit?' At which point, my knees sag, and I sense the lights starting to go out.

32

Samira is still with me. The basement lock-up is more prison cell than a room: one lumpy mattress on the floor, a small basin and a stinky toilet in one corner. I still have my phone, but the battery has died. Neither of us has a watch. The cable ties may be gone, but the door is locked and bolted. We're not going anywhere. Everything aches. My insides feel sore, battered and bruised. The cut on my face has stopped bleeding, but my jaw and cheekbone hurt when I speak. My left arm feels raw, the muscle throbbing when I tense it, the upper arm area crusted with dried blood where the chain tried to rip me.

They slide a tray of food into the room at one stage. The food looks edible, considering. Right now, though, I can't face a thing. Instead, I try sipping water from the tap. My stomach complains angrily when I attempt to keep fluids down.

Bit by bit, Samira and I talk. I tell her about Baz and she weeps genuine tears of joy. She wants to know about his leg, asks how he is able to walk. So, I show her my two prosthetics, her eyes wide. She then tells me her story. The journey with her brother, the things not even Baz has felt able to tell me. When she describes the woman at the Turkish border, I know it has to be Irina. Her description of the ferry crossing is so vivid, so real, I find it hard to imagine what they had to endure. Hearing about her enslaved life of enforced prostitution makes me sick to my core.

'Promise me one thing.'

'What?' I reply.

'Never mention this to my brother. If he needs to know, I want it to be me who tells him.'

We doze side by side on the lumpy mattress.

'Why they are leaving us alone?' I mutter out loud at one stage, talking more to myself than Samira.

'Gregor is busy tonight,' she answers, to my surprise. 'I heard him discussing it before they put me in the van to come and find you. Important business, he called it.'

'Why are you here, though?' I ask, my brain slowly cranking.

'They needed me to get to you, I suppose.'

'I don't get it. Why would they do that? I was coming after Gregor, frankly, whether or not you were here. Okay, yes, I was also trying to find you. It hardly warranted them taking the trouble of bringing you here.'

Which is when she tells me about what Irina had said. About how she wanted Samira to be 'generous with her body one last time'. The penny is dropping. I have the same uncomfortable feeling I had when I was speaking to Claudette in Paris.

'Has anyone asked you to give blood, recently?'

She looks at me, puzzled.

'Why, yes. Twice. First, it was blood, urine, loads of measurements too. Then more blood two days ago. How did you know?'

'Measurements?'

'Yes, all over. Height, waist, arms and legs, even hands.'

‘Just a wild guess.’ This is not the truth. However, I’m not sure this is the time to tell her. It had seemed only a vague possibility in Paris. Now, I’m convinced. Bad news for Samira. Though, perhaps, not altogether bad news. For the time being, it’s probably the only thing guaranteeing her safety and keeping her alive.

Sometime later and I’m feeling a little better. I even swallow a little water without too much difficulty. I nibble on a stale bread roll and tell Samira about the charity. She’s intrigued, loving my description of Grace and Kels, but is undecided about Freds. She’s not a fan of Alsatians, she says. With her help, I stand up and try to move around. I feel sore all over, my arm hurting the most. I bend to touch my toes and my stomach and ribs respond angrily. Nothing appears broken.

Some say pain is good. It keeps you alive and keeps you focused. I need my energies focused on getting us both out of here. The trouble is, I’m running out of options.

We are dozing fitfully, propped against each other, our backs to the wall, when without warning the door is flung open. Standing there, bold as brass, is Irina. I’ve never wanted to hit a woman, but right now I realise I would be capable. Having heard what Samira has been through, it might even be a pleasure.

‘You’re not good at taking advice, Baxter.’ She has a small pistol in her hand. I’m not good with weapons, either. A gun is usually enough to make me think twice.

‘Nice to see serial abusers making house calls, Irina.’

‘Gregor and I have been discussing you over dinner. It’s the end of the road for you, I’m afraid.’

‘But not for you?’

‘Don’t make me laugh. No, Gregor’s just attending to something upstairs. Then he’s coming down to deal with you personally.’

'I'm quaking.'

'You should be. Samira, are you ready to go? We're leaving.'

'Where to?'

'Back to my house. I need you to rest for the next few days.'

'Got something planned, have you?' I say. 'Something suitably perverted?'

'I've had enough of your self-righteous crap, Baxter. You beat people up to within an inch of their lives, then lecture me about abusive behaviour. You should have paid me the money when I offered you a way out. If you had, you and the girl would now both be free.'

'That's bullshit and you know it. I told you. I never negotiate.'

'It's academic now. Come on.' She points at Samira. 'Get a move on.'

Samira gives me one last, frightened look, then heads out of the room. In so many ways, she's like her brother.

'See you in the next life, Baxter.' Irina slams the door as she goes, turning the key in the lock and sliding the bolts top and bottom.

Time ticks by. Two or three hours have passed since Samira left. Gregor will play a waiting game. Wanting me at my most vulnerable. Which is likely to be at about two or three in the morning. The time when he and his crew are ordinarily awake, the nightclubs winding down for the night. If he's not distracted by a woman, about this time Gregor would be reviewing the takings. Seeing which clubs were up and which were down. Counting tip money. Working out how much his bar staff were cheating him. Or reviewing which girls were worth keeping and which ones could earn him more money in other ways.

I hear voices outside the door and I'm quickly on my feet. One of them is male. The sound differs from what I was expecting, the accent slightly French. The other is female, her words spoken more softly. Bolts top and bottom are slid open, and the key turns in the lock. As the door swings open, in walks the North African, Scorpion-Head. Behind him, to my surprise, is a platinum blonde. Lisandra!

'So, Baxter. Ready for round two?' Scorpion-Head is dressed in a simple T-shirt and jeans. It shows off his muscles to full effect. Any side effects from my earlier punch to his face are no longer visible. The bike chain is gone. Instead, his right hand is holding a baseball bat, identical to the one his crony used recently. Possibly the same one. 'Time to see what you're made of.' He turns, fleetingly, to Lisandra. 'Stay out of the room if you don't want to get hurt.'

Scorpion-Head holds the bat in one hand and advances towards me. I move in closer, creating a circle of imaginary space between us, about six feet wide. The bat swings lazily in his hand, first one way, then another.

'Run out of people to do your dirty work?' I ask.

'No, Baxter. I wanted this pleasure to be all mine.' We are walking around each other, circling first one way and then another.

'No, I get it. This is the hour when the others are upstairs back at the Pink Geranium, enjoying the perks that go with the job. Screwing the girls before they can leave for the night, isn't that right?'

'Don't push your luck.'

'You probably can't get it up any more without a blue pill, isn't that right, Lisandra?'

'Shut the fuck up!' I take angry outbursts as a good sign.

'How many times have you tried to screw her?' I nod in Lisandra's direction. 'Thrust your grubby little digits up her skirt in the hope your puny windsock might get a raise.'

'I'm warning you!' He swings at me with the bat, first one-handedly, then using both hands to steady the weapon. I duck out of range, jolts of pain from my sore ribs and chest screaming at me to go easy.

'Tariq and Besim were good at that. Groping the girls. I'm guessing the entire team are impotent, just like you, eh?'

Which is when Scorpion-Head really loses it. Both hands on the bat, he lashes out, left and right, as if he were some intergalactic fighter. I duck and dive, first one way, then the other, as we step sideways around each other in a circle. I want his growing rage to make him careless, hoping my legs don't give way first. His problem is his choice of weapon. The harder he swings the bat, the more its momentum delays the counter-swing. Which is how I land my first and only real punch, a charging right elbow to his exposed neck. Followed by a knee into his groin. Both of which cause him to trip and fall backwards onto the mattress, with me rolling on top. The bat goes flying. Dazed, he recovers, grabbing my throat with both hands. I reciprocate, but his neck is too thick for my fingers.

Instead, I go for his eyes. He's wise to this and keeps his head moving, his own hands tightening around my throat. We wrestle, both of us struggling, me at a disadvantage because my damned prosthetics won't let me do what I need them to. In contrast, he uses his feet to good effect, allowing him to flip me onto my back. I don't have the power or strength to reciprocate. I try twisting my body, but it doesn't work. Breathing is fast becoming a problem and reality is dawning: I'm fighting a losing battle. He raises himself on his forearms, using bodyweight to add pressure on my larynx. I rain blows with my fists onto his exposed neck and chest but to no effect. Scorpion-Head senses victory. Desperate to turn the tables, I try a last-ditch knee to his groin, but it lacks power. The man doesn't flinch. I feel nauseous, a red haze beginning to descend telling me that I'm already slipping into unconsciousness.

'Not so clever now, Baxter,' is what I vaguely hear him say, a sadistic, triumphant grin leering at me as my eyes roll backwards.

Which is when I hear an almighty cracking sound. Instantly, his body goes limp on top of me. Instantly able to breathe, I take several painful gasps of air before opening my eyes. Lisandra is staring down at me, a worried expression on her face, baseball bat in one hand.

‘Ricky, are you okay?’

‘Good shot,’ I mumble.

‘I hate that bastard. Did I kill him?’

‘Help get him off me and we can find out.’

Once on my feet, just about breathing, I survey Lisandra’s handiwork. The bat connected directly with the side of his skull. He never stood a chance. I check for a pulse.

‘He’s dead,’ I pronounce.

‘Oh, my God.’

‘I owe you. You saved my life. Thanks.’

‘We should get out of here.’

‘Too right.’

‘Can you walk?’

‘Do you know the way?’

‘Sure. We might even find a car waiting.’

We head out of our small room and back into the underground garage. The place I had taken three out of five men down until Gregor showed. The outer garage door is closed, but there’s a button beside the ramp which Lisandra presses. Slowly, the louvred metal shutters rise. On cue, a black Chrysler Voyager materialises from somewhere close by. Lisandra slides open the rear door and the two of us climb in, me with more difficulty than I’d been expecting. Sitting behind the wheel is a man I don’t recognise.

‘What’s going on?’ I ask Lisandra, the car already underway. We’re in a quiet backstreet, part of a smart neighbourhood somewhere in London. I read a street sign as we turn at the junction. London Borough of Brent. Sounds like Kilburn and beyond.

'I'm your get-out-of-jail card, Ricky.'

'Are you one of the good guys?'

'In a manner of speaking.'

'You're working for Saunderson, right?'

'Not directly.'

'But you've been working undercover on Blacksmith?'

'You know about Blacksmith? Yes, Guilty as charged.'

'Thank you. I thought I was about to say goodbye back there. What happens now?'

'That depends. What's the time? Four-thirty in the morning. Saunderson would like a conversation, but I guess it can wait. Do you need a doctor?'

'It, too, can wait.'

'In which case, where would you like to go at this weird hour of the morning?'

I give her Inés's address and the driver keys it into the navigation system.

'Should be there in fifteen, this time of the night.'

'Can I borrow a phone? I need to call Inés and forewarn her.'

Lisandra hands me her mobile and I dial the number from memory. When a sleepy Inés answers, I close my eyes and talk. The relief in her voice is palpable. I end the call and hand the phone back.

'I feel terrible about Alisa.'

'Not as bad as me,' Lisandra says, tears welling. She looks at me and

I feel a need to touch her arm in support. 'Sometimes, this job is shit.'

'Tell me about it,' I mutter, more to myself than to her.

'What next?' says Lisandra. We're standing on the curb outside Inés's apartment.

'It's time to take down the Blacksmith gang, once and for all.'

'That means stopping Irina and the other woman. Not to mention Gregor. He'll be so pissed after tonight.'

'Finding Samira is just as important,' I point out.

'I should have done more to help her. I'm sorry.'

'It would have been too risky. Don't worry, we'll find her.'

'Saunderson's keen to speak.'

'I'll call him later. What about you?'

'I think a deep bath and a long sleep is called for,' she says. 'I'm overdue a lot of holiday.'

'No, I mean work-wise. Now your cover's blown.'

'Back to my old life, I guess. I'm glad, in a way.'

'Listen, Grace and I usually help women in different circumstances. However, it doesn't mean we wouldn't be pleased to see you. Come by the charity and say hello, sometime. We'd like that.'

'You know, I might. Next time, I promise I won't bug your offices.' She hugs me gently, my mind picturing Grace's disapproving look. Then she gets back in the car and it disappears into the night.

Inés is amazing, even at five in the morning. Hair frizzed to bits, no make-up, skimpy nightdress, flimsy cotton wrap-around: just pure, raw Inés Keller. I like this woman more and more. We enjoy a lingering embrace on the doorstep before heading upstairs. Baz is awake, keeping a watchful vigil. Marta sleeps through my arrival. I tell Baz the good news about Samira. The bits about her being alive, at least. Not yet about the transplant business. He listens, a shocked expression on his face, then puts his hands together, prayerfully, tears flowing. All three of us embrace. It's a powerful moment.

'Where she now?'

'With this woman, Irina.'

'Yes, but where?'

'I don't yet know. We'll find her, Baz. I can feel it, we're close.'

Baz is touching my arm and sees me wince. 'What happened here?'

'I got in the way of a bicycle chain. Gregor's men play rough.'

'You kill Gregor?'

'Not yet. There are a few less of his men to bother us. He's still at large.'

'Let me look at that arm of yours,' Inés says. 'Then, I don't know about the two of you, but it's Sunday. I'd quite like some more sleep.'

Before heading back to bed, however, she cuts the torn material around my upper arm, washes away the encrusted blood, sprays the area with an antiseptic powder, then puts on a dressing. Having examined the bruising on my cheek, she declares nothing broken. The gash on my face is closed and warrants only a small plaster. I promise to see a doctor about my ribs and abdomen, and that seems to satisfy her. Enough to allow her to slip into bed beside me and then fall instantly into a contented sleep.

33

I doze, my mind spinning while Inés sleeps. We wake at nine and Inés says she needs to head out, for reasons she won't explain. I ask Baz to go with her. I couldn't bear it if something awful happened. I promise to stay with Marta. In his current mood of optimism, Baz would most likely agree to anything I ask. My body seemed able to cope with the coffee I'd drunk earlier so, over another mug, I plug in my phone to charge and call Grace. She is overjoyed to hear from me. Even more so on hearing the news about Samira, though not when she hears what Irina has in store.

'My God, Mister Rick, that's terrible. Does Baz know?'

'Not yet. I want to break it to him gently.'

'What happened to Gregor?'

'Still at large.' Which is when I tell her about my near-death experience and how Lisandra came to the rescue.

'The blonde woman? The one who had eyes for you?'

'Yes, her – and no, she didn't have eyes for me. She was working undercover.'

'Oh, my Lordy. Well, I never.'

I explain I want another team meeting. She suggests finding rooms at a hotel for a few days. I like this idea, although I suspect an ulterior motive. The dehumidifiers are driving her nuts. There's plenty of Murray's money still burning a hole in my pocket, so I agree. Grace says she'll get on to it right away.

I check my phone for texts, remembering someone buzzing me the previous evening. I had thought it might be Saunderson. In fact, it was Antoine Laroche. He's found details of Irina's recent flights to the UK. Nearly all are to the same airfield. A grass strip at a place called Fowlmere. I'll ask Kels to research the place later.

While Marta sleeps, I call Saunderson. He wants to come around in person. Twenty minutes later, he's sitting opposite me at Inés's breakfast table, looking as tired and gaunt as ever. What he wants is for me to back off for a while. With Gregor's team depleted, Operation Blacksmith is about to crank up a few gears. Saunderson thinks they'll be able to make some arrests in the next week, or so he hopes. Then he stops, seeing the look on my face.

'You're not interested in hearing this, are you, Baxter?'

'Yes and no.' He arches one eyebrow at me. 'Yes, I like to hear what's going on. No, I'm not particularly interested because there's a young Iraqi woman whose life is in danger.'

'And you're going to find her?'

'Maybe.' I shrug.

'How do you propose going about doing that?'

'Depends on whether you and I are on the same side.'

'Our undercover operative saved your life, didn't she?'

I shake my head and smile.

'She did. I owe Lisandra. Or whatever her actual name is.'

'Let's combine forces, Baxter. You share what you know. Together we can wipe this operation off the face of the earth.'

'You mean go after the two sisters?'

'Them and the whole shebang.'

'What do you have in mind?'

'That, my friend, depends on what you know and how much you're prepared to share.'

'Fancy a coffee?' I need a distraction, a little time to think this through.

'White no sugar works every time.'

The kettle boiled, the coffees made, I take courage in both hands. I tell him the main bits. Not everything, just what I feel is essential. About Baz and Samira, about Irina and Tanya's mother.

'You had someone speak with her? In Bratislava?'

'Sure. Why not?'

'Bloody hell. You're unbelievable, you are.'

I tell him about Elena Moravková's kidney problem. Not, though, about her imminent arrival at Joubert's clinic.

'Is that why you went to Paris?'

'Your babysitters seemed confident they'd find out. Are you saying they were over-optimistic?'

'Perhaps. Answer the question.'

'Moravková's medical team in Bratislava have been consulting with the Paris Transplant Group about her case.'

'She's heading to Paris for a transplant?'

‘Maybe.’ It’s a delicate balance between telling the truth yet being scant on certain details.

‘While we are on the matter, you went to Beauvais. Why?’

‘An old friend of the family flies out of there. He promised to give me a lift back home.’ Again, true, but not the complete truth. I look at the bags under Saunderson’s eyes and feel some sympathy.

‘What now, Baxter?’

‘According to this chum of mine, Irina owns a small plane.’

‘Which explains how the two sisters slip in and out of the country undetected.’

‘Here’s what I suggest. You give me free rein to find Samira. You also promise not to give me or her brother, Baz, any grief about their immigration status. In return, I hand the two women to you on a plate. Hopefully Gregor as well. Are you prepared to run with that?’

‘Alive?’

‘To the best of my abilities.’

‘Unharmed?’

‘Able to answer questions.’

‘You’ll keep me informed the moment you’re ready to pounce?’

‘Part of the deal.’

‘And you say it’s going to happen imminently?’

‘If I have my way, at some stage in the next forty-eight hours. Seventy-two tops.’

‘If you deliver that without screwing up, the whole bloody Blacksmith team will be lifetime members of your fan club.’

Just before noon, Marta emerges.

'Where's Mum?' If she knows about my overnight run-in with Gregor, she doesn't show it.

'Out. She didn't say where.'

With that, the front door opens and in walk Inés and Baz, both grinning broadly.

'We have a surprise for you,' Inés says, handing me a small suitcase. I peer inside. It holds my things: clothes, new stump liners and a few bits and pieces.

'What's going on? You both look guilty. What have you been up to?'

'Your apartment has magicked itself back to normal. Even the door's been repaired.'

'Are you serious?' I'm so flabbergasted, I don't know what to say.

'Baz and I were worried about you. We wanted to do our bit to help.'

'Bloody marvellous,' I say, kissing the top of her head and giving Baz a hug. 'Thank you. That was above and beyond. There is one snag.'

'What's that?'

'Now, only the pair of you will know where everything is.'

'Not me.' Baz shrugs, a smile on his face, his hands upturned. 'I only mending door.'

34

Grace has pulled out the stops. We have access to a suite of meeting rooms for the next few days. She claims the hotel wasn't busy, but I sense she's twisted arms. She's also sent a message to everyone to turn off all mobiles. In case what remains of Gregor's team is feeling in the mood for revenge. Grace has replenished the supply of burners and Vince has been sent to deliver them. Late morning, he drops off several: two for me, one for Baz and one each for Inés and Marta. Only Marta complains. She finds being disconnected from her social media accounts unbearable. As if a human right has been breached. We argue, I win the day and she sulks.

'I hear you only just made it?' To be fair, Vince sounds concerned.

'It was touch and go, I admit.'

'Despite all the gym work.'

'I've only so much power in my lower legs. Pinned to the deck, I get in trouble. I wasn't able to flip the guy onto his back. He was a big brute and all.'

'Next time we're at the gym, I'll try to help you with that. I'm glad you're safe.' He bumps my shoulder with a fist and heads off.

Baz appears. I feel bad not telling him the entire story about Samira.

In particular, Irina's designs on his sister's kidneys. I see the beaming smile on his face and dread what I have to say. I take a deep breath and dive in. He receives the news in silence: frowning, jaw set, and eyes staring.

'A kidney? We stop this, yes?'

'I promise.' I wish I felt this confident.

'This woman is evil. In Turkey, I see with my own eyes. My God, now this.' Inadvertently, he grabs my sore arm. 'We find her, please?'

'Of course.' I try not to wince, jangled nerve endings sending shooting pains everywhere. 'We'll find her. We're meeting Grace and Kels shortly, to brainstorm ideas.'

Before leaving for the hotel, I make a few calls – one to Kels and one to my mother. Then I remember another on my urgent list. The line at the other end rings but switches through to voicemail. I leave a message: 'Ring me back urgently.'

Grace convenes the meeting for mid-afternoon. Vince arrives last, together with Kels and Freds. The hotel doesn't allow dogs, the manager only relenting when Grace explains he's a medical assistance animal for two disabled people.

With everyone settled, I start with a precis of the last forty-eight hours. I also report we have a new objective with the clock ticking: finding Samira.

'No joy with Tanya's phone?' Too late, I realise my question to Kels sounds downbeat.

'Been disconnected for days. Ever since your visit.'

'How about Irina's?'

'Sorry, her phone's a mystery.' She sees the despondent look on my face and shrugs.

'I've a better idea, Mister Rick. One or more of us should go to the Paris clinic. All we then need to do is wait for Samira to show up.'

It's not a bad suggestion. I check my watch. Moravková should have arrived there by now.

'I doubt the two sisters will travel to Paris.' It's Vince speaking. 'Not when they know Ricky's still alive. They'll want the loose ends tied up here, make sure Ricky's not about to cause more trouble. I'd be sending a couple of heavies to act as Samira's protection escort. I'll volunteer to go to Paris and sort things if you like?'

'Even better, why not let the police handle it?' Grace has the bit between her teeth. 'The moment Samira turns up at the clinic, let them intervene.'

The truth is, if the French police apprehend Samira, she's in trouble. She has no passport. They'll discover she's an illegal and refuse her entry into the country. The UK won't want her back either. She'll be deported back to Iraq. Once they have pumped her for information about Irina and Tanya. Sure, the Moravková woman might be in Paris, but she'll be there legally. As an EU citizen, she can't be detained in the vain hope her two daughters might show up. No, I'm convinced. We have to find Samira before she leaves the UK.

'Grace, international police operations are never predictable.' I look at Vince. 'Do you have a passport?'

'Sure.'

'Then I like Grace's first suggestion. Would you mind going to Paris?'

'Who am I to refuse such a request?'

'What do we think Gregor's likely to do next?' I turn to Kels. 'I don't suppose his phone is active?'

'Dead as a dormouse.'

'I'd love to know where he is.'

'If he's any sense, he'll be lying low,' Grace mutters to no one in particular.

Baz looks up sharply, his face beaming.

'Maybe, Ricky, you and I visit minibus driver, Lennox. He knows where Tanya is, for sure.'

'That, Baz,' I say, giving him a warm smile, 'is genius thinking. We could go first thing in the morning. We'd be back by lunchtime.'

Other thoughts are soon being kicked around. Vince wonders about the two of us visiting the nightclub once more. He thinks we might find clues to Irina's whereabouts, perhaps in Gregor's safe or somewhere in his office. We might even find Gregor himself. A contact phone number for Irina would help. One that hasn't been disconnected. I'm not convinced, but don't rule it out. Instead, I make a case for exploring options near the airfield Irina keeps flying in and out of.

'Do we know where Fowlmere is yet, Kels?'

'South-west of Cambridge.'

'So, we're looking for a house or farm next to a large green space that could also be a private airstrip.'

'That sort of thing, yes.'

'Only a few thousand of those that might fit the bill, then.' Vince, blunt as ever, calls it as he sees it. The room falls silent. He's right, of course, his words deflating any lingering mood of optimism. The truth hits hard. Without more information, finding Samira is going to be nigh-on impossible.

Baz and I are up with the sun, arriving in Boston sometime later with no holdups. We drive to within two streets of Lennox's house and park up. According to GPS data, Kels believes Lennox is back home after some early morning driving in and around the Fenland area, presumably taking workers to their respective farms.

'You ready?' We are standing outside Lennox's front door, in a hurry to get things moving.

'Sure.' Baz hasn't been to the gym for three days. That aside, after my brief run-in with Gregor and his gang, I've little doubt he's in better shape than me. I press long and hard on the bell, keeping my thumb on the button. With the bell still ringing, I eventually hear sounds of someone approaching.

'Hold on, hold on. I'm coming, dammit.'

No sooner does the door open than Baz is forcing his way past Lennox, heading directly to the kitchen out the back.

'Hey! Where the hell do you think you're going?'

Lennox, flummoxed by this brazen invasion of his privacy, is in a quandary. Chase after Baz or prevent me from entering? He achieves neither. I'm in the house, standing in front of the closed door with my arms crossed before he can react. The hallway once again reeks of foul odours and stale air. If I needed a reason to get out of here, this man's personal hygiene is enough of an incentive.

'I have a good mind to call the police,' he says, then has a lightbulb moment. 'You were here last week. You're the ones that pissed off Tanya.'

Loud noises are audible from the kitchen. Baz is throwing pots and pans around in the manner we had agreed. Lennox storms off to investigate and I follow in his wake. Once in the confines of the small kitchen, Baz and I quickly overpower him, pinning him hard against one of the kitchen chairs. Time for yet more cable ties: one around the wrists behind his back and another around each ankle. The exertions cause Lennox to sweat profusely.

'What do you want?'

'Information.'

'You can both fuck off.'

Which is a dumb thing to say to Baz, given all the stress he's been under. Out of character, maybe. Today he reacts by stepping forward and delivering a hefty punch, fair and square, to Lennox's face.

'Way to go, boy.' Baz smiles coyly, wriggling his shoulders as if limbering for another.

'Listen, Lennox. The less time any of us have to spend in this shithole of yours, the better. Be under no illusion, you are going to give us what we want. The choice is yours whether you give it voluntarily. I'd recommend that you co-operate.'

An agreeable amount of blood is dribbling out of Lennox's nose and down his chin. It's probably why he's helpful. The downside is I have to reach into the man's trousers to retrieve his mobile phone. Not something I relish doing.

'I gave you Tanya's number last time.'

'Cut the crap. We both know she's got a different number. How do I get into this phone of yours?'

He's about to give me a bullshit answer. I can see it in his eyes and so can Baz. When I nod at Baz, to encourage him to swing a second punch, Lennox relents and tells us everything. I find the number and commit it to memory before placing Lennox's phone in my jacket pocket along with my own.

'Heh, I'd like my phone back.'

I turn to look at Baz.

'Did someone say something? I heard nothing.'

'Nor me,' Baz says.

'You bastards. Untie me and give me back my phone. I'll call the police.'

'No manners, some people,' I say and take a greasy tea towel off the rail by the cooker. I tie it around Lennox's mouth. 'That should keep you quiet for a bit. Look on the bright side. It'll mop up some blood.' I give Baz a nudge. 'Ready?'

We leave Lennox whining and whimpering, and make our way outside. Out on the street, I call Kels and give her Tanya's new mobile number.

'Give me a second.' I hear fingers flying rapidly over a keyboard.

'The phone looks to be heading south. On the A1, just beyond Peterborough.'

'Ring me back when you have an idea about the destination.'

'Sure.'

'One more thing. Any progress on those bike number plates? The one Inés snapped a picture of the other night?'

'I'm sorry, Ricky. They completely slipped my mind. Too much going on. I'll get onto it right away, I promise.'

Sometime later, back in London finally and having dropped Baz off near his home, my phone goes. It's the friend of mine I tried calling yesterday. We speak for several minutes. The caller seems happy to help. He'll do his best, he tells me. If not personally, he thinks he'll be able to find someone reliable. I stress to him that people's lives are depending on this, before ending the call.

As I sit stuck in heavy traffic near Mile End, I know I'm taking a gamble with what I've just put in motion. Who knows whether it will really work? It depends on what we find in the next twenty-four hours.

There are too many unknowns. Which is when my phone rings. It's Vince, on the Eurostar.

'Bad news.'

'Tell me.'

'Bloody train's broken down. We're stuck outside Lille. Plus, the French engineering union is on a go-slow, can you believe it?'

'What time do you think you'll get to Paris?'

'We've been sitting here for two hours already, twiddling our thumbs. At this rate, we'll be lucky to arrive by nightfall. I'm sorry, Ricky.'

It's an unwelcome reminder: the best-laid plans and all that. I was nearly killed the other night. I take it as a reminder. My naturally optimistic, self-confident disposition is suddenly feeling battered.

35

Twenty-four hours after our team meeting and we're no further forward. No sooner had Kels begun tracking Tanya's new number than the phone disconnected from the network, somewhere outside Cambridge. I suspect Gordy Lennox may have had something to do with that. So, once again, we've no idea where she is. It feels like we're back at square one. Even Vince isn't faring any better, his train having only recently been towed back to Lille station. With a fair wind, he should be in Paris by five in the afternoon. Not entirely catastrophic, but we've wasted a day getting not a lot further forward. I call Saunderson once back at the hotel. He has nothing to report either. An air of despondency is settling in.

'Why are you so gloomy, Mister Rick? You'll find the girl, I know it.'

'I hate failure.'

'Don't be so ridiculous. I've told you once, none of us believes you are failing. What are you planning next?'

'Vince suggested he and I should go back to Gregor's club. It's a pity Vince isn't here. I'd feel much more comfortable taking him than Baz.'

'That's a crazy idea. Going back to the club, I mean. They'll be expecting you, trust me. There has to be a better way.'

'If there is, I can't see it.'

'Wait for Kels. She'll find something, she usually does.'

'*Bonjour. Cabinet du docteur Joubert.*'

'*Bonjour. Claudette*?'

'*Oui.*'

'*C'est Rich Somers*. We met at the weekend.'

'*Bien sûr*. I remember. How are you today?'

'Fine. More to the point, how is Madame Moravková?'

'All testing is complete. It's too soon to be one hundred per cent, but everything is looking positive for the donor matching. Very positive indeed.'

'Excellent. Any decision on date and location for the procedure?'

'We will know later tonight, once the last test results have been confirmed. I understand the donor is expected here tomorrow, sometime late morning. Assuming everything is positive, the operation can happen without delay.'

It hits me hard that we're almost out of time. I desperately need Vince's help. I scan the list of burner numbers Grace assigned to everybody and dial his number. Thankfully, Vince answers and we speak briefly. He's reached Paris, finally, and is on his way to the clinic. I explain that I've got something more urgent I need doing. When I mention what it is, he asks loads of questions and we discuss options. Not entirely convinced he'll be able to help, he promises to text if he has any news.

All I can do now is wait. Truth is, I'm not very good at waiting.

'Where's Baz?' I ask Grace.

'On his way over. He wanted to know if you were going to the gym?'

I shake my head in disbelief. After months spent trying to locate his sister, we finally know she's alive, but the clock is ticking if we're to save her from the surgeon's knife. We're becoming desperate, struggling to think of ways to find her whereabouts. It's a race against time, we're still not making progress – so no, Baz, the two of us are not about to swan off to the gym!

'He's got to be joking!' I try to keep my tone measured. 'Send him out to get some food for us all and make himself useful. Change of subject, any news from Kels?'

'Not a squeak. What do you fancy eating?'

'Surprise me. While you and Baz make your decision about the food, I'm going to speak with Saunderson.'

Ten o'clock at night and we're still in the office. After much agonising, Baz and I are preparing to return to the Pink Geranium. We've run out of options. Grace is trying her best to dissuade us, but we're already in the last chance saloon. Just as we are on the point of leaving, my phone rings and Grace's faith and persistence are rewarded. It's Kels. I sense from the outset she's found something.

'The motorbike number plates. Good and bad news,' Kels begins in a rush. 'They belong to a limited liability partnership registered in Jersey. That's the good news. The bad news is it's impossible to discover who's running the business. There are many layers of corporate structure acting as a smokescreen. I've spent hours searching but found nothing. A total blank.' I sense there's a *but* coming. 'Except,' she announces after a dramatic pause, 'I had a brainwave. Perhaps there was a partnership registration document on file? The one lodged with the Jersey registrar when the partnership was established. Lo and behold, I found it. Guess who's one of the founding partners?'

'Irina Moravková?'

'Correct. There's more. Because these are the registration documents, it notes an address. Hers is stated as Abbot's Farm, Langley. It's on the border between Hertfordshire, Cambridgeshire and Essex.'

'How far from Fowlmere,' I say, holding my breath.

'Nine miles as the crow flies.'

I sense her beaming with pride down the other end of the phone.

'Kels, you're a genius.'

'This is it, isn't it?'

'Wait. There's one other thing. I've checked the map. Abbot's Farm is next to a place called Nuthampstead. And Nuthampstead was the location of a US bomber base in the war. It closed sixty years ago and they broke up the runway, but here's the thing. These days, there's still a grass strip. Suitable for light aircraft only.'

'Runway length?'

'Seven-twenty-five metres.'

That was plenty, given that Kit Myers had said the Skyhawk could land on a sixpence. This news, taken together, feels like one giant leap forward.

'Bloody amazing, Kels. You might just have saved our bacon.'

I ring off and check my watch.

'Baz.' I yell as I gather my things. 'You ready? Time to go and rescue Samira. You coming, by any chance?'

36

I never carry a gun. This may be naïve. Perhaps foolhardy. However, what's the point in me having something I've no intention of ever using? I hate the things. God gave me hands, feet and a fit body. Through my stupidity, I lost both feet. So now, when I'm in a scrape, I have to make the most of whatever body parts I've got left. I'm finding, more and more, that I'm quite good at using what I've got to my advantage. Not always, as I found with my near-death experience with Scorpion-Head. That's when I feel inadequate. When having something extra could level the playing field. If not give me the edge. I rarely feel the need. However, I've been worrying more recently that there might be occasions, like when walking into something potentially dangerous, when having something up my sleeve would be reassuring. Would make the difference between life and death. As in when visiting a strange property in the middle of nowhere at night. Somewhere secure, a place probably patrolled by armed guards.

Which explains why, in the glove box of the car, I've taken to carrying one or two extra items. Besides the spare burner and, more recently, the cable ties. One is a mini-taser. Mine looks and feels slightly larger than a standard cigarette lighter. Don't be deceived; this baby can deliver several thousand volts at the touch of a button. No one's going to ignore that when it zaps you on the side of your neck. The second is a telescopic baton. This is a thin tube about six inches long, made of a super-strong, lightweight metal. At the end is a heavy metal ball the size of a marble. Hold the tube in your hand, press the button with your thumb and, when the need arises, lash out. Three tapering inner tubes shoot outwards, the weight of the metal ball pulling them one by one until they click into place. Suddenly, I have a weapon as long as a baseball bat. Powerful enough, I'm hoping, to stop a few opponents dead in their tracks. All it takes is one direct hit. The metal ball at the end packs a terrifying punch. Not that I've ever tried it in anger yet.

By the time Baz and I reach the village of Nuthampstead, it's way after two in the morning. I stop the car just beyond a pub called the Woodman, grabbing the mini-taser and telescopic baton from the glove box. I stuff the taser in my pocket. The baton fits into clips I've fitted to the rear of my left prosthetic. Hidden from view and yet quickly accessible. Kels has sent me screenshots of the area around Abbot's Farm, both as a map and aerial image. As the crow flies, we're about half a mile away. To get there, I'm planning to skirt around the grass runway and approach the property from the rear. This is like walking three sides of a large rectangle to cover the distance of the shortest side, but I reckon it's the safest way.

'You ready?'

'Sure.' Baz is beaming. He's excited. I hope I am not about to lead him into something we might regret.

'Best turn our phones to silent.' Baz follows my lead and toggles the mute button. As I'm doing this, a text arrives from Vince. 'Mission accomplished' is all it says. Excellent. Couldn't be better timing.

The weather is kind to us as we make our way along a rough dirt track. The sky is mostly clear, save for the occasional cloud. It's a new moon, meaning the light intensity is low. Enough for us to see by, but not too bright to make us stand out. After a few hundred yards, the path forks left and right. After consulting the map, Baz and I take the left fork. Sure enough, a while later, we approach the end of a long, well-mown strip of grass.

'Is this runway?' Baz asks, doubt in his tone.

'Looks like it to me.' There are no markings, lights, or any of the accoutrements you'd find on a grown-up airfield. This is just a grass strip, with a rough track down one side. There are no fences or signs either, the only buildings being two barns in the distance at the far end of the strip. 'Those look like they were once aircraft hangers,' I say, pointing. 'Come on, let's take a peek.' It's only as we set off that I see the windsock, hanging limply at the edge of the grass strip. This definitely feels like we're at the right place.

A while later, and we're peering through cracks in the locked barn doors, unable to see much of anything. There's no way in without a crowbar or busting open the padlock, and I don't think either is on our 'must-do' list for the evening. Instead, we skirt around the end of the runway and head towards a clump of woodland. I point to a small gap in the trees.

'That must be the rear entrance to the property.'

Even though we're exposed to the elements, there's barely enough light to risk being silhouetted against the night sky. Someone watching with night vision goggles might see us, but not anybody peering in our direction with naked eyes alone. Only when we reach the trees do we spot our quarry through the foliage: a large, two-storey country property positioned in the middle of an expanse of lawn.

The house looks quiet, with no lights visible anywhere. The grounds extend from a long, gated driveway in the far distance to the woodlands Baz and I are standing in at the back. It's hard to estimate in the dark, but the property is about two hundred yards away. Around the perimeter, hidden amongst trees, lies a three-metre-high steel fence. This is a serious boundary, built to a high professional spec. Nothing flimsy that would rattle in the wind. This one has sturdy metal fence posts sunk into concrete, with close-packed chain links, the holes too small for finger- or toe-holds. By the gap in the trees lies a metal gate with electronic locks on the top, middle and bottom. A device most likely triggered remotely. Nothing that might easily be bust open, that's for sure.

'You think this is the place?' The whites of Baz's eyes gleam at me in the dark.

'With a fence like this? It has to be. No ordinary farmer needs this much protection.'

'How we get across?'

It's a fair question. A pole-vaulter could do it. It would be a tough landing without a safety mat, but that would be one way. With our prosthetics, there are fewer options. I am running out of ideas when I see something that might work.

'Follow me a moment.'

I've spotted a large oak tree, close to the fence about fifty yards away. If Baz gives me a leg up, I think I might be able to crawl along one branch and jump to grab hold of the top of the fence. Not the easiest manoeuvre for either of us, given our legs. I'm keen to avoid landing full-force on our pins since this can cause severe damage to our leg stumps. Sometimes there's little option. In the event, I needn't have worried. I pull myself up into the tree with Baz's help, sit astride the branch to get my bearings, and then give him a hand up. Next, inching our way, one by one, along the branch, we take it in turns to leap to the fence top before lowering ourselves to the ground. What hurts most is my abdomen. I'm still suffering the effects from all those punches.

Whether the fence has inbuilt motion sensors or because we made too much noise, at that moment, two guards appear from around the side of the house. Baz and I hasten towards a shrub bed a short distance away and drop to the grass, face down. The guards are heading in our direction, one of them holding a powerful torch and systematically scanning the area alongside the fence.

'Baz, when I give the word, make a move towards the house and let them see you. When that happens, stand still, got it?' My friend gives a thumbs-up gesture and I pause, waiting for the right moment.

'Okay, go!' The guards are looking away. Baz makes about forty yards' headway when there's a shout.

'Heh, you!' The guard locates Baz in his torch beam, and the pair run towards the spot where Baz is standing like a deer, frozen in the headlights.

'Face down on the ground, now!' The other guard is holding a gun and Baz needs no further persuasion. I, meanwhile, am on my feet, crouching low and waiting. In my hand is the pocket taser, my thumb toying with the button. One simple depression will unleash its massive voltage. With both guards distracted by Baz's prone form, I make my move. I am ten yards away before the man with the gun senses something. By the time he turns around to peer into the darkness, I am already upon him, the taser jabbing hard into his throat. The hideous effects of a high-voltage discharge to his neck stun him. The gun goes flying. Without a pause, I ram my elbow into the neck of the second guard, the one with the torch. This is followed by a thumping left-hander to his solar plexus. Both men go down. Baz, meanwhile, is back on his feet. I hand him a pair of cable ties.

'Tie these two up,' I say, retrieving the torch and turning it off. No point in telling the world we're here. Baz makes quick work of their hands and I do the same with their feet. I realise I recognise one of them. The man with the gun. He's got tattoos on both forearms – the same guy who threw the first punches at me in Gregor's garage. I grab hold of his jawbone in my right fist and squeeze hard.

'Recognise me?' People tell me I've got a powerful grip. 'How many other guards are there?'

'Two,' he gasps.

'Where?' I squeeze harder and he grimaces.

'Inside the house,' he says with difficulty.

'Are there cameras?'

'Everywhere.' Inwardly, I groan. This is bad news.

'Is the front door locked?'

'There's an entry code,' he squeals.

'I'm waiting.'

'Four-two-seven-zero.'

'What about the young woman?' I glance at Baz, but he can't have heard this.

'She'll be sleeping.'

'And the Moravková woman? Or her sister?'

'They arrive in the morning.'

'What about Gregor?'

This time, I get no response. I try again, squeezing harder, the jawbone close to breaking point. Still no reaction.

'Don't say I didn't warn you.' I let go of his jaw and slam a clenched fist down hard onto his nose and face.

'Payback for what you did to me in the garage.'

He's about to utter something obscene when I land a follow-up onto his jawbone. The noise is not pleasant.

'Now we're about evens, don't you think? Let's try one more time. Gregor. Is he here tonight?'

He thinks about not replying, then reconsiders. Finally, he shakes his head.

'Will he be here in the morning, too?'

He nods but doesn't speak. I take it as a yes, on balance.

'Okay,' I call to Baz, who is beside the other guard. 'Off with the belt. Stuff a handkerchief in his mouth and hold it in place with the strap, as I'm doing.' Tattoo Man lets out a muffled cry of pain as I pull the belt buckle tight against his broken jaw.

I check my phone. Four in the morning. There's another text from Vince: 'Moravková has moved. Don't yet know where,' is all it says. Bugger! This could be disastrous. If we're unable to stop Samira from leaving the country, then my plan for Vince to save the day could well be in ruins. I type: 'CRITICAL YOU FIND HER' and press send. The block capitals should speak volumes.

I debate taking the gun but decide to toss it over the fence, out of harm's way. If Tattoo Man was speaking the truth, it'll be two against two inside the house. In normal circumstances, I'm happy with those odds.

Baz and I encircle the house from the protection of the trees, spotting four sets of cameras, one on each rooftop corner. Save breaking a window, the only way in appears to be through the front. We make a dash to the side wall and, with our backs hugging the brickwork, inch our way around. I'm hoping this is the best way to avoid the cameras. I key in the four-two-seven-zero code, and the front door clicks open. The house is in darkness as we step inside.

We stand stock-still for what feels like an age, listening, senses charged, not hearing anything untoward. Just when we think we may have got in undetected, bright lights flood the hallway.

'Neither of you make a move.' A bouncer type steps forward, a gun pointing directly at us. Not someone I recognise, but this one's part of the A-team. Muscles bulging, trim physique, he holds the gun in both hands like a pro, left hand steadying the right wrist. Magna cum laude at training school. 'Eat the floor, the pair of you. Arms and legs wide like a starfish.' So far, grade A*'s all round.

We do as we're told. Holding the gun barrel hard against our torsos, he pats us down, finding the mini-taser but not the telescopic baton. He also finds Baz's phone, but not mine. That earns him a grade reclassification. More like an A than an A*. He pockets the confiscated items and tells us to get to our feet.

'You must be Baxter.' He shifts his gaze from me to Baz but doesn't seem to recognise him. 'Gregor warned us about you. He should be here soon after daybreak. He's going to be so happy to see you again.'

The door opens, and another man emerges. I know this one. It's Black T-Shirt from the garage the other night, still sporting a whopping bruise on his face from where I hit him. He too is holding a gun, though only in one hand. If I were guessing, he's just woken up. He gives a cocky smile when he recognises me, sauntering towards Baz and me as if about to give us a long lecture. I don't let him have the chance. The moment he's in range, I deliver an uppercut to his jaw, and Baz, bless him, punches him equally hard in the stomach.

Almost in unison, two guns go off. One is Black T-Shirt's, the gun flying out of his hand, a loose shot hitting the ceiling. The other comes from the first guy – the A-Grader. The shot was most probably aimed at me but, in the mêlée, the bullet nicks Baz's forearm. My friend cries out and there's a commotion from one of the upper rooms. Next thing we know, leaning over the upper floor balustrade is Samira, her frightened face peering down on the scene below.

'What's happening?' she yells, then screams. 'Baz?' She says something in Arabic I don't understand. Baz, clutching his arm, now dripping with blood, replies.

The first bouncer shouts, 'Get the fuck back to your room, do you hear?'

'My brother. You've shot him.'

'It's a flesh wound,' the A-Grader says, more hope than fact.

'I need to help him,' she pleads, already halfway down the stairs. At which point, the A-Grader lets off a second shot into the air and the room goes silent.

'No, you don't. Back to your room. You'll be leaving in a few hours.' He kicks the injured Black T-Shirt guy, who's still on the floor. 'Keep an eye on the girl. Make sure she stays upstairs.' He turns his venom on Baz and me. 'You two are coming with me. Any more trouble and I'll not hesitate to use another bullet. Is that understood?'

Black T-Shirt gets to his feet unsteadily. He considers taking another pop at me but rethinks when he sees the A-Grader watching. Reluctantly, he climbs the stairs, Samira yelling something to her brother in Arabic as she retreats to her room. Baz manages a reply whilst the two of us are being frogmarched along the hall. Then it's through a sturdy door and down steep stone steps to a cold, musty cellar beneath the house. We've hardly had time to get our bearings when the lights go out and the cellar door is slammed and bolted firmly from somewhere above.

Sealed in our private tomb. Not a sliver of light from anywhere. Baz wounded and his arm still bleeding. Although we've found Samira, it doesn't sound as if she's going to be here for much longer.

Once more, it looks as if I've well and truly cocked things up. The clock is ticking. As of right now, there seems little prospect of us being able to do anything to save Baz's sister any more.

37

Despite us fast running out of time to save Samira, I suddenly have a much more pressing problem on my hands: how to stem the flow of blood from Baz's wound. This predicament is made worse by the complete and total darkness. Armed with only the feeble screen light from my burner phone, I somehow need to construct a crude bandage if we're to stop the bleeding. I have this crazy idea, but putting it into action proves a struggle. It takes forever to tear a single long strip of material from the back panel of my cotton shirt. I repeat the procedure to create a smaller strip that I then fold over itself a few times to produce a crude wound dressing.

'I guess this might hurt,' I say, placing the smaller piece of material on top of the open wound.

'At least I see Samira.' Baz grits his teeth as I wrap the longer strip of material around his upper arm, on top of the wound dressing. Satisfied that it might just about do the trick, I secure everything in place with a double knot.

'What did she say to you?'

'She loved me.' He smiles and gives a coy shrug. 'I said we rescue her. She told me not to be foolish.'

'Did you tell her you loved her too?'

'Sort of,' he says, embarrassed.

Using the light from the burner, I fumble my way around the cellar. I have to believe there's a light switch somewhere. Sure enough, after nearly stumbling over the stone steps we came down, at the very top, next to a firmly locked and bolted cellar door, I find what I'm looking for. When I flip the switch, the cellar becomes instantly bathed in murky light. I stare in hope at my phone. Fifty per cent battery, but no signal. Not even at the very top of the stairs. Bang goes any idea I might have had of calling Grace for help.

With the lights on, I inspect the dressing on Baz's arm. The material is matted in blood, but at least the wound is no longer bleeding. We explore the cellar, hoping to find a way out. There is none. The underground space is entirely empty. No boxes, no cases, no unwanted furniture. Nothing to give us any hope. The only way out is the way we came in. I peer hard at the door and its hinges, giving everything a good shake, but to no avail. The door is set rock-solid. For the moment, we're going nowhere.

Four hours later, there are noises from above. The time is eight in the morning. There's a lot of activity suddenly. Heavy footsteps back and forth; sounds of furniture being moved; and voices. Several voices. Baz and I move closer to the stairs to listen, but the sounds are muffled. We learn nothing. About to give up hope, we hear a man's voice immediately overhead. Then, the sounds of bolts being slid back, top and bottom. I reach behind my prosthetic leg for the telescopic baton. Finally, the door opens.

First down the stairs, gun in hand, is the A-Grader. Following closely behind is someone I recognise. Two people, in fact. Both women: one with long, blonde hair, the other with much shorter, dark brown hair. They stop halfway to look down at the two of us. The A-Grader is by now down at our level, the double-handed grip redeployed, his gun pointing unambiguously.

'The Moravková sisters.' I glance at Baz. Seeing Irina in the flesh will be bringing back all the wrong sort of memories.

'Thanks to you, Baxter, my sister and I are being forced to leave the country.' It's Irina talking. 'We're not particularly happy about that, but no matter. We've made our fortune. We'll be back. Once the police case against us fizzles out. Next time, we'll be unstoppable. Especially since you won't be around.'

'You think so? How are your mother's kidneys?'

'God, Baxter, you really are an annoying little shit.' This time it's Tanya.

'Holding up well,' Irina chips back in. 'Once Samira has donated both of hers, she'll be even better.'

'Both? Your mother surely only needs the one.'

'In Slovakia, we do things differently.'

'I hear your mother's been moved out of her clinic. Found a black-market surgeon back home who's happy to accept a substantial payment in cash, have you?'

'I'm puzzled, Baxter, how well informed you appear to be.'

'I told Gregor. There are police undercover operatives all over your repulsive little organisation.'

'I don't believe you. Anyway, I'm not sure what the fuss is about. Samira will get at least one kidney in return.'

'Just not one that works.'

'Life's a bitch, Baxter. Perhaps her darling brother can donate one of his? If he's alive by then. After Gregor's finished with you both.'

'When does the plane get here?'

'In about twenty minutes. First, Tanya and I were going to watch my friend here put a bullet in your head. Then my sister came up with a different plan.'

'Don't tell me. A long, slow, painful death.'

'You should have been a clairvoyant, Baxter. Perhaps in your next life.' She glances at her sister. 'Come, let's find Gregor. It's his show from now on. Bye, Baxter.'

Tanya casts me one last appraising look.

'Too bad, Ricky.' She gives me the full-on lip-licking treatment, knowing that it's yanking my chain. 'For you, maybe I'd even hang around a bit more, but ...' She blows an air kiss. 'Sadly, we've got a plane to catch.'

38

Which leaves just the three of us. All alone in the cellar, waiting for Gregor to make an appearance. Tanya didn't bother locking the door behind her. That was either foolish or else a signal that Gregor's arrival was imminent.

The guy with the gun has the upper hand. He's armed, and Baz and I are not. There's an air of anticipation among the three of us. The A-Grader wants to look good in front of his boss whenever Gregor deems it's the moment to visit. Because of this, he continues standing, arms outstretched, the double-handed grip deployed to the full. Looking the part. Ready to react. Just as his boss would expect. Baz and I, meanwhile, are desperate to escape. The clock's ticking, with the plane expected to leave sometime soon. The distance between the A-Grader and us is about five metres. Not even an amateur gunman misses at five metres. So, we're compelled to wait. Wait for Gregor to appear or wait for an opportunity. Whichever comes first. In life, sometimes you have to make your own luck.

Which is why I start to pace. Back and forth, small figures of eight. Nothing aggressive, nothing to challenge the man with the gun. Enough to be annoying, not enough to compromise his advantage. Or so I want him to think. The good thing is, with just one wink from me, Baz joins in too. Not in unison, each of us making our own random figure-of-eight movements. Two men, two blurry targets.

'Stop moving, the pair of you,' he yells.

It's probably dawning on him we're in a concrete cellar. Firing a gun in this space is going to be random. Loud as hell and dangerous. If he fires twice, the opportunity for a ricochet is huge. When neither of us takes notice of his command, he edges nearer to exert his authority. Which is precisely what I wanted him to do.

'Last warning. Hit the deck, or one of you will get hurt.'

Turning clockwise at the end of what I plan to be my final figure-of-eight, I make as if to scratch my left shoulder with my right hand. Instead I press the thumb button on the telescopic baton secreted in my palm. Next moment I lash out at his gun hand, watching with satisfaction as the metal ball bearing works its magic.

'Get out of here!' I yell to Baz as the man's wrist disintegrates, and the gun goes flying. I drop the baton and charge at the wounded man, headbutting him in the face and swinging a massive fist as a follow-through. It's a knockout punch, which does what it says on the tin. I grab the baton, collapse it back down again, and then hurry up the stairs to see where Baz has got to.

I have just locked the cellar door when I turn around and see someone advancing towards me.

Gregor! In his hand is my mini-taser.

'Baxter!' he growls. 'You've missed your chance. The plane's about to arrive and your luck's run out. It's just you and me left, I'm afraid. Now,' he says, holding the taser in front of him, 'I am fascinated by this device of yours.'

Too late, I hear someone else behind me. Before I can turn around, something hard hits me across the back of the neck and shoulders. My vision starts to flicker and my knees buckle.

When I come to, Gregor and the man I tasered in the garden earlier are kneeling on my arms, pinning me to the floor. I'm wide awake because Gregor, whether conscious of it or not, is pressing down right next to where Scorpion-Head's bike chain cut into my upper forearm. It hurts like hell. Gregor has no interest in how I'm feeling, though. He's intent on ramming the mini-taser against my neck.

'I warned you the other day, Baxter. Perhaps it's time to enjoy a taste of your own medicine for a change?'

I try to remain impassive. Instead, my eyes give away my terror.

He gives a sickly smile and presses the button. Involuntarily, I let out a loud howl of pain, my body jerking furiously. Every nerve, every sinew feels frazzled and weakened.

'Not so much fun on the receiving end, is it?' He nods at the colleague pinning my other arm. The one I had zapped earlier. 'Want to have a go?' He looks at me with an evil smile. 'Wait, I have a better idea. This is the man who poured boiling water over Tariq's privates. We should reciprocate. How would you like a few thousand volts on your dick, Baxter?'

'It'll save on the blue pills,' the other man counters. They roar with laughter, both tugging hard at my trouser waistband. Not a second too late, out of the corner of one eye, I see Baz tiptoeing towards us. He's holding a heavy wooden chair in his hand, and he raises it above his head, ready to strike. The blow, when it comes, whacks Gregor with a massive clout to the skull. The strike is so powerful, it makes Gregor's head collide with the other man's with force. Both hit the floor, out cold.

'Excellent work and just in time,' I say with heartfelt gratitude. 'I was beginning to think you'd abandoned me. Thanks.'

'You okay?'

'Just. That taser was evil. You saved my life. Again.'

'It's good to help each other.'

'Come on, let's use some cable ties on them both and then throw them in the cellar. Saunderson can have them later. We haven't much time if we want to stop that plane before it leaves. Assuming we can work out a way to open the locked gate out the back.'

'No need, Ricky. It's open. I look already. It's what took me so long.'

'Baz, you're a bloody genius.'

We look like a couple of battle-weary soldiers as we half walk, half run towards the airstrip. From this distance, the runway looks barely distinguishable from a mown lawn in the morning sunlight. Baz was right about the rear gate being open, both of us grateful we don't have to struggle over the fence this time. Staggering out the back of the woods beyond the gate, I am finishing a brief call with Saunderson, telling him about Gregor and the house, when my heart sinks. Touching down on the grass strip in the middle distance is a small, propeller-driven aircraft. Samira and the two sisters are about three hundred yards away, waiting for the plane to taxi to a halt. We need to move fast if we're to stand a chance.

The prognosis does not look good.

In our condition, it's an almighty struggle. If I had my blades, I might have been there already. But I have a pounding headache and my legs aren't moving as I'd like, courtesy of the taser. Baz is never a fast runner at the best of times, especially when suffering the effects of a gunshot wound. One-third of the way there and the plane has already come to a halt. The engine dies, and the pilot is quickly out of the aircraft to help the three women climb aboard. He's doubtless spotted us, under instructions from the sisters to get a move on.

I try a burst of speed, but my legs feel like jelly. With one hundred yards to go, the pilot is climbing back on board. The cheeky bastard even gives a brief wave in our direction as the door closes. Myers said it was cosy in a Skyhawk with four people. When I see the pilot wriggling his way back to the cockpit, it looks like he wasn't kidding.

Down to the last forty yards and the engine is firing back to life.

I imagine Irina or Tanya yelling at the pilot to get going. Ten yards to go, and the handbrake comes off, and the plane starts to roll. I see Tanya turning in her seat, leering at me in victory as Baz and I fail to catch them. This is when I should have had a gun. Instead, the pilot opens the throttle and the plane races away.

So very close. As it turned out, not close enough.

In no time, the plane is airborne. I come to a breathless halt and collapse onto the grass runway. Baz joins me seconds later. We watch the plane amble into the sky, conducting a sweeping turn over the airfield as it heads into the clouds. If I'm not mistaken, I even see the pilot giving a friendly wave. What a bastard!

'What happens now, Ricky?' Baz looks crestfallen. Burner already in hand, I compose a brief text message and hit 'send' before replying.

'We lost one battle, Baz. However, unless my eyes deceived me, the end of the war may be closer than we think.'

39

'Bloody brilliant, Sarge.'

'What is, boss?'

Saunderson winks at Wellby but says nothing, picking up the open-channel microphone and toggling the transmit button.

'Listen up, everyone. They should be landing any minute.'

Scattered around the airstrip at Fowlmere are several unmarked police vehicles, including one high-security van with metal grilles over its glass windows, front and back. Saunderson and Wellby's own vehicle is blocking the taxiway off the airfield's only runway.

'How come you know what's happening?'

Saunderson passes Wellby his mobile and shows him the text he's just received.

'Baxter? I don't get it.'

'You will, Sarge, trust me.' He scans the horizon and sees in the distance what looks like a plane, descending through the clouds. 'Hand me the binos, will you?' He places the powerful lenses against his gaunt face and stares at the distant speck. 'Yes, that looks like our baby. Here, look for yourself,' he says, handing the field glasses back to his colleague.

'I'll be damned,' Wellby says a few moments later, eyes straining against the lenses. 'It is them. How did you ...?'

Saunderson says nothing. Instead, they stare at the sky, transfixed. The plane's approach looks unstable – what Saunderson later describes in his report as a 'stuttering descent', jerking right and left at random, only just in control.

When the wheels hit the runway, it's Wellby who spots what's happened.

'Bloody hell. No wonder he's wobbling all over the place. The engine's not working!'

Saunderson smiles as various vehicles swarm onto the tarmac in pursuit. The Skyhawk brakes gently, surrounded by cars the instant it comes to a halt. Armed officers leap out and take up positions encircling the plane, in the process yanking open the rear door. One by one, the frightened passengers are dragged into the open air. Two of them are immediately placed in handcuffs.

'Come on,' Saunderson says, the cue for him and Wellby to climb out of their car and walk to the aircraft.

'Irina and Tanya Moravková. Finally, we meet.' Saunderson turns to Wellby. 'Read them their rights, can you, Sarge?' He then looks at the terrified young woman standing beside them. 'You must be Samira?'

'Yes.'

'I'm glad we found you before it was too late. You'll be pleased to know your brother is at the other airfield. Now,' he says, looking towards the man climbing down from the Cessna. 'Would you be Kit Myers, by any chance?'

'Guilty as charged.' Myers beams and steps forward to shake Saunderson's hand.

‘Quite a neat bit of flying, if you don’t mind me saying.’

‘Thanks. I rarely find an opportunity to fly these babies any more.’

‘Spot of engine trouble, was it?’

‘Yes, it was weird. The fuel pump stopped working. I was compelled to make an emergency landing. Probably just a fuse. You never know, I might have inadvertently knocked the pump switch to off when I was hurrying to get back to my seat at the other airstrip. Wouldn’t have been the first time I’d been clumsy.’

‘You bastard!’ Irina spits at Myers, venom in her eyes. ‘What happened to François, my pilot? Did you kill him?’

‘Me?’ Myers exclaims, genuine surprise on his face. ‘I’ve never killed anyone in my life. Your pilot phoned in sick this morning. I was around and said I’d fill in.’

‘You think you’re so bloody clever,’ Tanya hisses, struggling in her cuffs. ‘I want a lawyer. Myers, I won’t forget you in a hurry. You’d better look over your shoulder from now on, I’m warning you.’

‘If I were you, Miss,’ Saunderson chips in, ‘I’d shut it. Making threats in front of an arresting officer is not usually a clever move. Sarge, get them in the van, will you?’

‘Sure thing, Boss.’

‘Tell me, Myers. Do you think you might be able to fix the fuel pump?’

‘I’m hoping a simple flick of a switch might be all that’s required.’ He says this with a grin on his face.

‘Good. Because I was wondering whether you could give Sergeant Wellby and I a lift back to Nuthampstead?’

‘Sure. But then I need to be getting back to Paris. There’s a private charter to Nice that’s been booked for this afternoon with my name on it.’

'That's kind, thank you. There's an evil bastard called Gregor who is locked in the house's cellar there. I want him in custody before he discovers a way to get out. I figured we might get there faster by air. The others can follow in the cars. Samira, if you're up for it, why don't you tag along for the ride? That way, you'll get to see your brother even quicker.'

40

The good bits in life, when they come, sometimes come big. Today is one of those days.

Saunderson, thankfully, has sent a brief text. Baz and I were about to head back to the house. Now we're staying put.

'Let's just wait,' I say cryptically. The two of us remain sitting despondently on the grass runway. Baz looks too crestfallen to argue.

I hear the plane before we spot it. Then I catch a glimpse of it coming in low on the down-wind leg. It performs a crop-dusting farmer's hard banking turn to land on the grass strip using only half the available runway. The plane taxis towards us and Myers cuts the engine. If Baz knows what's happening, he doesn't show it. I rush to the side door and yank it open, offering a helping hand to Wellby, who is first to get out.

'Great job, Kit!' I find myself shouting, even though the engine has stopped.

'I enjoyed myself. Got to rush, though, mate. I need to be back in Beauvais by lunchtime. Can you manage on your own back there?'

'Sure, thanks. I owe you, big time,' I say, helping Saunderson to the ground. 'Baz, come here a moment.' I call out, giving a silent signal to Samira to stay put and wait. She senses what's happening, sitting patiently in silence for her brother to appear.

Baz comes across to the plane, looking first at Saunderson then Wellby, bemused. He then sees me beckoning and walks to the aircraft door. He has a big scowl on his face.

'What is it, Ricky?'

Only then does he peer inside, his face a picture. The lightbulb moment dawns slowly, his face cautiously bursting into one enormous smile. Awkwardly, painfully, Samira emerges. For these two, there are no loud whoops of joy, no screams of happiness. Theirs is a soft and gentle reunion. Full of love, warmth and honest emotion. They embrace for a long time, the moment tender. It's a wet-eyed occasion, me included. Samira steps forward to hug me, and I have to warn her to go easy. Various parts of my body are already complaining loudly.

This is what it's all about, why I am doing the things I do. I feel an odd pang, wishing Cath could see this moment. Maybe somewhere she might be, looking down approvingly, who knows?

Baz steps away from his sister and comes towards me. Now it's our turn and the two of us hug.

'Thank you,' he whispers in my ear. I feel his warm tears on my cheek. We have become like brothers, Baz and me. For once in my life, I feel content.

'Good things come to those who wait.'

I step away, wiping my eyes and peering once more back inside the aircraft.

'Thanks again, buddy,' I say to Kit. 'I guess you have to get going. Call me soon, promise?'

I shut the door and almost immediately, Myers hits the starter.

'Right,' I say to Baz and his sister. 'It's time for DI Saunderson and Sergeant Wellby here to make some arrests. We don't want Gregor breaking out of the cellar if we can help it.' As we stride out for the gap in the trees, Myers lifts the Skyhawk into the air and performs a sweeping turn over our heads. All of us give a gigantic wave, watching the aircraft turn south and head for Paris.

41

On Grace's instructions, I am told to take a few days off. To recover, as she puts it. I suspect she really wants me out of the way, so she can get the place organised the way she likes it. Who am I to argue? I spend the time with Inés and Marta at a rented house by the sea. The holiday is a great success. So much so, Inés and I agree we might even repeat the experience – this time on our own. The three of us arrive back late at night, exhausted but happy.

Next morning, Marta is back to school, and Inés calls in to her office saying she'll be in late. Her story is that someone's coming around to check the new boiler. I don't need any encouragement. This has become our special euphemism. With Marta no longer in the house playing gooseberry, the two of us enjoy a long and lazy morning to ourselves. I am not even aware that something is up until I get to the office around lunchtime. It transpires that Inés had been conspiring with Grace all along.

My first impression, as I cross the threshold, is that we have a new reception desk. Nothing fancy, but Grace tells me later that the old one had become damp and mildewed because of water damage. I only half believe her, but no matter. Freds's sofa is where it usually is. Freds, however, is not, and I'm aware of more noise than usual, a distant sound of chatter and glasses clinking. It's only when I reach the conference suite that I realise what is happening.

'Mister Rick. Welcome back.' No sooner has Grace spoken these words than the entire room bursts into spontaneous applause.

'What's going on?'

'We thought a surprise celebration party was called for.' Grace steps forward to envelop me in a vast embrace.

It turns out everyone is here. Baz, Samira, and Kels. Plus Vince. Even Kit Myers. Then there's Saunderson and Wellby and a few other police hangers-on. Most surprising of all, sitting in one corner with Freds looking doleful at her feet, is my mother. I make a beeline for her.

'I'm so proud of you, Ricky,' she whispers as we embrace.

'How did you get here?'

'That young man of yours, Vince. He drove up yesterday and collected me. I'm in a very nice hotel, which I need to thank you for.'

Grace has organised everything. Why does this not surprise me? In just one week since the nightmare at the airstrip, the office is looking good as new. If not better. We have new furniture and carpets throughout. Even my office has been tarted up. The shiny new table in the conference suite is laden with food and drink. I'm about to grab a beer when I spot Baz and his sister looking at me. I head across the room.

'How are you both?'

'We're doing okay,' Baz replies, his face a mixture of emotions.

'How about you?' I direct my follow-up question at Samira.

'I still can't believe it's over.'

'I promise you it is. You look great, both of you.'

'When I left you in that room the other night,' Samira begins, her voice so soft I can hardly hear, 'I felt so guilty. I was convinced they would kill you. That it was all going to be my fault.'

I place a finger against my lips.

'Hush. It's history. We're here, we're safe, and there's no need to revisit any of it. We escaped, and the bad guys are going to jail. How have the police been towards you both?'

'Okay,' Samira says, but there's something in her tone.

'What is it?'

'Baz and I are worried. We don't want to be deported. Not now. Not after all this.'

I catch Saunderson's eye across the room and beckon him and Wellby to come and join us.

'Thanks for coming today,' I say once they arrive. 'It's good to see you both. I presume Blacksmith has been disbanded?'

'Wound down,' Saunderson replies. 'We're hoping for some swift prosecutions. If we're lucky, we'll find a judge who'll be in the mood to dole out long sentences. Especially Gregor. God, he's a piece of work.'

'Trust me,' Baz intervenes. 'The two women are worse.'

I clasp Baz around the shoulders.

'I know, Baz. But like I just said before these two arrived, you're going to have to find ways to put all of that behind you. It's history.'

'On that point,' Wellby intervenes, 'if anyone would find counselling helpful, we can put you in touch with several excellent people.'

'That could be useful, thanks,' I say. 'This charity is what it is because of all the great people I have around me. Not just Grace, but Baz too. I couldn't have done this without him. He saved my life. Literally.'

'Twice,' Baz says, beaming proudly.

'Look, folks, I need to ask a favour,' I say, my arm still on Baz's shoulder. My gaze, however, is fixed on Saunderson. 'It would help these two enormously –' I nod at Baz and then his sister '– if you could remove one particular issue from their worry list. They are incredibly anxious that, if they help the police convict Gregor and the two women, they might well end up being deported. I don't know what you feel, but I can tell you this. Baz and Samira have suffered way more than most people on this planet. I think they deserve the freedom to choose a life here if they want. I need Baz to continue working for me. If Samira is interested, Grace and I would love her to come and work at the charity here too.' I glance across and see the look of surprise on her face. 'We just don't need the authorities, be it the police, Border Force officials, or anyone else connected with the Home Office, hounding them just because they might be easy targets.'

'Baxter, I hear you. My position is simple. Sergeant Wellby and I joined the police to track down criminals. We're not particularly interested in innocent people's immigration status. I promise you this. I'll have a quiet word further up the tree. Nothing official and I can't give guarantees. However, when this gets to court and the Blacksmith crew are prosecuted, none of us needs an immigration issue to flare up and cause embarrassment. I hear what you're asking. Officially, I can't comment. Unofficially, I'm not interested in pursuing this and I promise to be helpful. Does that answer your question?'

I look at Baz and Samira, and they nod in agreement.

'Which reminds me, Baxter. I wanted to ask you something.'

'Fire away.'

'Blacksmith turned out all right, in the end, all things said and done. Wellby and I were wondering whether you might be interested in doing something similar in the future? On a case-by-case basis, naturally, and only if circumstances allowed. It would have to be an unofficial arrangement. Off the books and off the record, naturally. But we thought it could work to both our advantages.'

'Funnily enough, I was wondering more or less the same thing myself. I don't see why not. We have similar objectives, even if we approach things using slightly different methods.'

'Let's think it over and kick it around more when we next meet.'

'Good idea. Tell me, different subject altogether, but that person over there,' I say, nodding towards the woman talking to Kels and Vince. 'Is she the person I once knew as Lisandra?'

All of us turn our heads. The woman in question has long, dark brown hair, but her face looks familiar.

'No longer the platinum blonde, but yes, that's her.'

'Well, excuse me, but I think it's time I went and said hello. That woman saved my life.'

Lisandra beams when I come across to join her conversation with Kels and Vince. Grace, never slow to watch my back, arrives at the same time bearing a plate of food, which she offers around.

'I nearly didn't recognise you. I don't suppose Lisandra is your actual name?'

'It's Hayley,' she says, and we embrace under Grace's ever-watchful eye.

'This is the lady who saved my life. My advice, though: if you ever see her holding a baseball bat, I'd steer well clear.'

'Sandwiches, anybody?' Grace says, catching my eye and making me smile.

Kels has made a big effort. Today her hair is blonde and super frizzy. Almost Afro. It's the tidiest I've ever seen her. Ignoring the denim dungarees and piercings for the moment, that is. From the way she keeps smiling at Vince, I'm certain the two of them have become an item.

'I'm glad you've met these two,' I say, indicating Kels and Vince. 'Without Kels here, we'd have never found the airfield location. As for you, Vince, that was neat work in Paris. What happened, exactly?'

'You mean taking care of the pilot? It was easy. No permanent damage. He just became unavailable for work for a few days.'

'It's a good job I had someone reliable to step in. Have you met Kit

Myers?' I say to Grace, beckoning to my old friend to join our little group. 'Kit, this is Grace. Without her, the charity simply wouldn't begin to function.'

'Pleasure to meet you.' He beams at Grace. 'If you ever want the dirt on Ricky, he and I go way back. Just tip me the wink and I'll tell all.'

'Don't you dare. It works both ways, just remember that, buddy. Changing the subject, nice job with the broken fuel pump. How soon after take-off did you pull that stunt?'

'Almost immediately. Dad used to do it to me all the time. It was his little joke. You just have to flip a switch; the engine splutters, then conks out. Had them all bricking it in the back, that's for sure.'

'I'd have loved to have seen Irina's face.'

'She was utterly terrified. Convinced we were all about to die.'

'Nice job, buddy. I owe you. Don't think I didn't see your cheeky little wave as we were trying to catch up with you at the airstrip.'

'I wondered if you'd spotted that.'

'You were lucky the sisters didn't twig what was going on. Thanks, mate.'

'Always happy to help an old friend.'

'Different subject, have you seen Mum's here?'

'I was chatting to her earlier. She hasn't changed much. Seems pretty smitten with your Inés.' He glances over my shoulder and nods his head. I turn to look. The two of them appear to be getting on like a house on fire.

'I think I'd better make sure they're not plotting something I might later regret. Great food, thank you,' I say to Grace, grabbing a mini-quiche from her tray before heading over to find Mum feeding Freds a corner of her sandwich.

'That dog is the most overfed Alsatian on the planet.'

'He's lovely,' Inés says. 'Your mum was asking whether we might go across one weekend soon and stay the night.'

'Only if you're sure,' I say, checking my mother's expression.

'Ricky, darling, seeing what you're doing here, what you did for me. It's about time we had a proper talk. I've been stupid. You have a right to know more about what happened to Cath.'

'It's the reason we had our falling-out, remember?'

'I know. It was totally my fault, and I apologise. Come and stay soon and let's have a proper conversation. All I'll say for now is this. It was complicated.'

'In what way?'

'There are things you are not fully aware of. The people she was with, and so forth. I think it's time for you to go digging. You're good at that. I've already apologised for not seeing that in you earlier. Now that the dust has settled, I'd like the record to be set straight. Once and for all. For all our sakes.'

It's only later, as I'm lying awake in bed reflecting on the conversation, Inés happily purring in bed beside me, that I work out what has been bugging me since the party. What on earth did my mother mean when she had said 'for all our sakes'? Why the sudden change of heart where before everything about the way my sister had died had been such a closed book?

I roll over, knowing that I will not solve this particular conundrum right here and right now. I shall call my mother in the morning and arrange a date to go and see her. I have this horrible feeling that after everything that has happened, firstly with Marta and then latterly myself, Inés will find me more of a long-term liability than an asset. I hope not, but I need to be realistic. I look across at her sleeping body, stroking her hair idly with a finger. Into my sleepy brain, I recall the words that my father often said.

'You have to make the most of what you've been given in life, son.'

He was undoubtedly right. Who can ever know what the future will bring? My sense, just from what little my mother has intimated, is that it's likely to be full of a few surprises. So, what's new, Ricky Baxter – why worry about it? With that, I close my eyes and wait for sleep to engulf me.

The End

WHY NOT TRY ANOTHER THRILLER BY THE SAME AUTHOR?

Visit: www.davidnrobinson.com

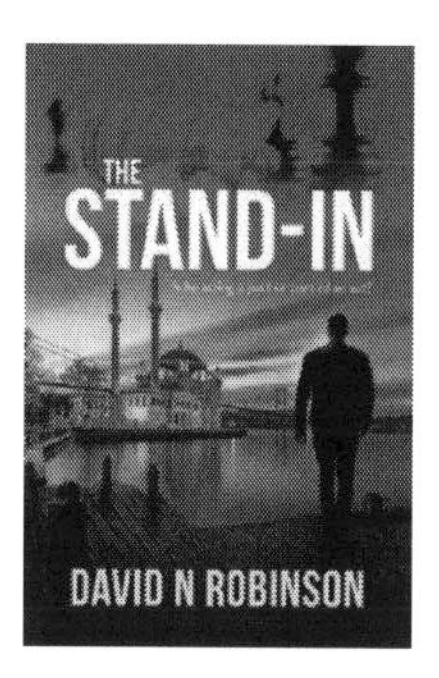

WANTING TO BE A SPY IS ONE THING: ACTING LIKE ONE IS QUITE ANOTHER

When stand-in teacher, Calum Ross, first locks eyes with Natalia, he can't quite believe his luck. Nor can the UK security agencies. They've been looking for a way to recruit Natalia's husband, Oleg Usmanov, a Russian spymaster and friend of the Russian President, for years. Ross might just be their man.

Except nothing about Usmanov is quite what it seems.

When Natalia is attacked, Ross finds the finger of blame being pointed squarely at him. With Russians out for his blood and his SIS 'minders' squabbling amongst themselves, Ross runs for his life, unsure who to trust, frantically needing to outwit the person secretly directing each of his moves around this deadly chessboard.

With Natalia's life on the line and Ross increasingly desperate to uncover the truth about Usmanov, this fast-paced thriller moves between Istanbul, London and the perilous canals of Venice. Only when you think the story has reached its climax do the twists and turns behind this fast-paced thriller finally reveal themselves.

Acknowledgements

Some authors write in their acknowledgements section about having a whole paid cast and crew behind them – publishers, editors, marketing people and the like. I am a little envious! When you're an independent author like me, you count yourself lucky if you have more than a handful of people to rely on to help take a manuscript from an initial idea to the finished book.

I am not grumbling, though. I count myself very fortunate. Over the short time I have been writing, a growing band of friends, supporters, and early reviewers have taken up my cause, many of whom freely give their time to read early drafts, offering advice and occasional course correction along the way. I'd like to thank them all, sadly too numerous now to mention individually. I couldn't do this without your support and affection for my writing.

A special thanks are due to my wife, Ginny, our two sons and our ever-expanding families, many of whom continue to rally around checking and re-checking and being supportive. Thank you. Writing isn't as straightforward as some think. We authors get things wrong, and we need advice and input from others to make it better.

Finally, two unsung heroes of my self-publishing world. My copy-editor, Carrie O'Grady of The Hackney Fiction Doctor, and my book cover designer, Peter O'Connor from Bespoke Book Covers. Both help me hugely and perform a fabulous job – thank you.

Author's Note

I have, in the past, tried all sorts of different methods to get my books in front of readers yet to discover me. I've tried Facebook and Twitter, I've tried free books to build mailing lists and spent money on book sites like Bookbub and Goodreads. I've even used paid advertising on both Amazon and Facebook as well. All these have helped, but the returns on investment can be meagre.

The funny thing is that whilst many successful self-published authors say that it is essential to build a mailing list of loyal fans, I've learnt over time that most readers rarely want to be bombarded, week after week, by yet more emails from an author they have only read a few times.

These days, I rely on people like you who read my books to do three things:

i) if you could leave an honest review on the Amazon page you bought or downloaded this book from, that would be the **very** best help you could give;

ii) next, if you enjoyed the book, perhaps you might help create a buzz and tell a few friends and family members about it?

iii) finally, perhaps I can persuade you to try a few other books that I have written?

Thank you for taking the time to read this book. I sincerely hope you enjoyed it.

In case you're wondering, I do offer a free book on my website, **www.davidnrobinson.com** – but you no longer need to subscribe to a mailing list to download it!

David N Robinson

For many years before COVID 19, I was a business leader: always out and about meeting people, travelling the world regularly. Endless plane and train journeys provided ample time for reflection. In between work, I would read books and plan for a different life.

These days, I am happy to be grounded, living my new life as an independent author. Working from home and living the dream. Writing thrillers, the sort of books I always hankered after on yet another long-haul flight. Fast-paced, contemporary page-turners – with plenty of twists and action along the way. Books about topical subjects that I love researching.

Most of the time, when I'm not researching a new book, my wife and I live in England, close to the fabulous city of Cambridge. The walks are fantastic, the bike rides not too challenging and the streets full of interesting and inspiring people.

Visit **www.davidnrobinson.com** to learn more about my writing.

Printed in Great Britain
by Amazon